SOFT AS STEEL

Donated
To The Library by

John
Heidersbach

© DEMCO, INC. 1990
PRINTED IN U.S.A.

SOFT AS STEEL

The Art of Julie Bell

FOREWORD BY BRIAN ALDISS

TEXT BY NIGEL SUCKLING

THUNDER'S
MOUTH
PRESS

This book is dedicated to my heroes – Boris, Tony and David.

Published in the UNITED STATES By
Thunder's Mouth Press
841 Broadway, Fourth Floor
New York, NY 10003

First published in Great Britain in 1999
by Paper Tiger
an imprint of Collins & Brown Limited

9 8 7 6 5 4 3 2

Library of Congress Catalog card number:
98-83189

ISBN 1-56025-191-3

Commissioning editor: Paul Barnett
Designer: Paul Wood

Reproduction by Global Colour, Malaysia
Printed and bound in Singapore by Craft Print Pte Ltd

CONTENTS

FOREWORD
by Brian Aldiss

SOME WHILE AGO, I was lunching in a Lebanese restaurant in Oxford, England, where writers meet. I fell into conversation with a young woman sitting across the table from me. We were talking about our interests in Pluto, the remotest planet of the solar system, and its large moon, Charon. The lady was so pretty that it took me a while to realize she was also clever, witty, well educated and skilled in the European game of flirtation.

Appearances count for much. They may not be of primary importance, but they remain the first elements of anything or anyone that meets the eye. Long before we smell, hear, touch, kiss a woman, we see her. The interior computer has immediately started on its complex calculations.

A memory of that Lebanese lunch returned as I gazed at the feast Julie Bell sets before us now. Her paintings are often fearsome and generally attractive. They have a strength beyond mere prettiness. They exist in regions beyond our ken, regions inhabited by giant snakes, immense suns, mountains, howling winds, lowering planets, arrogant banners. They delight with frank sensuousness in the human body – human or near-human.

We're plunged into a world of action. Would an ordinary human spine survive such poses? How many of these half-naked heroes have feet that never touch the ground? Julie presents a pure world of violence, of threat and triumph – of swords, sexual symbols, butts and breasts. Near naked the women may be, but, as Julie says, they may be exposed but they are totally untouchable. They emerge from somewhere amid the burning permafrosts of her mind and brush. They burst out upon us. Certainly they are no stay-at-homes.

These slay-at-homes are the vital ladies Julie admires. Many of them resemble her. And why not! Julie, on her own admission, has recreated herself: so why not recreate her image on canvas – that vibrant body, that sensitive face? So she comes clad as Lilandra, in gleaming body armour, or as a near-naked lady bearing a banner with a strange device, or with streaming dark hair she calls a robotic bird to her presence. As she says, she thinks in sensual terms. I have been particularly struck by an earlier portrait Julie painted of one of her sisters posing as a centaur. From the great carcass of the horse wells a luscious female body with ripe breasts. Above the body is perched a visionary head – a beautiful long-haired woman looks upwards into the distance, tenderly and intelligently.

To my prejudiced mind, this painting ranks with some of the works of the great symbolist and decadent painters of last century: Gustave Moreau, Odilon Redon, Franz von Stuck, and especially the Belgian master, Fernand Khnopff, who also liked to paint his sister. Julie's female centaur seems to rejoice in her own beauty and freedom in silence.

But Julie works in a commercial field where action is the order of the day. Her protagonists throw themselves from the page at life. Monsters may attack them, but they are beyond harm. Some come armed to the teeth, some leap from explosions, some use great wings, while others dance above lakes of tomato purée and gold. Many tote amazing armour, amazing hair-dos. The thongs between their thighs vibrate with their energy. Some indeed have liquid metal (one of Julie's trademarks) instead of flesh. What flows in their veins is some superfluid, maybe argon 38. They are transformed.

And here we have something of the story of Julie herself. She and I knew each other slightly, in days when we were both different people. She was then beautiful and energetic, immensely friendly, and getting into bodybuilding. But there was a nervous quality about her which puzzled some of her friends. Then she met and married the celebrated fantasy artist, Boris Vallejo. She transformed herself.

It seems, from what Julie has said, that she suffered from diffidence. However that may be, she was inspired by Boris to work hard and master the techniques which dazzle us here. Unusually, she is very frank and clear about the way she works. It's a wonderful life story which holds captive two seemingly opposite interests: bodybuilding and oil paints.

We all thrive on opposites. Seems that those great opposites, fantasy and reality, are two of Julie Bell's chief talents! Anyone gazing at these paintings can enjoy them in vivid display – and feel their batteries re-charged.

INTRODUCTION

JULIE BELL WAS BORN AND RAISED in south-east Texas but, after criss-crossing the United States, has finally settled in Pennsylvania within easy striking distance of New York City. Along the way, she married Boris Vallejo and startled the fantasy art world by stepping up onto the stage beside him and showing that she could paint her heart out along with the best of them.

Some people at first even muttered that Boris was painting her paintings himself, but as Julie forged her own distinct reputation, these doubters were silenced. There was no escaping that here was suddenly a new talent turning out stunning paintings as if she had been doing it all her life.

Julie and Boris have since begun to work as a team on some projects, staging joint exhibitions, sharing commissions from comic book publishers, and taking the platform at conventions together. But contrary to popular belief, they have so far never worked on the same painting. At most, they have helped each other out with minor details.Certainly their styles are similar because it was through Boris that Julie learned to paint and to bring her imagination to life, but there are differences. Julie: 'There are several ways our styles come through as being different. To start with, when we shoot photo references from models for an illustration, we will each aim for different results and often use entirely different lighting. Boris tends to focus on studying and celebrating the beauty of the form itself, whereas I often want to add the element of movement and dance. So we don't shoot at the same time because what we're looking for is so different.'

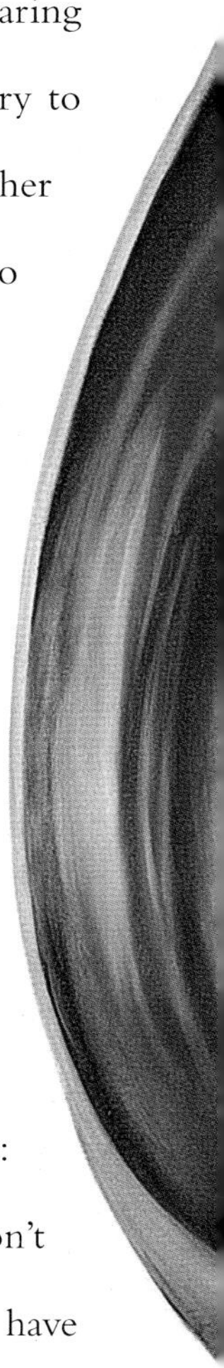

The seeming ease with which Julie leaped to fame is deceptive of course. She had to go through more than her share of pain, frustration and obstacles just like anyone who ever achieved anything. There was an enormous amount of hard work and talent behind her rise to stardom, but she was blessed with a bolt of pure luck when she found her companion and teacher who spoke the same language. Julie: 'It gives me a lot of confidence knowing Boris is next to me, and confidence magnifies your talent. I don't have to worry about getting stuck because he's so experienced and knowledgeable and always seems to have

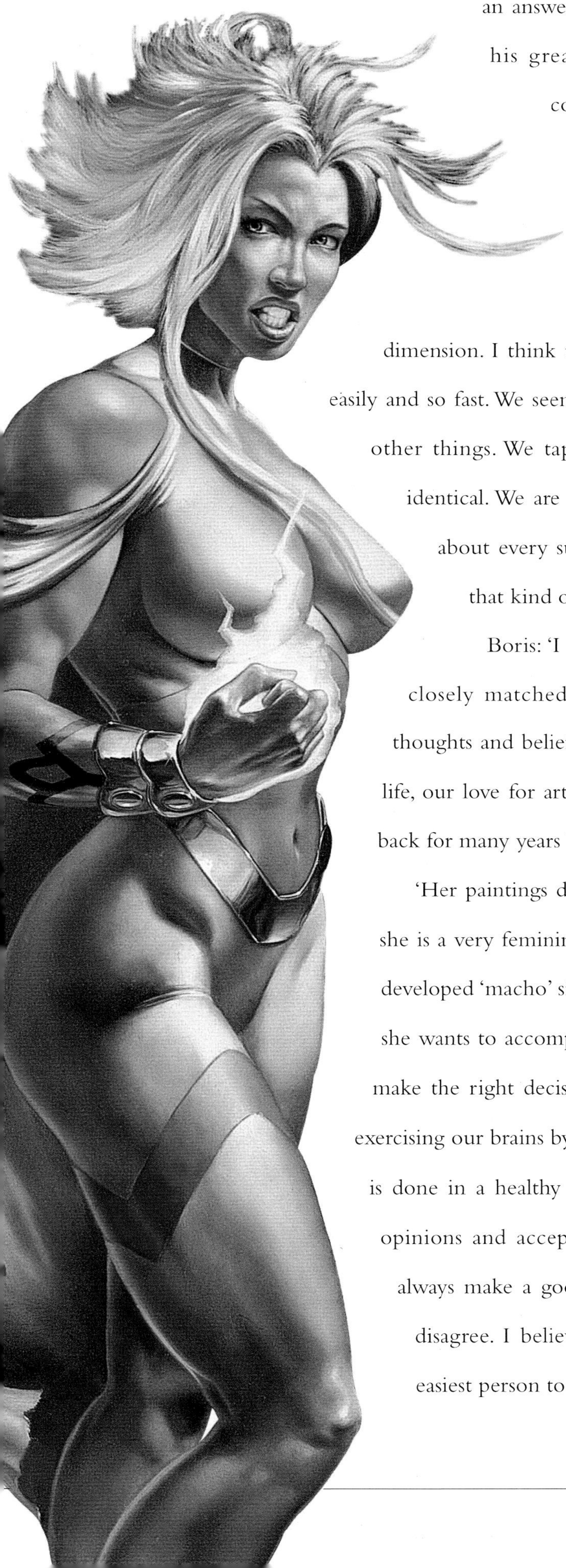

an answer. I can just go ahead and do the picture. I think one of his greatest gifts to me is to teach me to internalize that confidence so that I can draw upon it. Boris has such a wide range of talent – he's a once-in-a-lifetime genius. I'm in an amazing position to have that as a resource.

'As people, Boris and I have the same mindset. Our brains seem to come from the same odd dimension. I think that is one reason why we can learn from each other so easily and so fast. We seem to analyse things in the same way, both visually and in other things. We tap into the same place and our priorities are virtually identical. We are both perfectionists. Although we spend our days talking about every subject under the sun (and not under the sun!), we share that kind of communication that often doesn't need to be spoken.'

Boris: 'I could feel from the very beginning that we were really closely matched. It is not often that you run into somebody whose thoughts and beliefs you can identify with so remarkably – our ideas about life, our love for art and music. Our common interest in bodybuilding goes back for many years before we met each other.

'Her paintings definitely do have a more feminine touch than mine and she is a very feminine person, but then again, a very strong one, with a well-developed 'macho' side. She has a fierce determination. I know that whatever she wants to accomplish she will. She can, in addition, assess herself well and make the right decisions. Of course, there are also differences and we enjoy exercising our brains by arguing passionately about them from time to time. This is done in a healthy way because we have a mutual respect for each other's opinions and accept that we don't have to agree on everything. She can always make a good argument for her side, but will respect your right to disagree. I believe this is one of the reasons why she is just about the easiest person to get along with.'

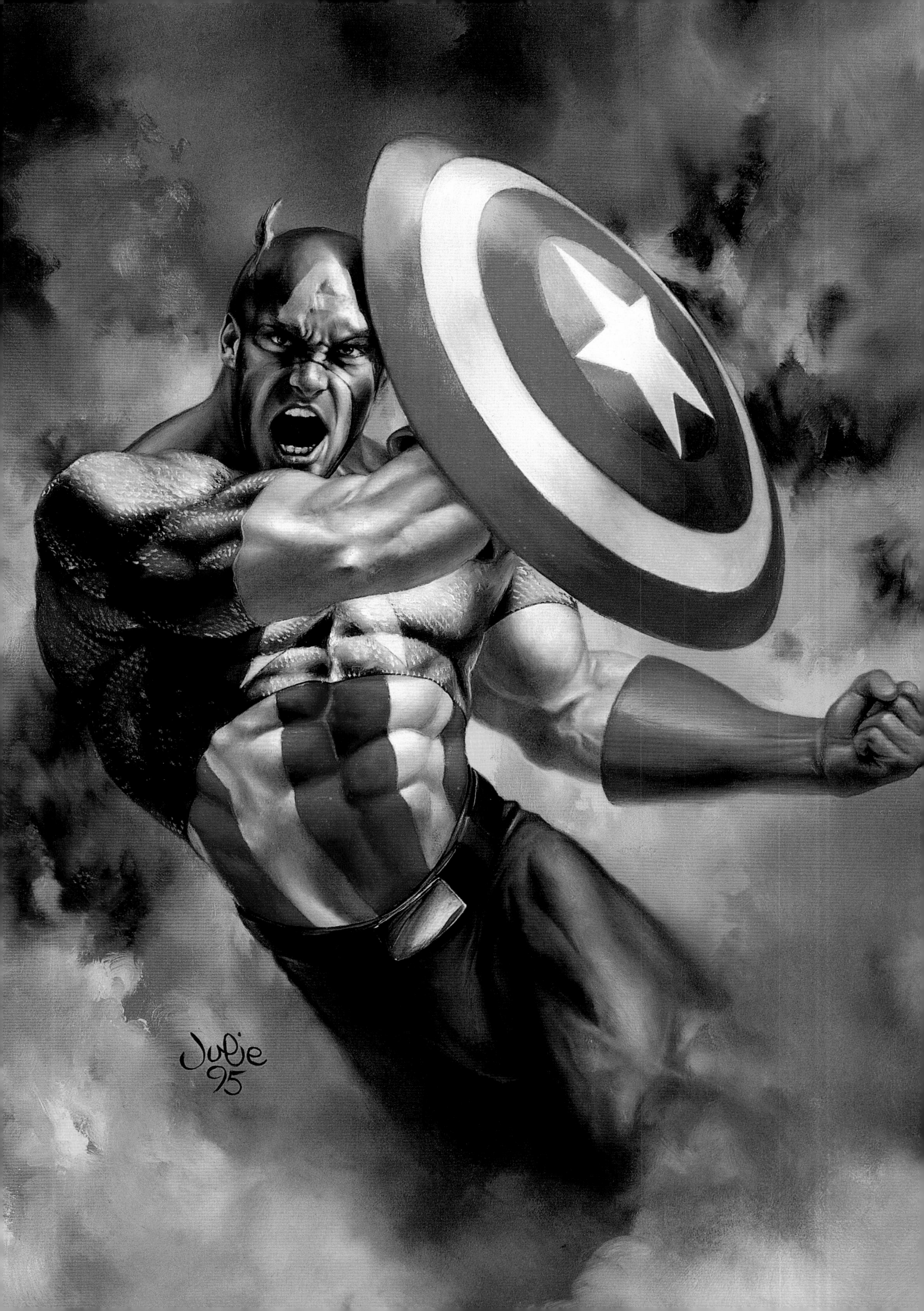
Julie
95

COMIC BOOK CHARACTERS

THE ATTRACTION OF comic book characters for Julie is that the driving forces behind these pictures are power, energy and movement. It is like trying to achieve the effect of a movie in something that is basically static and two dimensional. One trick is to place the characters deliberately off-balance in positions the viewer knows unconsciously they cannot hold, so they appear to be in mid-flow. Or the horizon may be skewed to give a dizzying effect, and there are many other little tricks that would be a shame to disclose.

ABOVE: *Spiderman vs. Venom, 1995*
Oils, 30 x 20 in (76 x 51 cm)
Trading card. Fleer Publishing Co.
TM & © 1999 Marvel Characters, Inc.
All rights reserved.

OPPOSITE: *Captain America, 1995*
Oils, 15 x 20 in (38 x 51 cm)
Trading card. Fleer Publishing Co.
TM & © 1999 Marvel Characters, Inc.
All rights reserved.

RIGHT: ***Marvel/DC Team-up, 1995***
Oils, 30 x 20 in (76 x 51 cm)
Trading card. Fleer Publishing Co.
TM & © 1998 DC Comics/1999 Marvel Comics, Inc. All rights reserved. Used with permission.
Marvel and DC Comics are great rivals with separate pantheons of superheroes, but because they are in the same business the success of each tends to help the other. Occasionally this is recognized when, as here, the two camps join talents. There is no conflict going on in this scene, the superheroes are exercising in readiness for some joint adventure in a 'virtual danger' room, like the holo-deck on Star Trek*'s 'USS* Enterprise*'. The scene was designed to be split up into nine equal parts, each viable as a trading card in its own right, but which can be fitted together like a jigsaw as an added treat for collectors. To tie everything together Julie devised the spiralling background with spiky elements radiating from the centre that only make sense when the cards are all together. In such cases it is hard to make each card quite as neat and self-contained as usual, but Julie enjoys meeting the challenge.*

FAR RIGHT: ***Silver Surfer, 1995***
Oils, 15 x 20 in (38 x 51 cm)
Trading Card. Marvel Comics.
TM & © 1999 Marvel Characters, Inc. All rights reserved.
In the 1970s when Julie Bell first started reading comics, the Silver Surfer was one of her favourite characters. 'Perhaps because he was a bit of an old hippy among superheroes,' she suggests. There was a rather sad, romantic tale to his background along the lines that he'd had to leave his true love behind and was forever searching to find her again. Julie has always preferred characters with a bit of romance in their history to those who simply make mayhem.

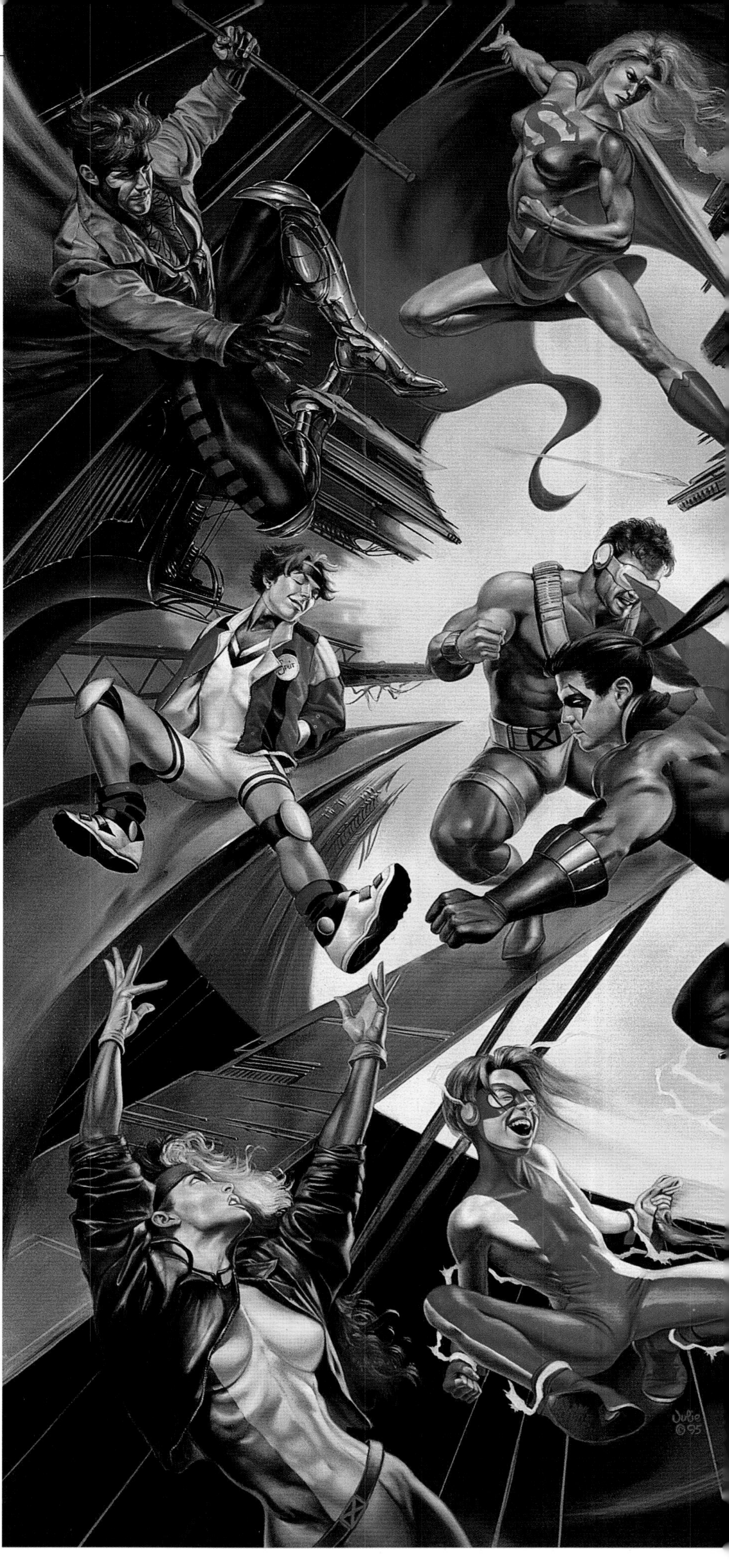
Julie
©95

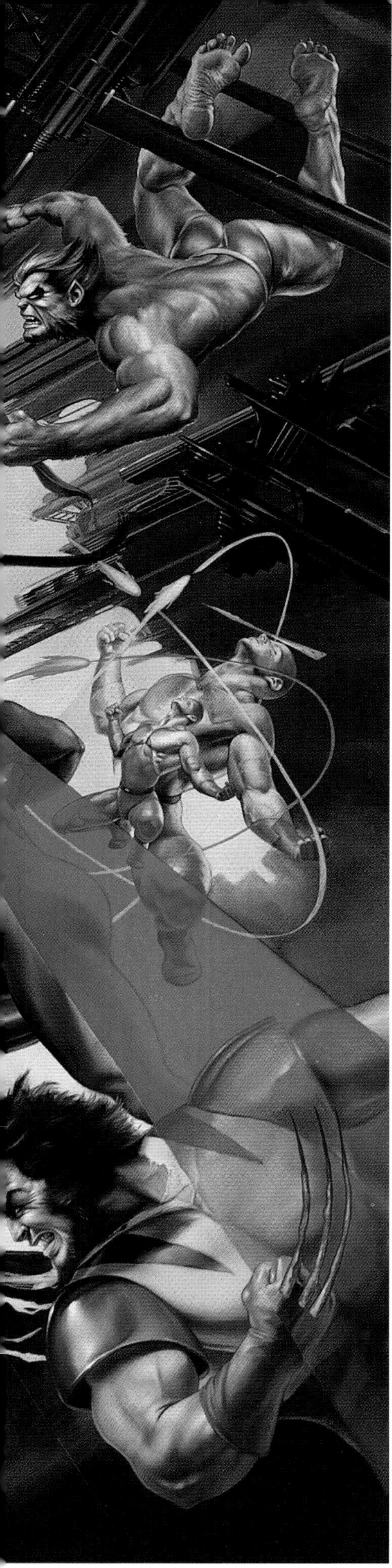

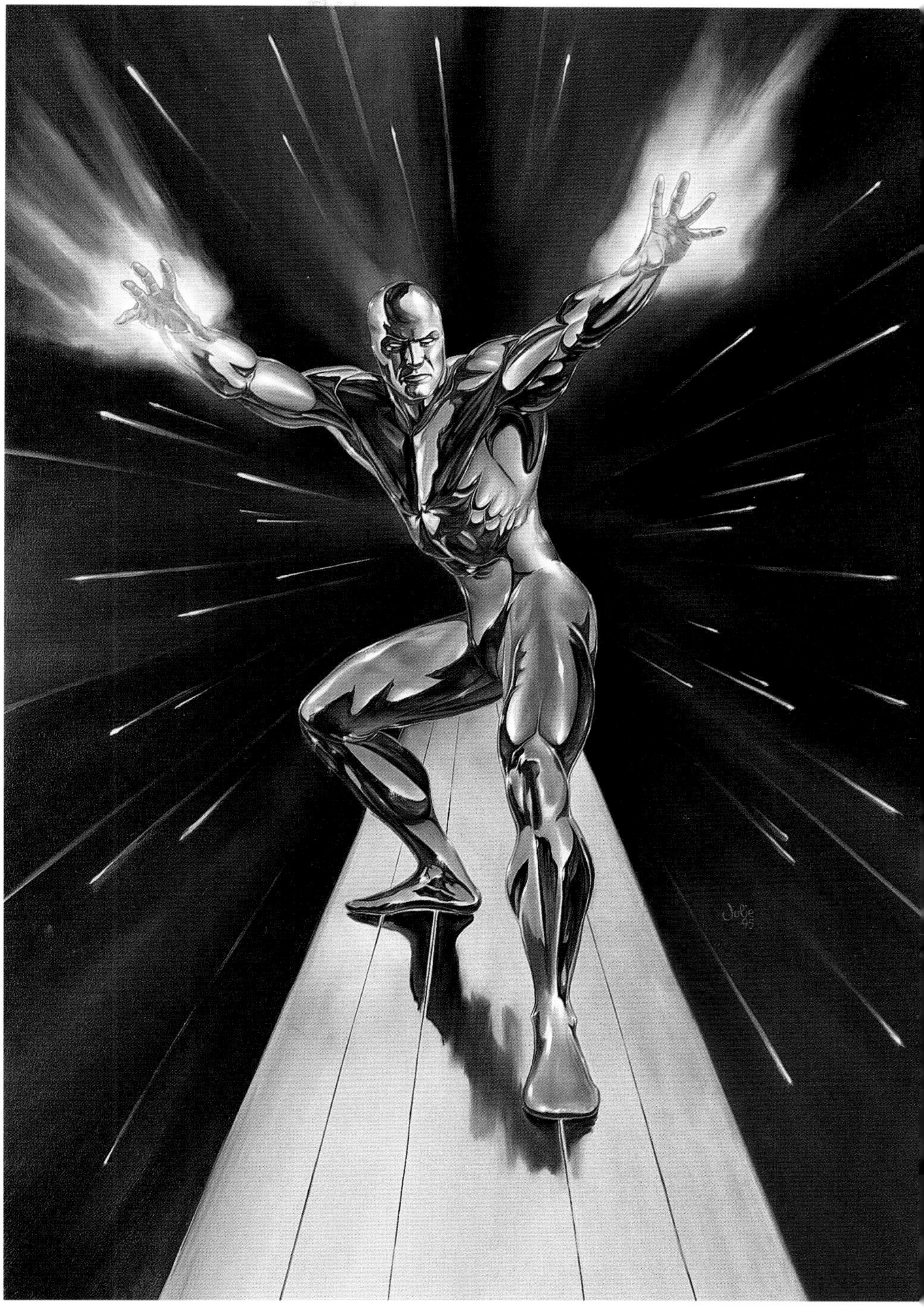

Julie's interest in bodybuilding and gymnastics is an obvious bonus when painting superheroes. She has also studied Tai Chi to an extent and has a general interest in the martial arts which she hopes to pursue in the future; but her action scenes owe as much to her interest in dance, which she practised avidly at school. She uses the language of classical ballet and modern dance to express the mood of her characters.

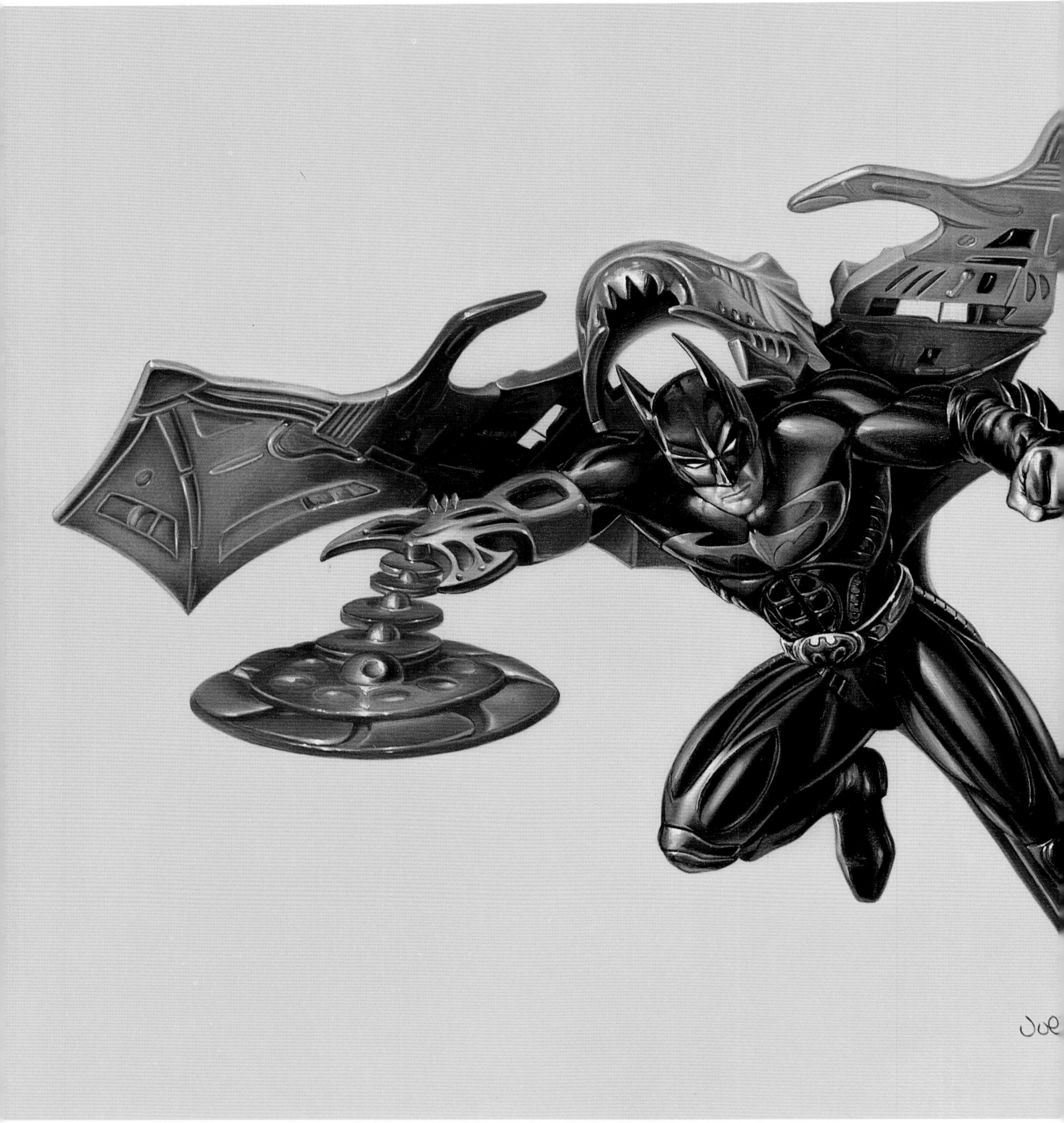

Batman, 1996
Oils, 15 x 20 in (38 x 51 cm)
Toy Box Cover. DC Comics/ Warner Bros.

The curious challenge of this image was to animate the toy within the box so it looked credible as a superhero in action. This was trickier than it sounds because it meant reworking someone else's concept from the inside out.

The degree of freedom an illustrator has in portraying comic book heroes varies. Sometimes the guidelines are very tight, as with characters like Batman or Superman whose costumes have been established over years down to the finest details. Besides capturing that established look the artist's imagination is then limited to the pose and setting. Sometimes there is more freedom, it all depends on the character and publisher. Whatever the case, Julie tries to find a model that fits her conception of the character both in looks and personality.

The great thing for Julie about superheroes is that because of their paint-thin costumes they are basically figure studies that allow her to express her love of the human physique. Life drawing is one of her passions. Strictly speaking, it should not be necessary for superheroes because they are generally pictured in action-packed positions that cannot be held for more than a split second, if possible at all. For these she relies on photos of models acting out the parts in the studio, which are exaggerated as necessary for the desired effect; but she sees life drawing as the basis of all her figure-work because she rarely just tries to repeat in paint what the camera has caught. This requires the intimate knowledge of physique which comes from regular figure studies, working in the round from a static model.

LEFT: *Rogue, 1995*
Oils, 15 x 20 in (38 x 51 cm)
Trading card. Fleer Publishing Co.
TM & © 1999 Marvel Characters, Inc.
All rights reserved.
This was part of a commission for 120
characters which Julie shared with
husband, Boris and which kept them
busy for the best part of two years. Rogue
is another of Julie's favourite characters
whom she has had the luck to illustrate
several times. The composition was
deliberately iconic so that with little
change it could be translated into a
jewellery design.

RIGHT: *Dr Strange, 1996*
Oils, 30 x 20 in (76 x 51 cm)
Trading card. Fleer Publishing Co.
TM & © 1999 Marvel Characters, Inc.
All rights reserved.
A rare chance to concentrate on a head
without having to get the whole figure
into the painting as well. Boris was the
model, though licence was taken with his
features to fit the part.

ABOVE: *Figure study*
Red chalk on toned paper.

Julie enjoys and is inspired by most forms of art but is naturally drawn towards those with an illustrative bent that tell a tale, because that is mostly what she does: 'The stories Boris and I tell in our pictures are kind of telling the viewers who we are. Not everybody has that need but I am one of those who really does.'

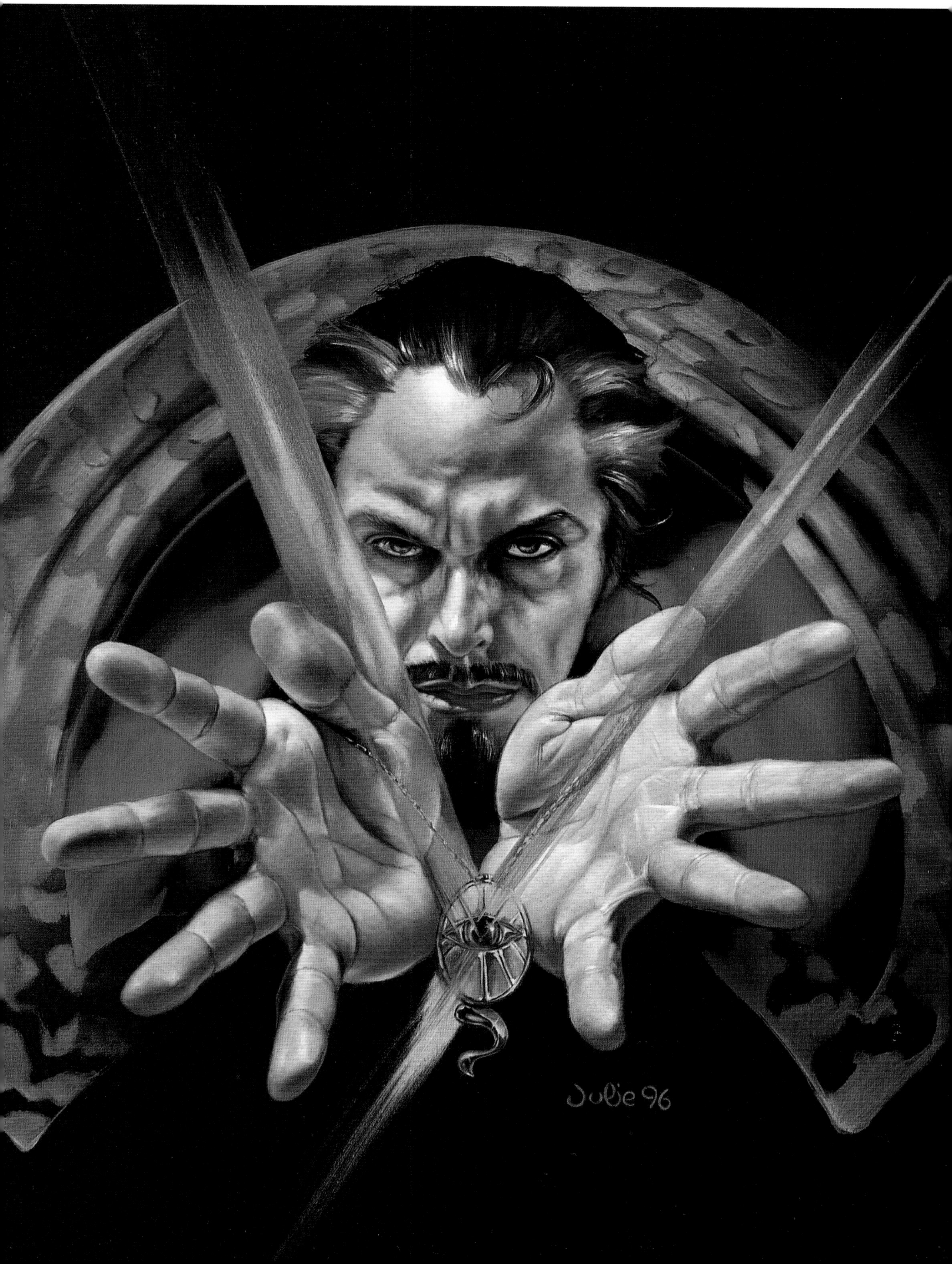
Julie 96

RIGHT: *Vampirella (sketch)*

FAR RIGHT: ***Vampirella, 1996***
Oils, 15 x 20 in (38 x 51 cm)
Comic book cover. Harris Comics.
The brief for this picture was to show Vampirella distraught at finding her home and loved ones destroyed by fire and demons, but the sketch was deemed a bit too close to reality. A general rule for comic book heroines is that whatever their situation, they should still look sexy and in control. So here Vampirella's grief is matched by rage and the urge for revenge.

Preliminary sketches are often drawn straight from the imagination, with reference material being used, if at all, just for the details. Once the concept is given the go-ahead, a model is booked to pose for the painting. The attraction of sketches is their spontaneity and dynamism, but working from live models injects a degree of realism that has become one of Julie's trademarks.

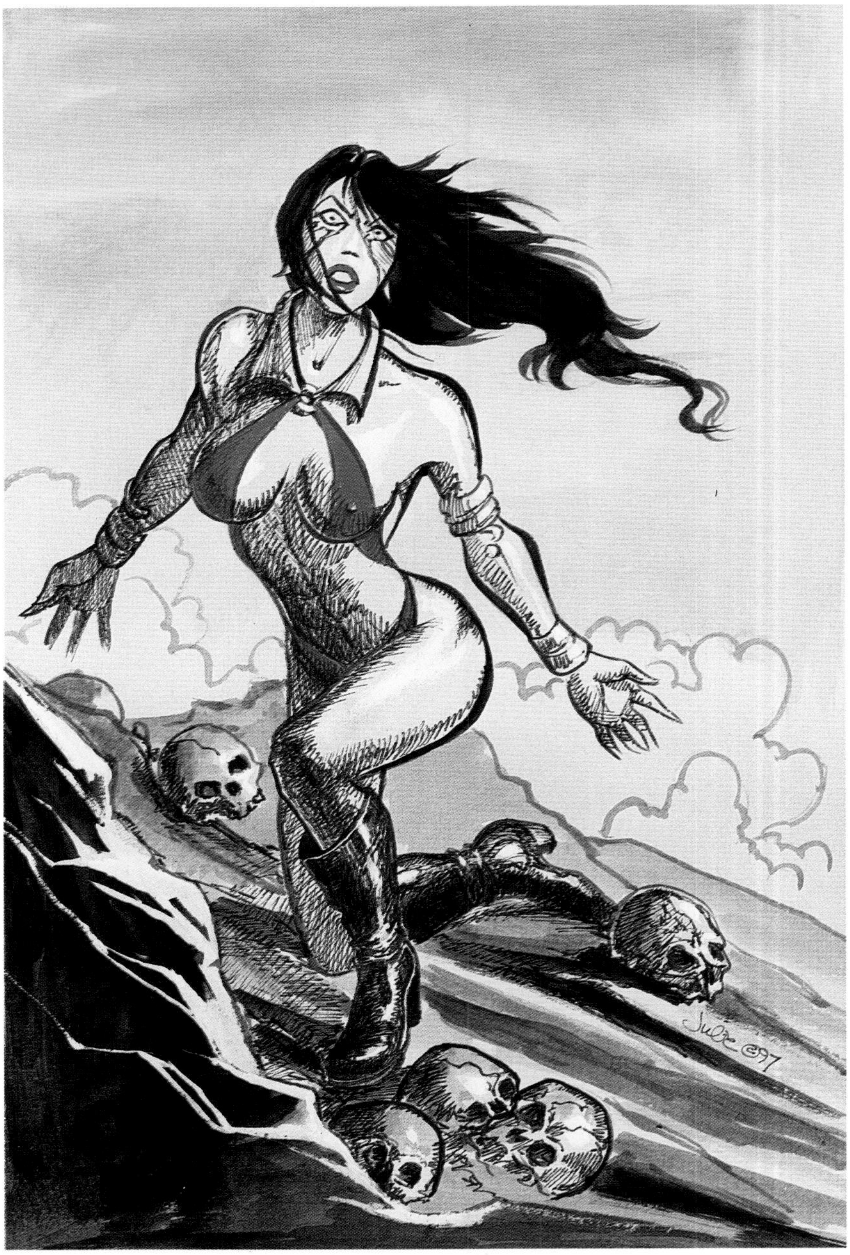
Julie ©97

Julie: 'I am a person who enjoys time to myself for reflection and sorting thoughts, and many of my pictures reflect this; but I also enjoy time with people. I tend to need time to process thoughts and try to put them into the "big picture". I know that sometimes people may have the impression that I am a kind of solitary person, but that's not really so. I have a comfortable balance between being a "loner" and being with company. I do get many of my best ideas while I'm alone, driving or walking or just doing some mindless task, but I also get a lot of my best ideas while I'm with people.'

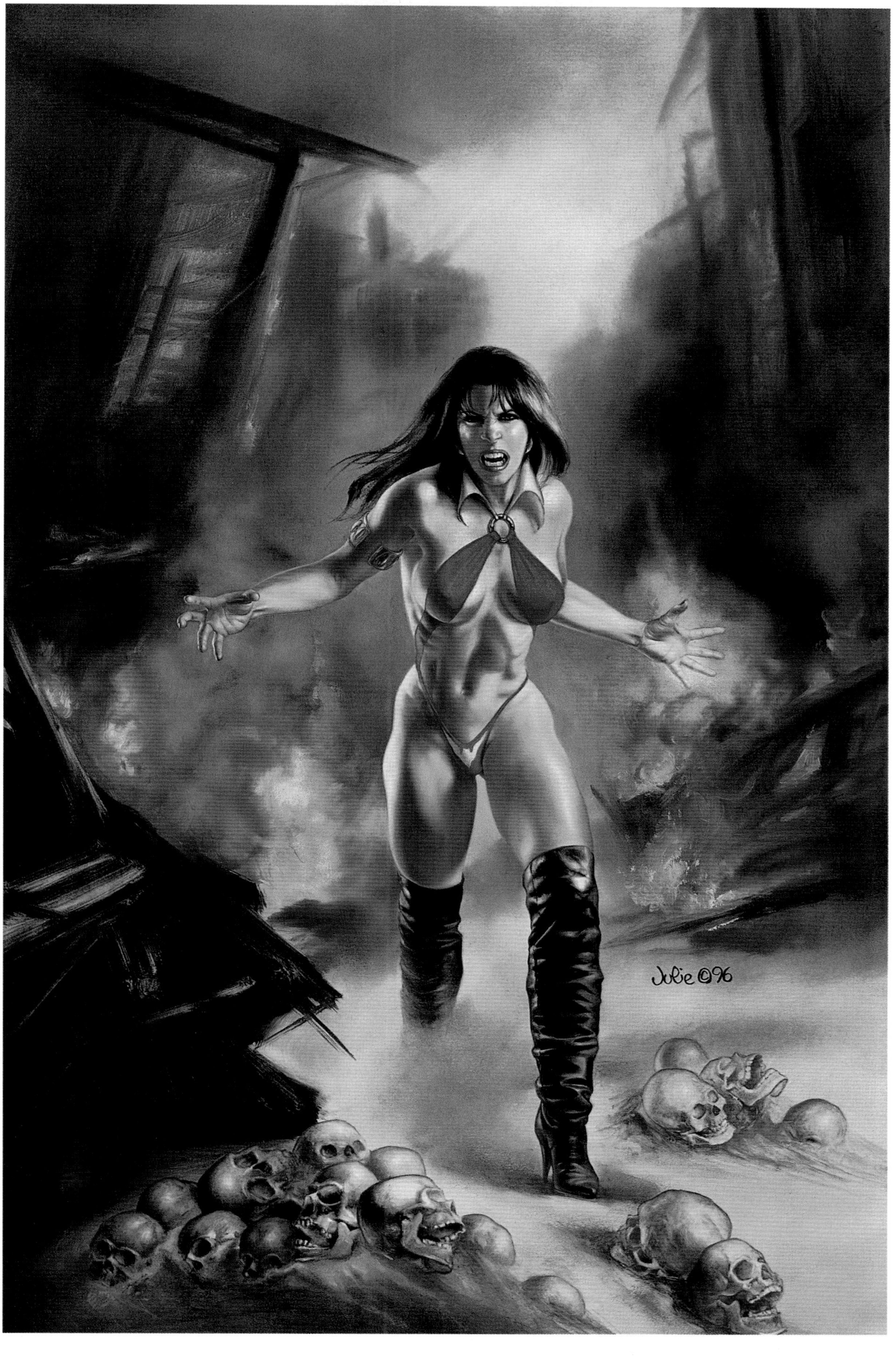
Julie ©96

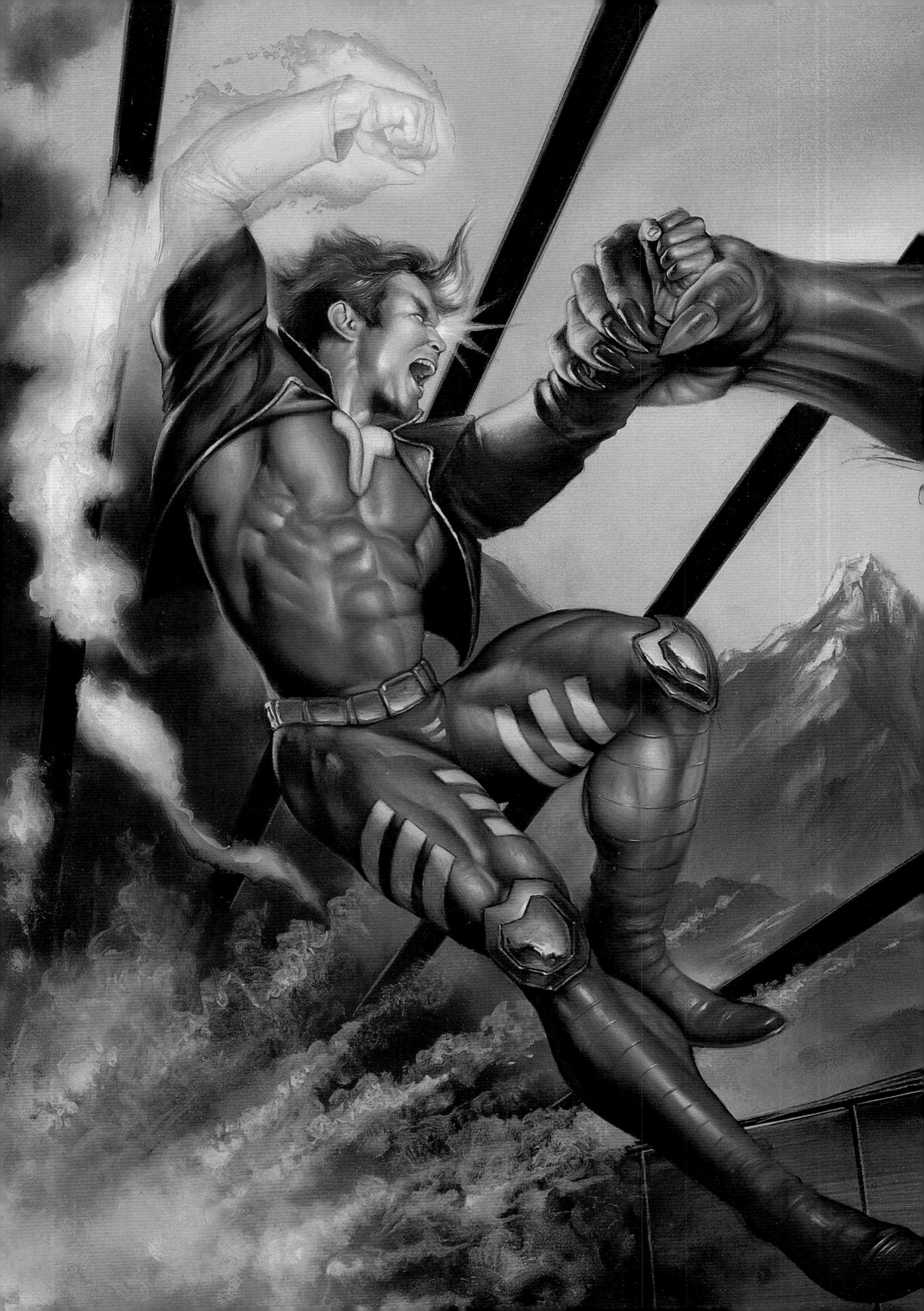

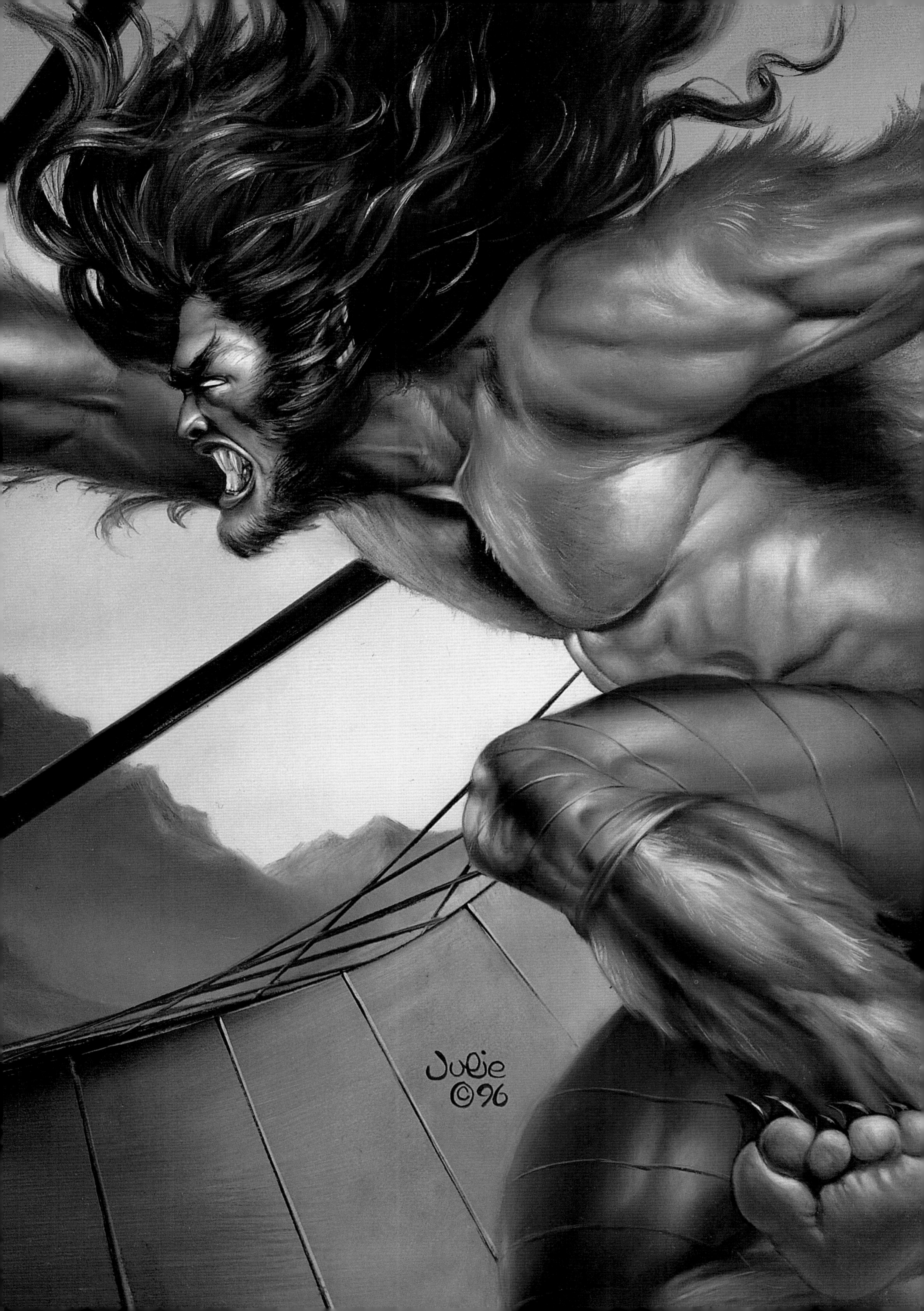
Julie
©96

PREVIOUS PAGES: ***X-Man vs. Dark Beast, 1996***
Oils, 30 x 20 in (76 x 51 cm)
Trading card. Fleer Publishing Co.

A scene designed to be split into two separate trading cards. With this series it was very much left up to Julie and Boris to come up with the scenes, working simply from a list of characters. The publishers kept the power of veto over the results but it was seldom exercised. With comic and book covers there are usually tighter guidelines for what is required and much discussion before the final painting goes ahead.

RIGHT: ***Spiderman in the Valley of the Lizard, 1997***
Oils, 15 x 20 in (38 x 51 cm)
Book cover. Byron Preiss Multimedia.

Byron Preiss specializes in paperback novels based on comic book characters. The covers are refreshing because they have different constraints to the comic books themselves or to trading cards. Julie liked the lizard character so although he is obviously meant to be scary she added a touch of humour.

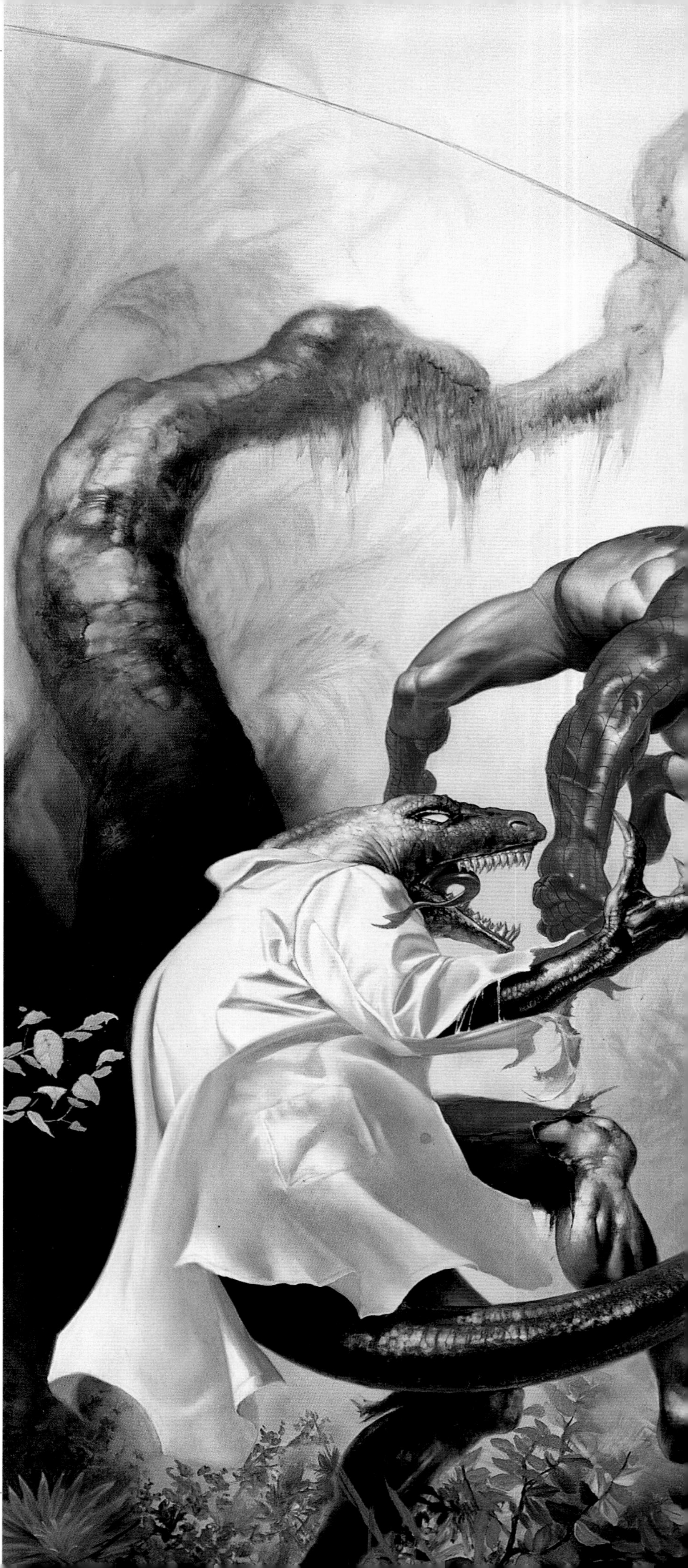

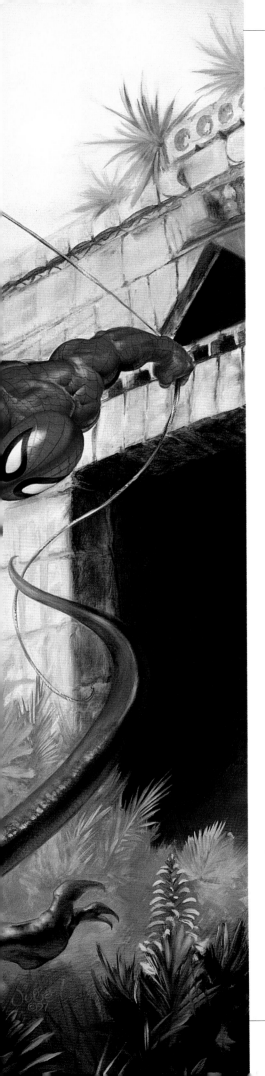

Julie: 'Nature is very soothing to me even when the weather isn't so calm, such as during a storm (I've been known to go to the beach in Texas during powerful storms just to see the weather, although I did recently pass up the chance to be there during a hurricane . . . I'm not that crazy!) and I enjoy being around nature when I'm alone in a different way than when I'm with company. When I'm alone with nature, I really feel like I'm some kind of wild energy spirit. When I'm with company in nature, I get to see how the people I'm with are affected by it and connect with them in a different way.

'In sports, my feelings are the same. I like individual sports more than team sports, but it wouldn't be any fun at all if there weren't other people involved. When I was in gymnastics, I enjoyed pushing my limits on the uneven parallel bars, competing with my own last performance, but the other girls in my class provided wonderful friendships and feelings of mutual respect. For the first year that I started bodybuilding, I worked out completely alone at home with free weights. When I started entering competitions and met some of the competitors, I realized what I was missing by being in training all by myself; not only fun and companionship, but inspiration, motivation, and the knowledge and experience that other bodybuilders could offer. So, I would say that while I'm extremely self-motivated, I am enriched to the point of THRIVING by having people in my life.'

Although no longer involved in competitive bodybuilding, Julie still trains with weights five days a week, really enjoying the whole process of working out and feeling strong. When younger her motivation was much more about how she looked than it is now because general health has become her priority. Within bodybuilding there comes a point where the two can come into conflict. Power-lifting weights can wreck

LEFT: *Captain Atom, 1994*
Oils, 15 x 20 in (38 x 51 cm)
Trading Card. DC Comics.
TM & © 1998 DC Comics. All rights
reserved. Used with permission.
Julie enjoys the focus of this kind of
picture, where the eye immediately knows
where to go and finds a single visual
statement that says it all. She was
particularly pleased with this character
and the way his fierce expression is
reflected in the pose.

RIGHT: *Lady Rawhide Rides, 1995*
Oils, 15 x 20 in (38 x 51 cm)
Comic book cover. Topps Co.
Lady Rawhide is an offshoot from the
Zorro comic books. Having appeared as
an incidental character she blossomed into
a star in her own right.

ABOVE: *Figure study*
Oils.

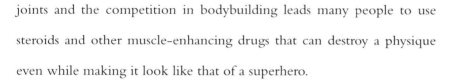

joints and the competition in bodybuilding leads many people to use steroids and other muscle-enhancing drugs that can destroy a physique even while making it look like that of a superhero.

These days training at the gym is combined with careful nutrition. For a few years she and Boris went through a junk food phase, but they are now very careful with their diet and have even become vegetarians. Before she met Boris, Julie was considering becoming a physical therapist and in a way she now acts out this vocation within the family. If she were not a professional artist she thinks she would be working in some medical field with art as a sideline. She really loves cooking and reading books on nutrition and health.

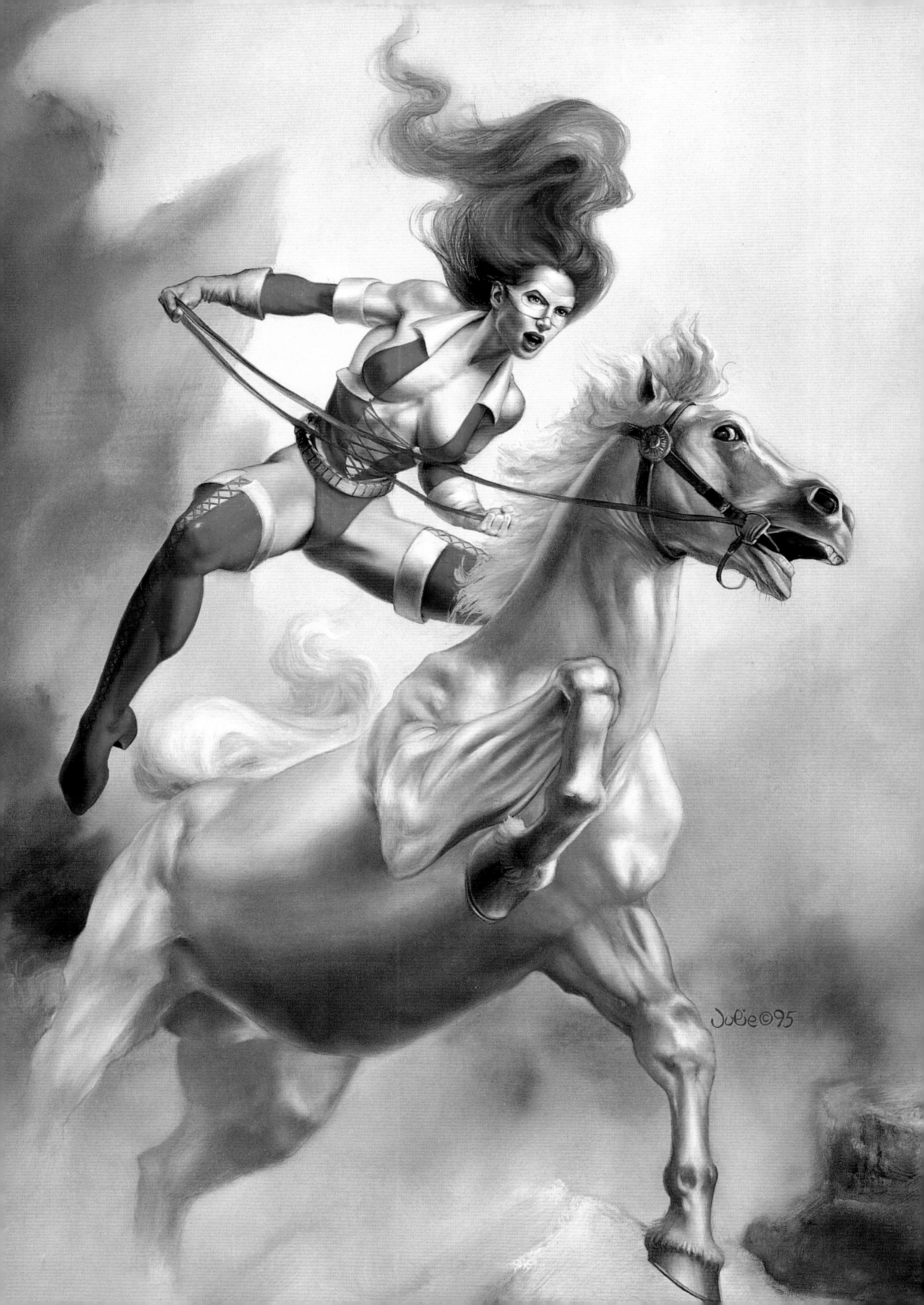
Julie©95

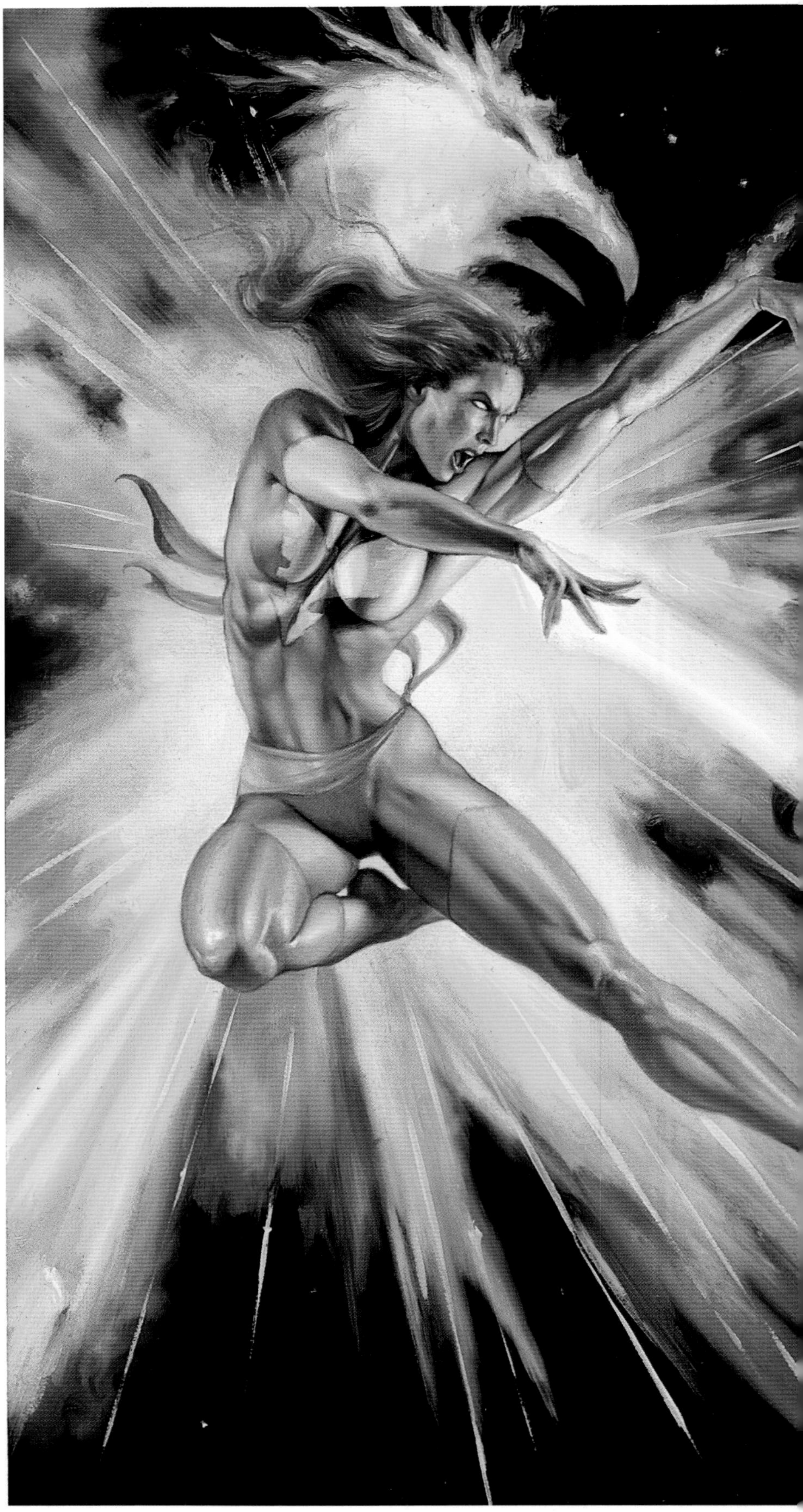

Phoenix vs. Magneto, 1996
Oils, 30 x 20 in (76 x 51 cm)
Trading card. Fleer Publishing Co.

This is another double trading card design. Phoenix, on the left, is the daughter of Jean Gray and Scott Summers. She was accepted into the X-Men when she went back in time to thwart their great enemies, the Sentinels.

Magneto controls magnetism and hence the atomic sub-structure of matter, which he can shape as he wills. Possibly the most powerful of the X-Men, he is the greatest champion of mutants against the hostile universe, but he so often gets carried away that it is hard to know if he is a hero or villain.

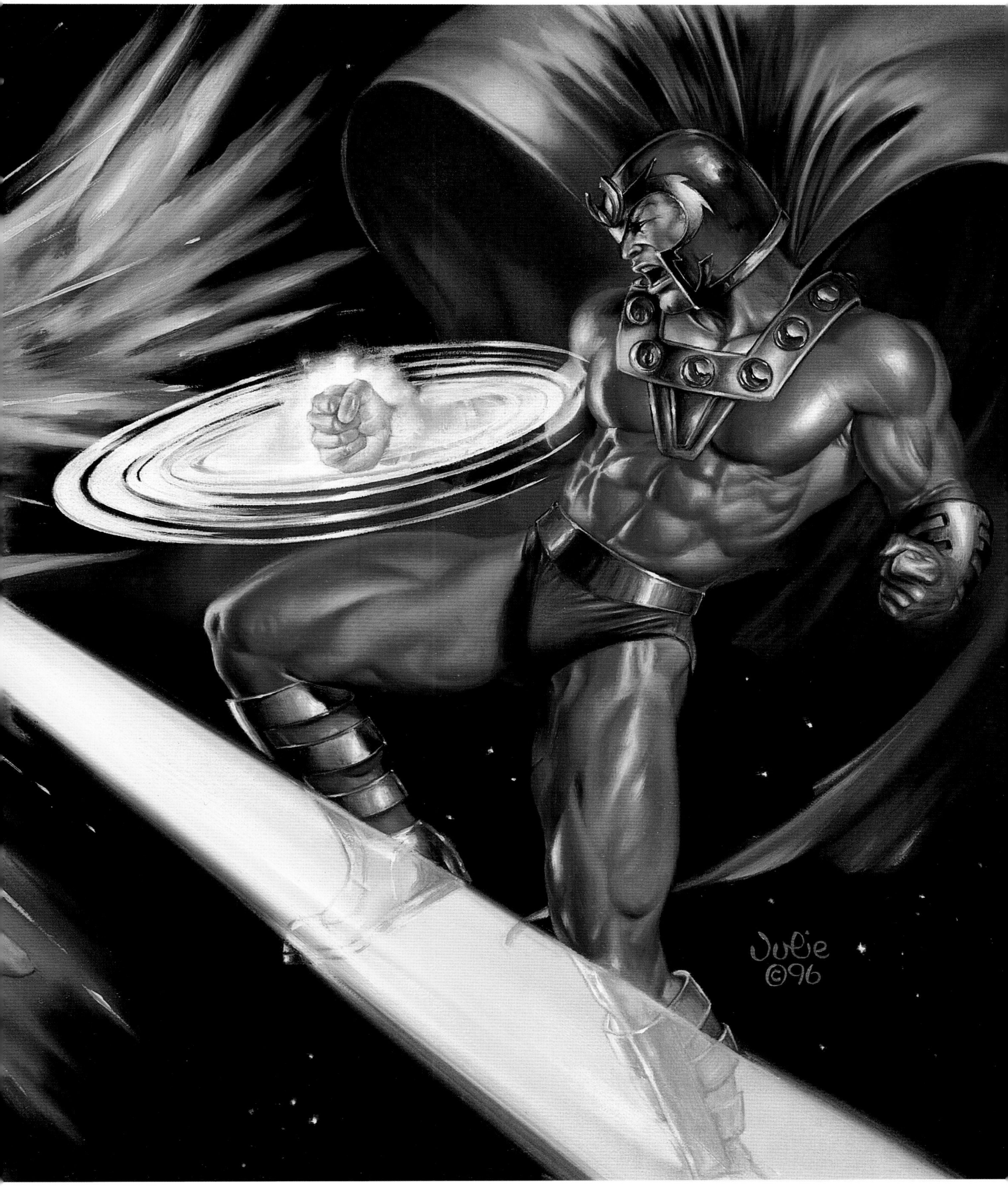
Julie
©96

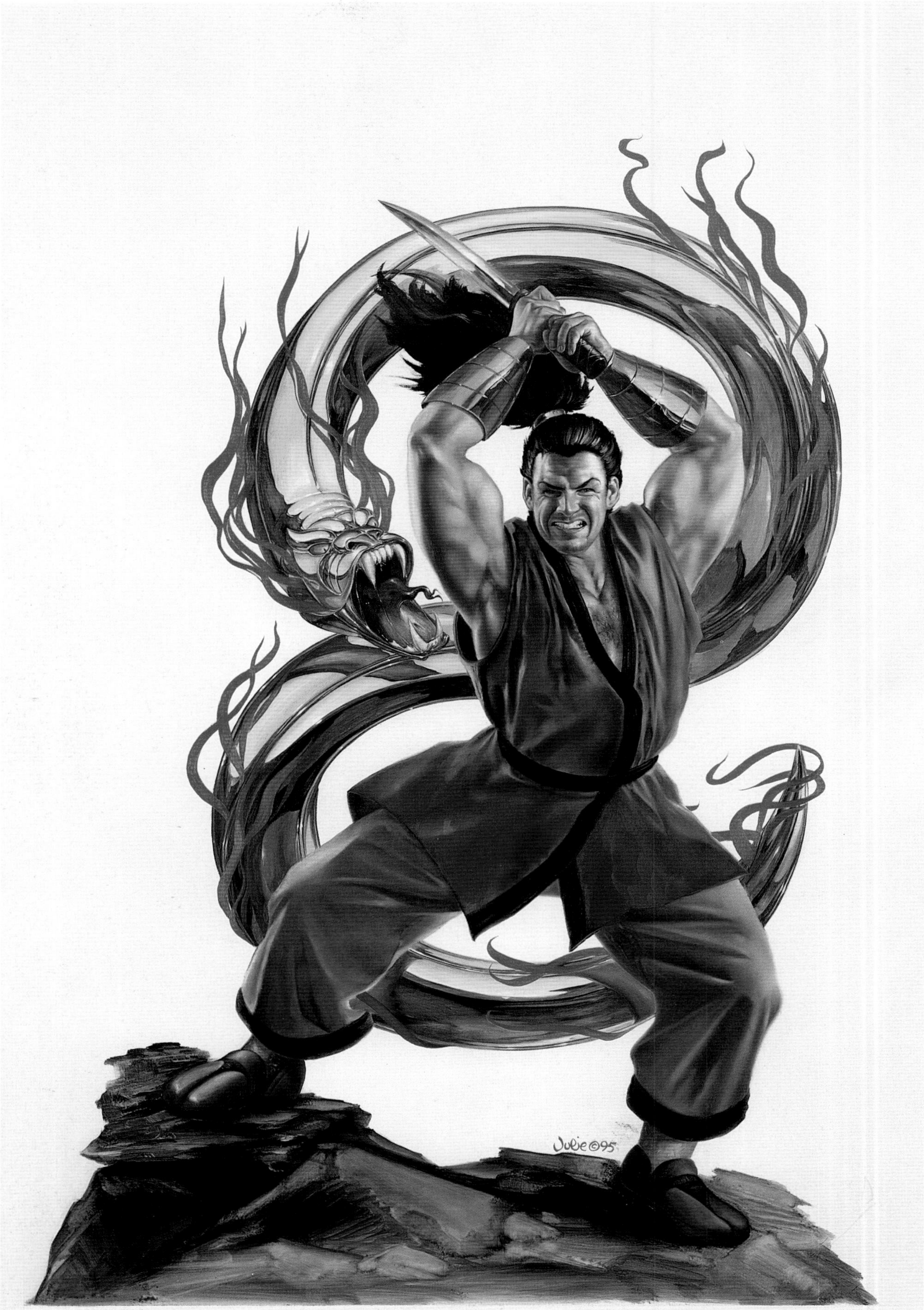
Julie©95

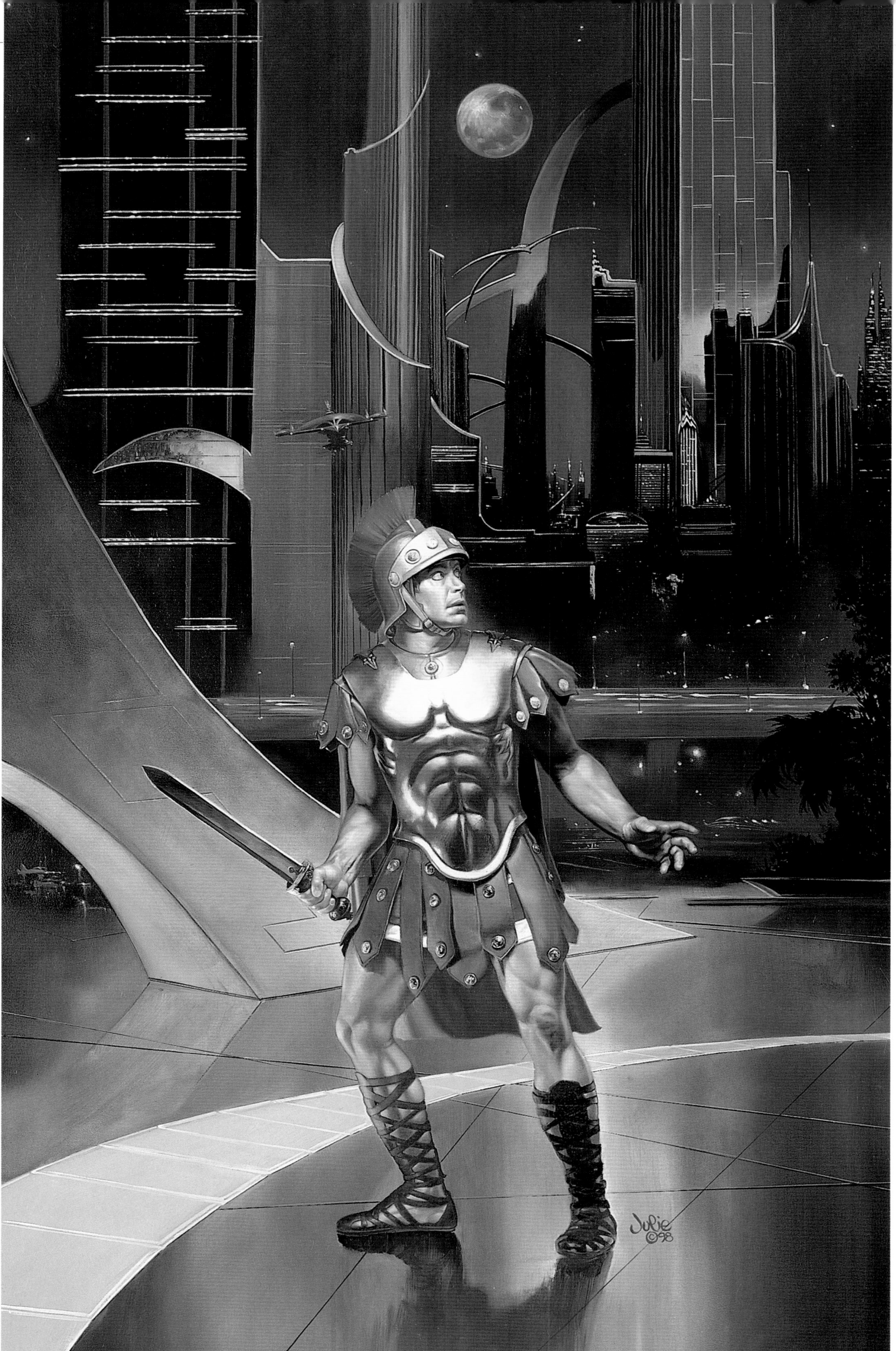
Julie
©98

PAGE 28: ***Uroborus, 1995***
Oils, 15 x 20 in (38 x 51 cm)
Trading card. Comic Images.
The samurai figure here was originally intended as a large cardboard cut-out display to promote a video game. The plan fell through, but later another chance came along to use it as a trading card by adding the background. The Worm Uroborus is a mystical serpent said to encircle the universe and eat its own tail. This was partly what attracted Julie, but she confesses it was equally because the name simply sounds like Boris'.

PAGE 29: ***Time Travel Mishap, 1998***
Oils, 30 x 20 in (76 x 51 cm)
Book cover. Tor Books.
This was designed for the tale of a Roman centurion transported to the future. The floor is deliberately hard, cold and shiny to give a futuristic touch, and also to throw in a little uncertainty, because it looks almost too slippery to stand up on.

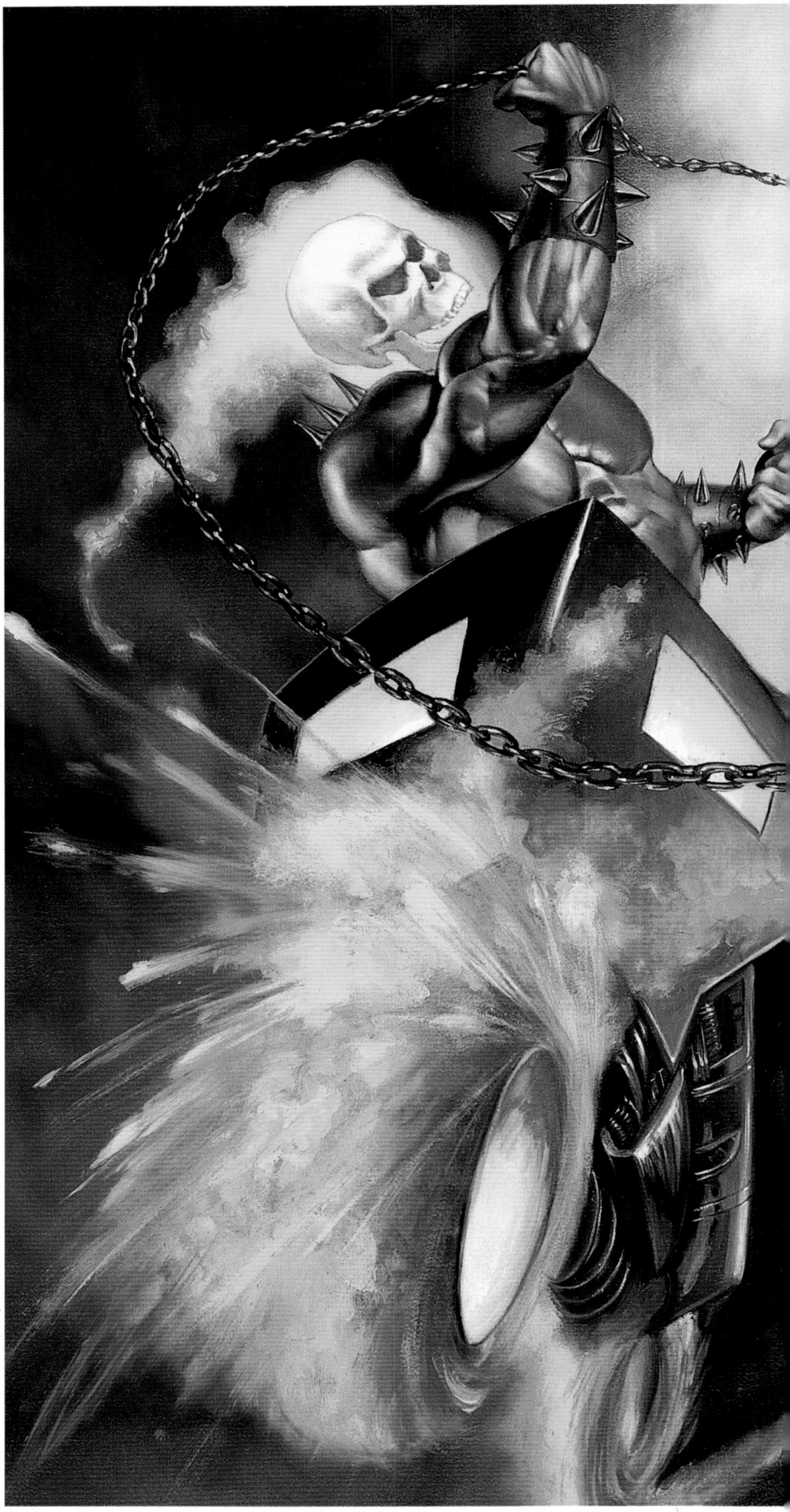

RIGHT: ***Ghost Rider vs. Blackout, 1996***
Oils, 30 x 20 in (76 x 51 cm)
Trading card. Fleer Publishing Co.

Boris was the model for Blackout when his hair grew down to the middle of his back. The scene was designed to be split into two separate trading cards. As in other cases Fleer suggested the pairing of characters to remind collectors of particular storylines, but beyond that it was up to the artist.

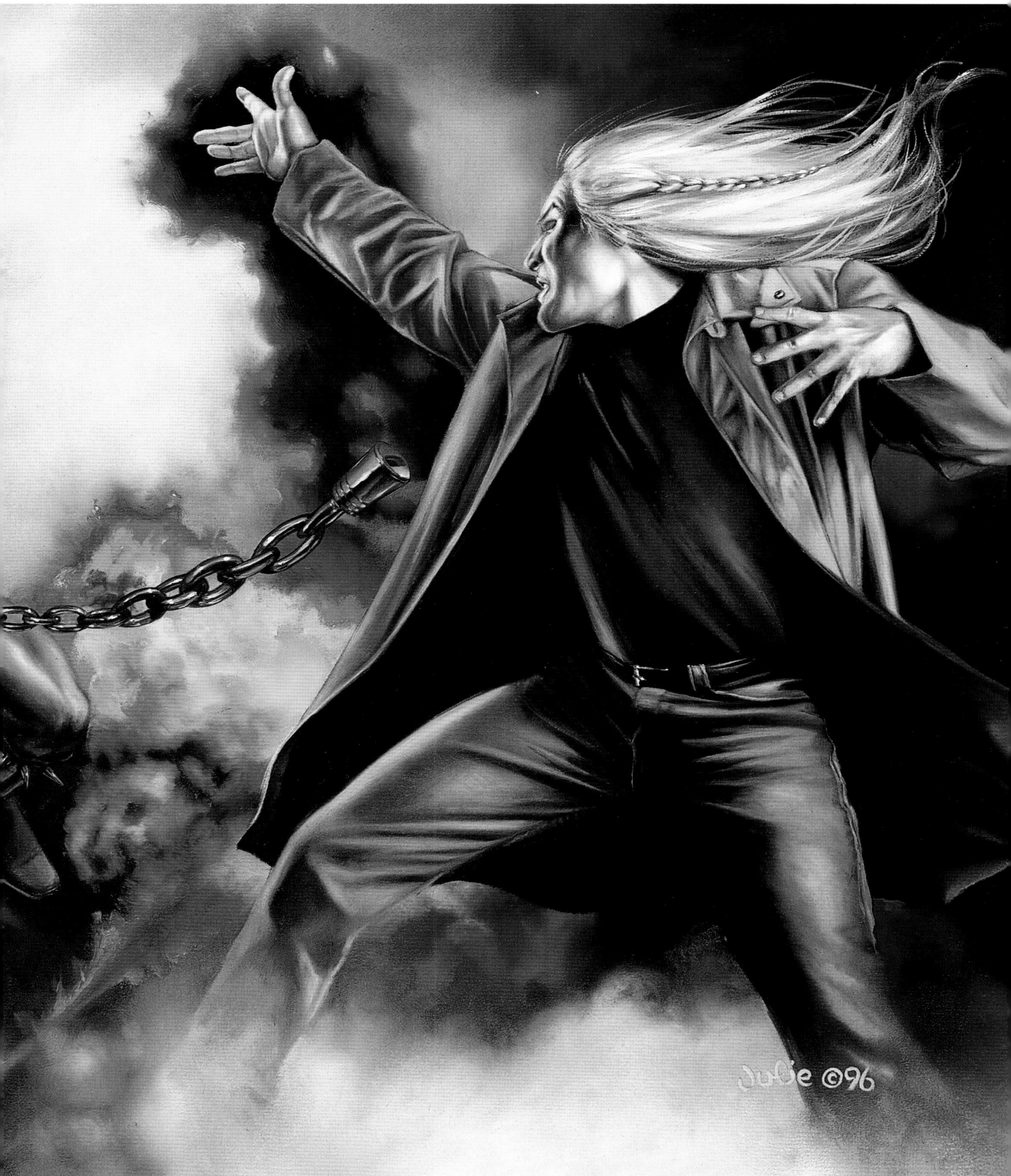
Julie ©96

Although she no longer competes in bodybuilding, Julie has not lost the urge that made her do so, the energy has just been channelled elsewhere: 'I am a very competitive person but it is sometimes misunderstood. I'm not really trying to beat other people. Of course I like to win because that's better than losing, but really what I am looking for is someone who will push me to my own limits. Like in tennis, it's very frustrating to play someone way above or below your own level.

'In art Boris and I challenge and inspire each other, but we're not trying to score points off each other. It's good, clean fun. We both are inspired by that kind of competition.'

With so much in common, they have many areas in which to compete, but they also have separate interests. One of them is Julie's love of drawing and painting in the open, whereas Boris feels more comfortable in the privacy of the studio. He is a self-confessed city boy, having grown up in the suburbs of Lima in Peru, and he developed an early

ABOVE: *Figure study*
Charcoal.

OPPOSITE: *Lady Rawhide vs. Scarlet Fever, 1996*
Oils, 15 x 20 in (38 x 51 cm)
Comic book cover. Topps Co. Originally this character's name was Anita Santiago and she became Lady Rawhide to avenge her brothers' mutilation at the hands of one Captain Monasterio. Her more usual weapon is a bullwhip. Writer Don McGregor invested all his talent in the series, which became his pet project and one of Julie's favourites too. She enjoys the stories for their soap-opera-like texture. Here we see Lady Rawhide about to duel with her great rival. As ever the suspicion and animosity between them is not carried beyond the point where they still look sexy.

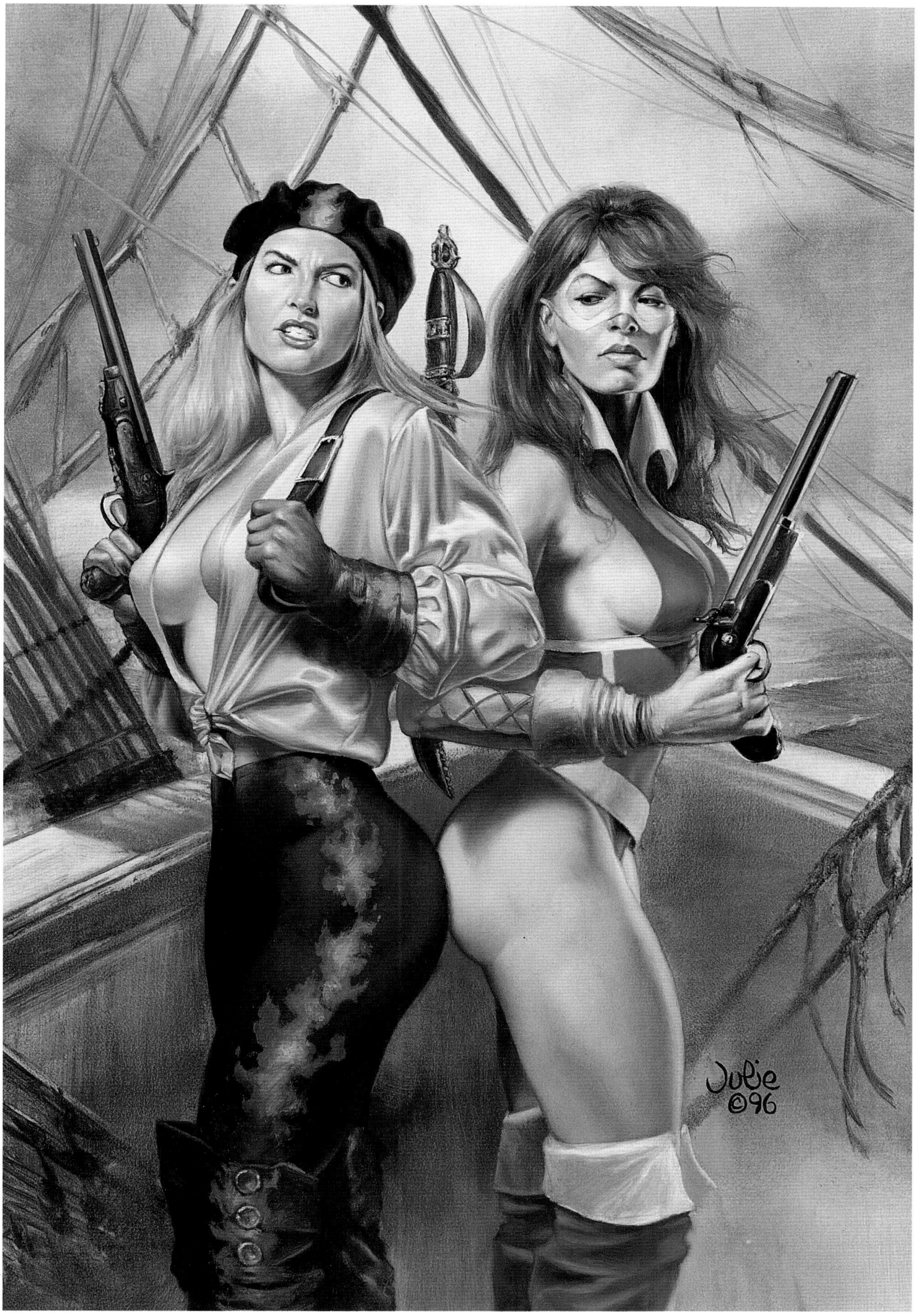
Julie
©96

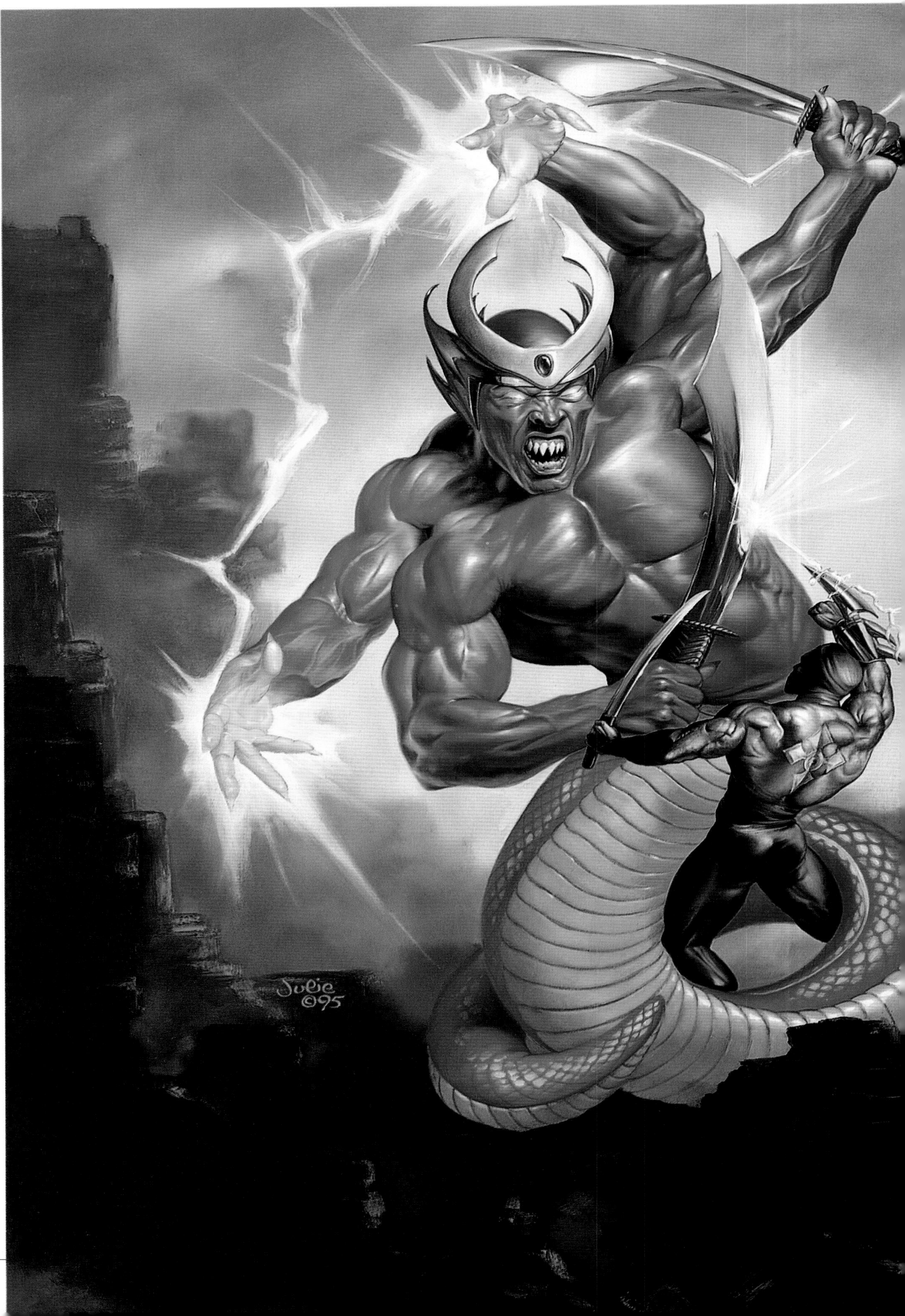
Julie
©95

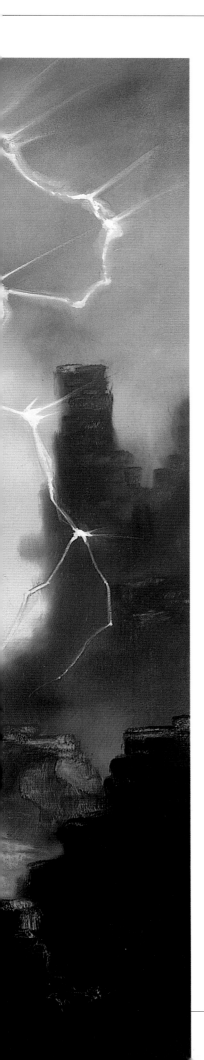

taste for the art and cultural life that only cities provide. When Julie feels like a day in the country, she generally goes off alone or with her sons. As they grow up, such moments are becoming increasingly precious and Julie would love the chance to be their parent all over again. Not because she would like to undo any mistakes, but simply because it has all been so much fun.

Julie's sons pop up in many of her fantasy paintings, which make an interesting record of their adolescence that is often more revealing than family snaps because they are more dramatic. Fantasy art is a natural home for Julie because she has always had an extremely vivid imagination. As a small child she believed cartoon characters were as real in some way as live action TV or movies. Of course, she could see there was some difference, but she did want to marry Mighty Mouse. This helps when it comes to slipping in and out of the fantasy worlds of her own paintings, but she has the great fortune of being able to keep one foot firmly rooted in reality and one in the mystical colourful world of fantasy. By bringing fantasy into the real world and bringing reality into the realm of fantasy, Julie gives us access to other dimensions through her art.

Another recurring theme in Julie's paintings is courage. This is not just because superheroes are what she is most often asked to paint, it also happens to be one of the themes she most enjoys painting. As in sports it is not just the victory that she wants to capture, though it is true we rarely see her characters in defeat; what she is more keen to show is

Red Demon, 1995
Oils, 15 x 20 in (38 x 51 cm)
Computer game cover.
An exercise in crimson skin.

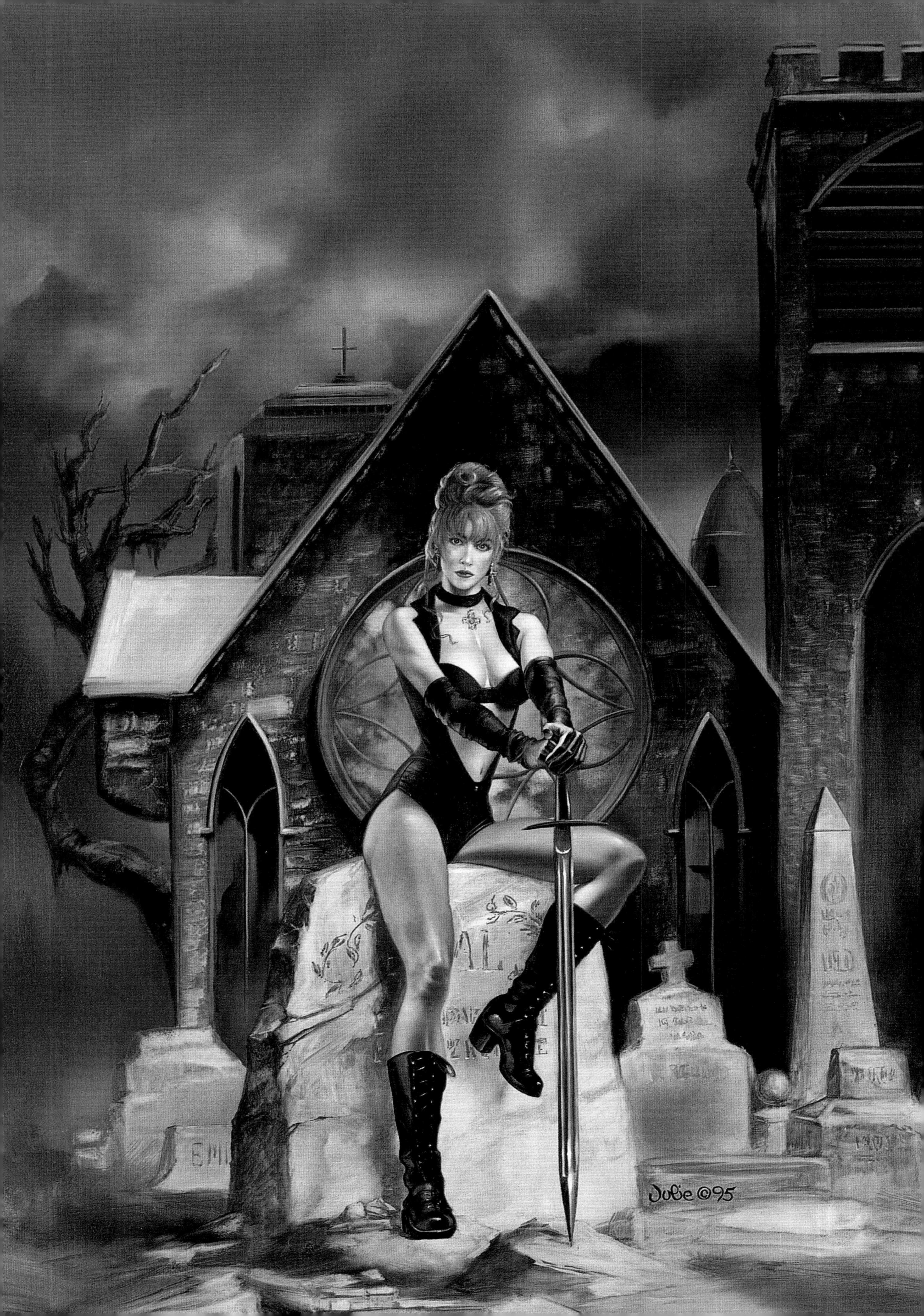
Julie ©95

The Guardian, 1995
Oils, 20 x 15 in (51 x 38 cm)
Comic book cover.
The model for this picture is the wife of the comic strip artist so both rather enjoyed having her portrayed here as the heroine Avengalyne. The church in the background is a real one in New York.

defiance of defeat whatever the odds. Courage means a lot to Julie as a person: 'I've had some really rough times to deal with in my life and learned the hard way the importance of keeping going despite everything.' What Julie has in a sense aimed for in her life is to become her own superhero, and this is something she always seeks to inspire in others, both through personal contact and through her paintings.

Julie feels that much of her urge to be strong on all levels comes from her childhood and the very difficult relationship she had with her mother, who was an alcoholic on top of having an unstable personality disorder and so was unable to provide the moral support most children get from their mothers. She died in 1985, but with hindsight Julie feels that in many ways her mother had, in effect, died years before and that there had never really been much chance of reaching a real understanding with her.

At the time it hurt a lot, but in the long run Julie feels much good has come out of the relationship: 'It forced a lot of acceptance on me and pushed me to make myself as strong as possible, which has helped in a lot of things. It was one of my greatest lessons. My mother was a big part of why it is so important to have all this heroism in my work, and self-sufficiency in my life. Other people can relate to that in the pictures.'

In everyday life it means that being a mother is one of the main things in her life, and not just to her own kids, but anyone in her circle who needs mothering.

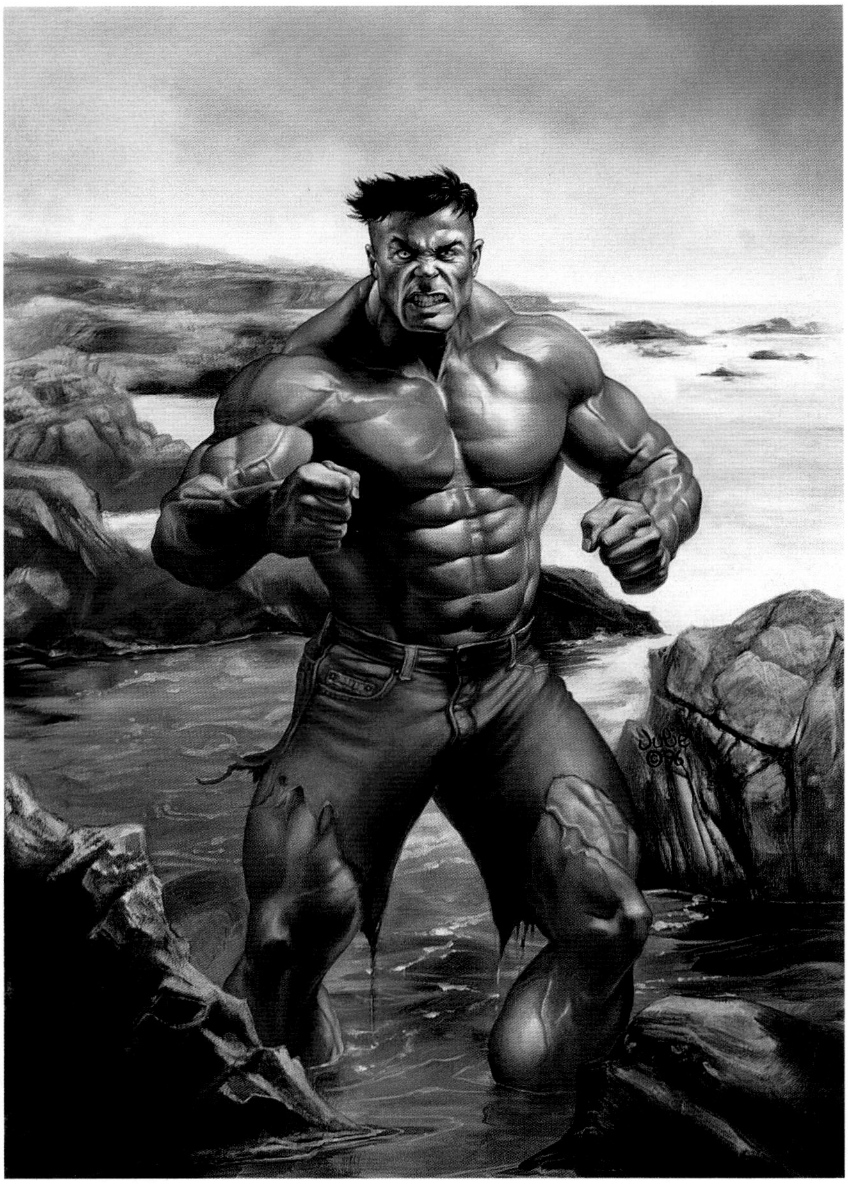

LEFT: *Gray Hulk, 1996*
Oils, 15 x 20 in (38 x 51 cm)
Trading card. Fleer Publishing Co.

The Hulk is a more complicated character than many in comics and his moods are open to a variety of visual interpretations. Having a free hand, Julie chose here to set him against the northern Californian coast which she had recently visited, hence the background being painted in a more specific way than usual.

RIGHT: *Shi, 1995*
Oils, 15 x 20 in (38 x 51 cm)
Comic book cover. Crusade Comics.
Julie: 'A lot of comic companies respond to the way I portray women. I give them strength and dignity as well as retaining their sexy look. In a way, it is a feminist statement of empowerment for me, that women can be both beautiful and in control of their lives. I do a lot of paintings with this message. I put in a lot of my own feeling of being self-sufficient.'

Colour is often as important as attitude and composition in Julie's paintings. The choice of colour can also reflect what is going on inside an artist as well as what is happening in the picture. At one time when Boris was going through a major upheaval in his life, he received a letter from a fan who said she had guessed from his latest calendar that he must be going through a bad period. This is great if the artist's mood matches the one they are aiming for in the picture, but it can otherwise cause problems. The trick is to make sure that you are in the mood of the painting and then just let the colours flow naturally from you into the picture.

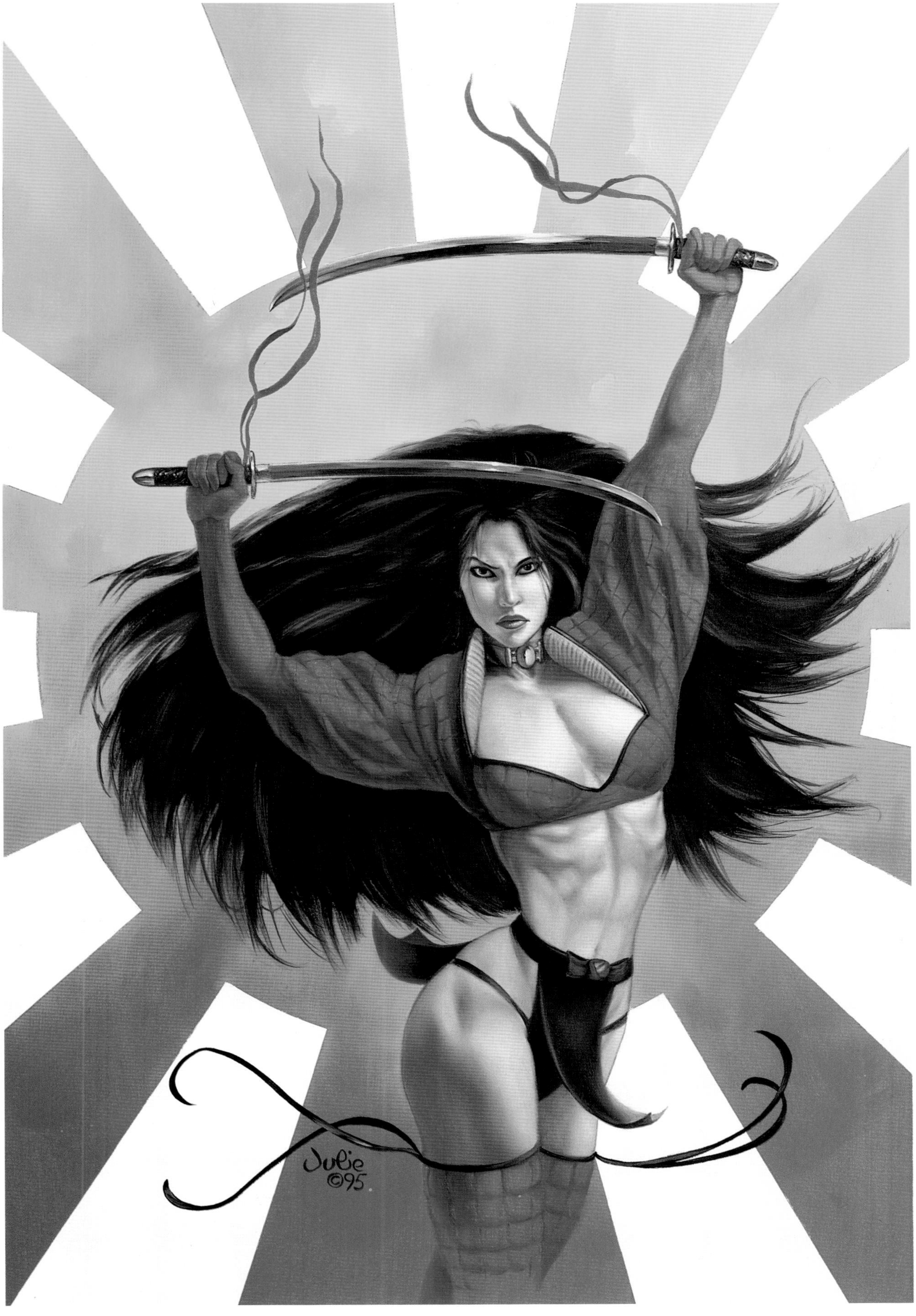
Julie
©95

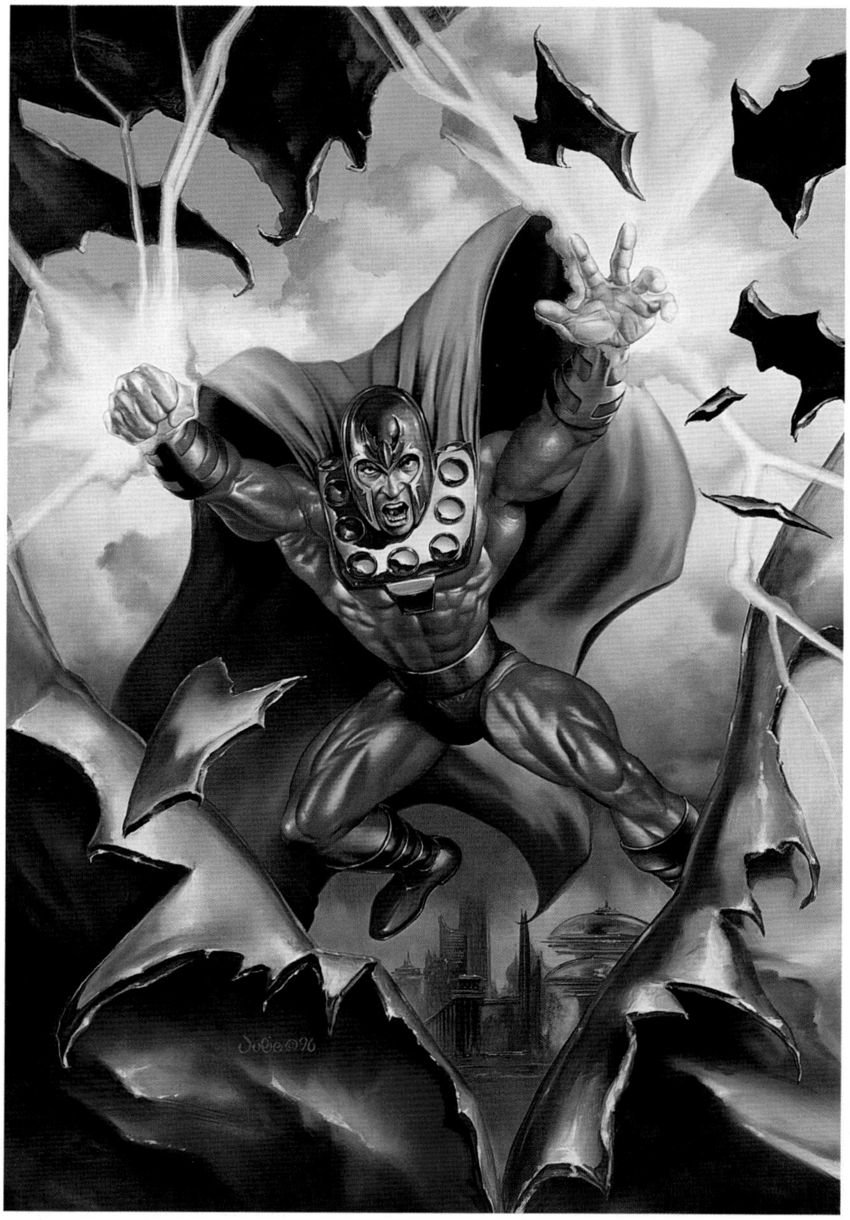

LEFT: ***Magneto, 1996***
Oils, 15 x 20 in (38 x 51 cm)
Poster. Marvel Comics.

One of two posters commissioned by Marvel just before they hit a patch of financial turbulence which sidelined the posters for a while. This is its first public showing, though the chances are that some time in the future it will be published as intended. The model was Ron Coleman, Mr Universe 1995 and gold medallist in the Pan American Games that year. Besides this, he is a versatile actor and appears in almost half of both Julie's and Boris' paintings requiring powerful male physiques.

RIGHT: ***The X-Women 1996***
Oils, 15 x 20 in (38 x 51 cm)
Poster. Marvel Comics.

Although still unpublished as a poster, this was enormously popular as a magazine cover, perhaps because it catches the current mood of 'girl power' in the United States which is apparent in all the media, particularly film and television. Originally it was less aggressive but at an art director's suggestion Julie beefed it up.

OVERLEAF: ***Hellspawn, 1994***
Oils, 20 x 15 in (51 x 38 cm)
Video game cover. Sega.
This is a gargoyle that comes to life in the game. The model for the body and general pose was again Ron Coleman. The rest of course was just imagination.

Colour can enhance the seriousness or humour of a picture. Mostly the choices are spontaneous and instinctive, but it helps to have a grounding in colour theory. Julie studied this at school and has built greatly on that knowledge since, especially over the past few years, but she rarely uses it in a totally calculated way; it just helps to speed up decisions and to check from time to time that the picture is going in the right direction.

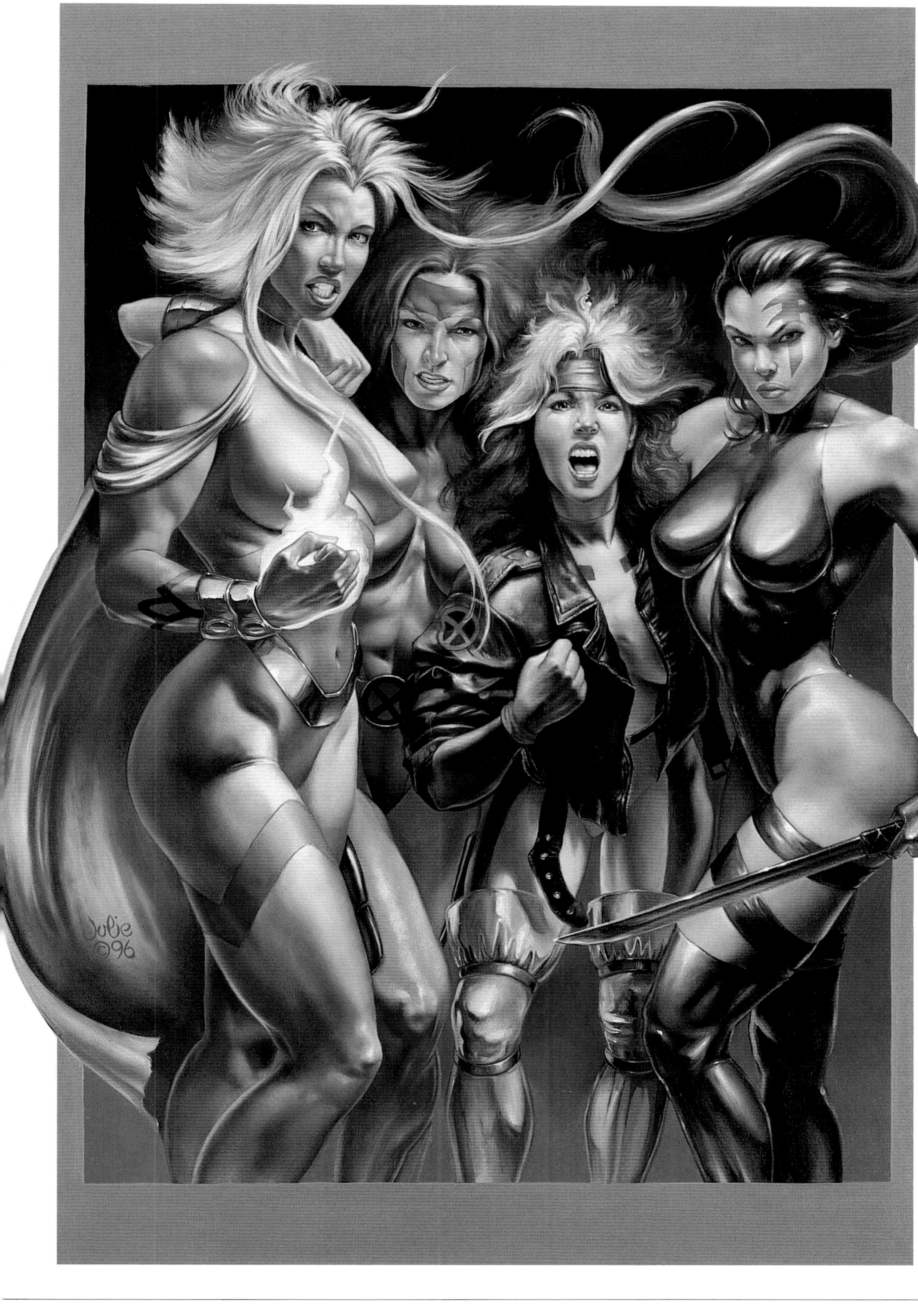
Julie
©96

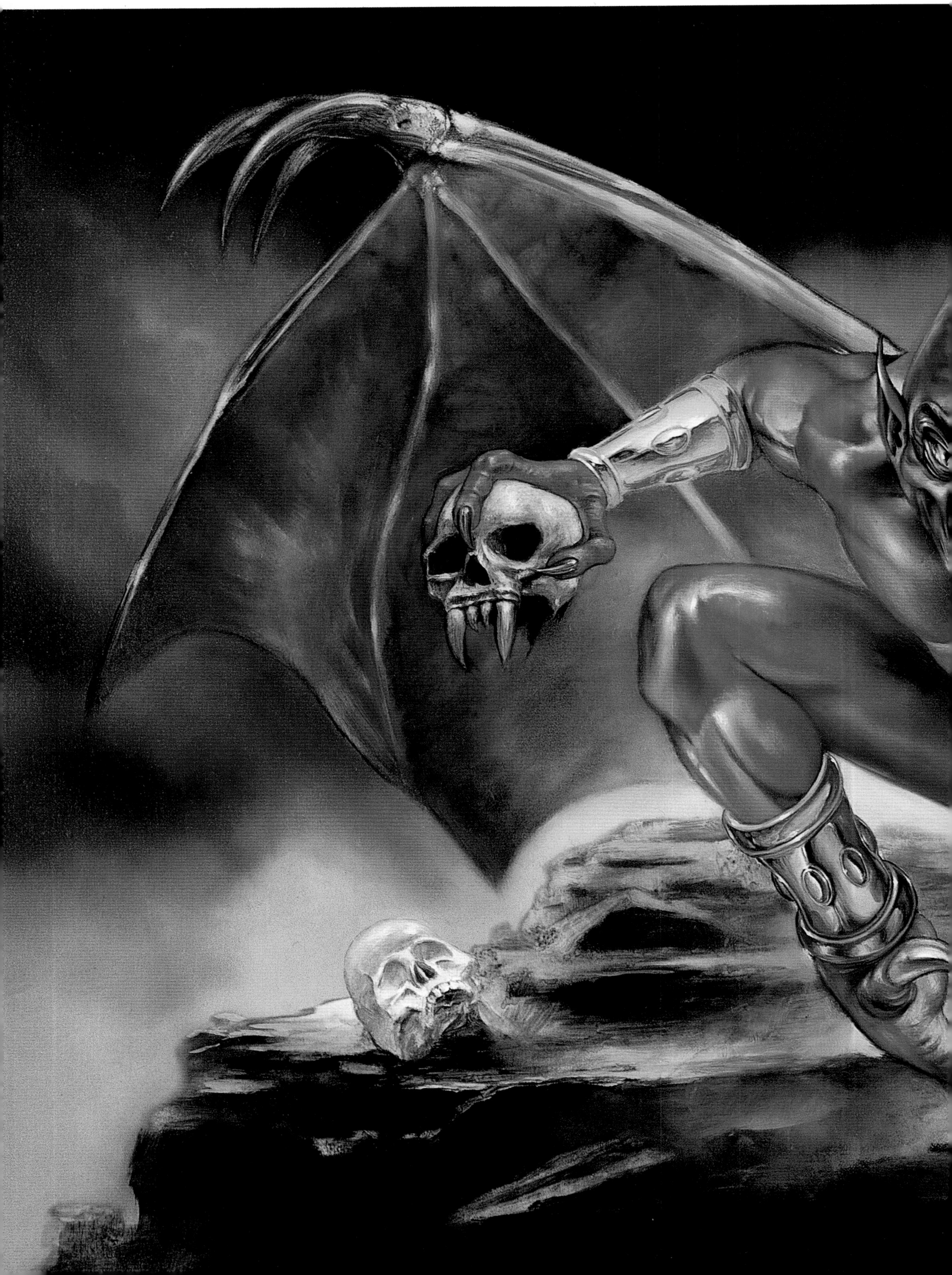

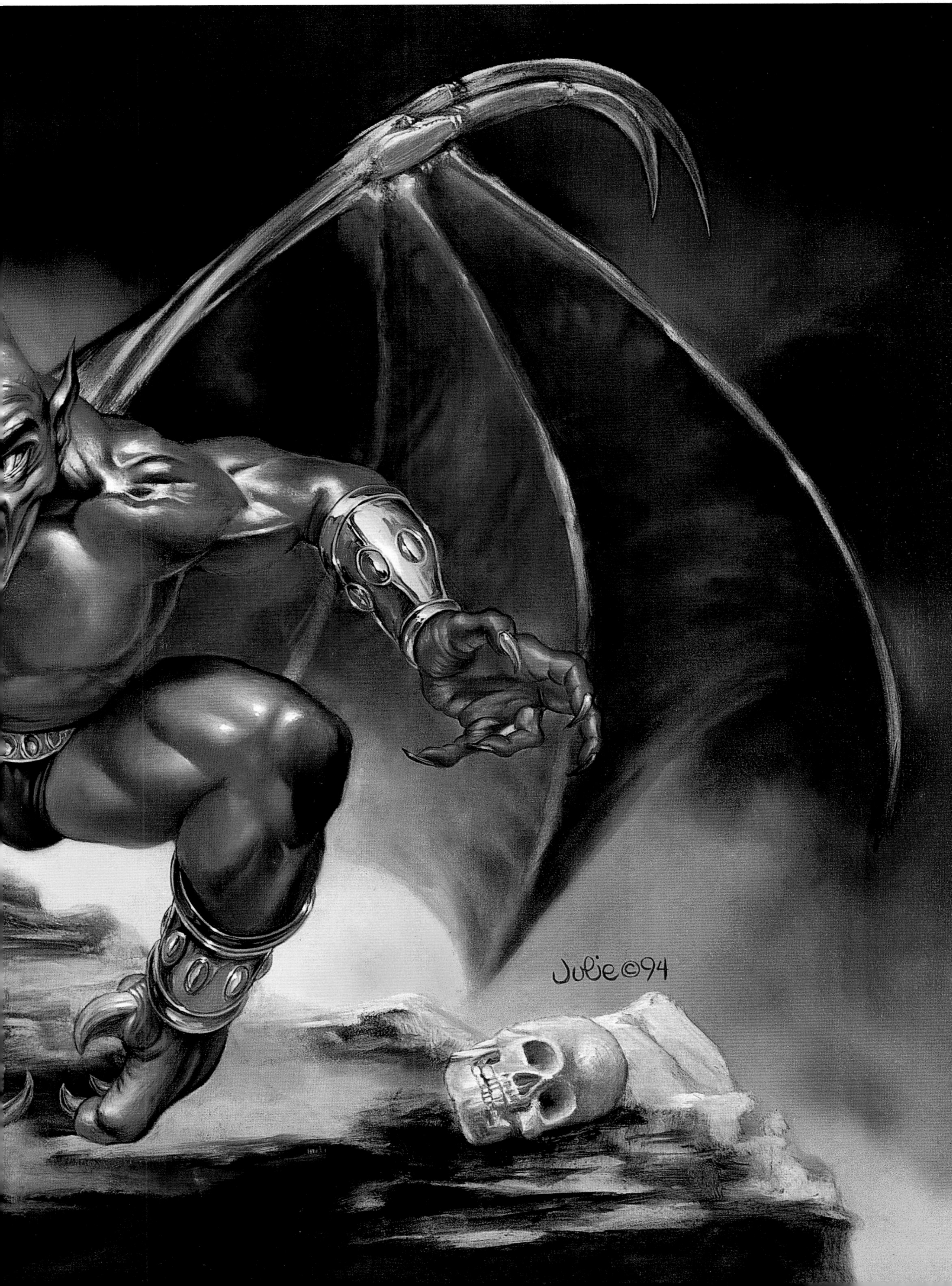
Julie ©94

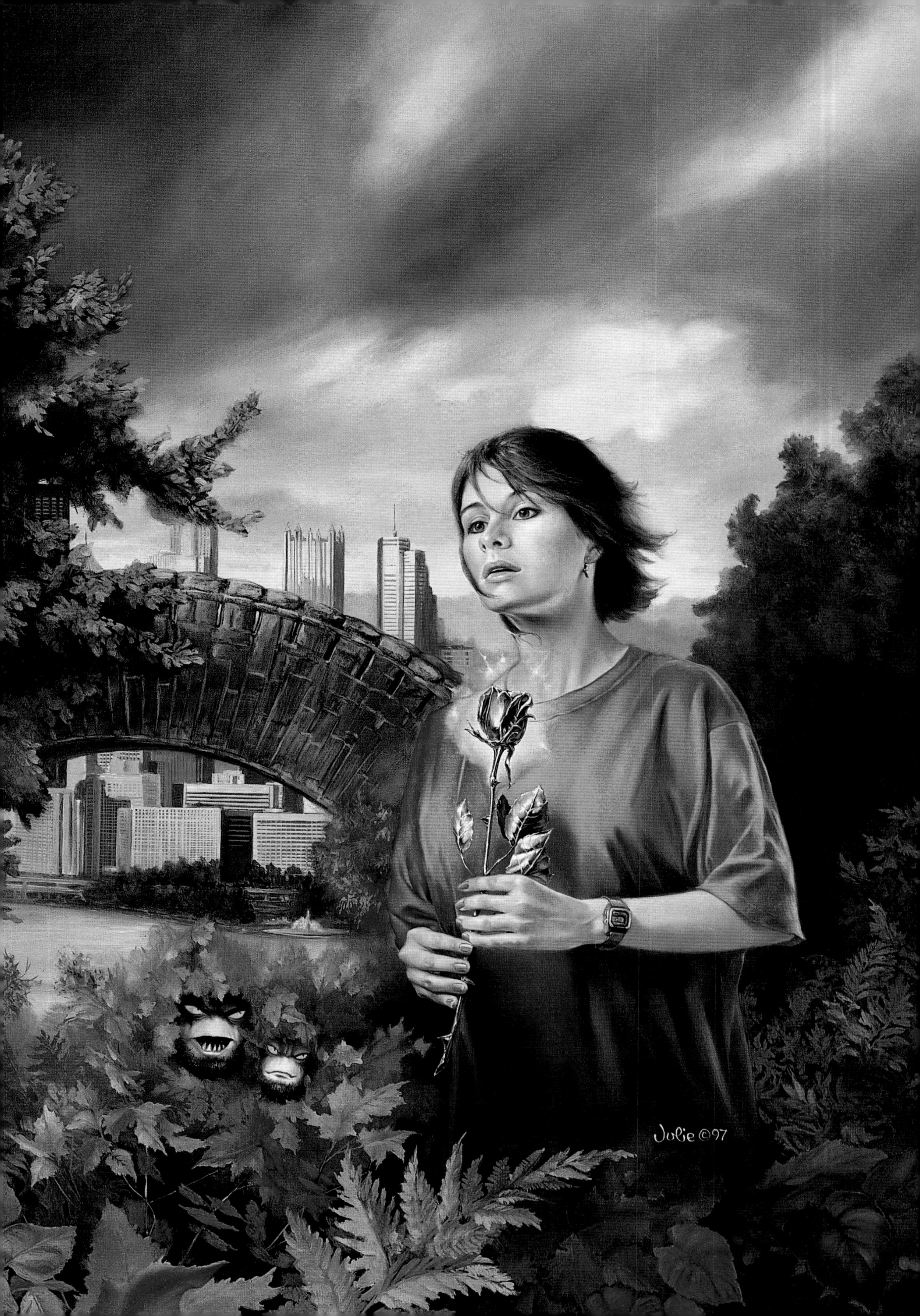
Julie ©97

2 WORLDS OF FANTASY

OPPOSITE: ***Shannon's Fantasy, 1997***
Oils, 20 x 15 in (51 x 38 cm)
Book cover. Penguin Books.
The story, Steel Rose, *that this illustrates is set in Pittsburgh, which Julie happens to know very well because her sons' grandmother lives there. She has visited the spot pictured here 'a million times' and the model is her niece, Shannon, who hopes one day to become a professional model. This is a happy instance of a commission providing the chance to paint something that is as personal to the artist as it was pleasing to the publishers.*

RIGHT: ***Soulmates, 1998***
Oils, 20 x 15 in (51 x 38 cm)
Dagger design. The Franklin Mint.
The Franklin Mint is one of the largest mail order suppliers of 'collectibles' in the world, with the manufacturing base to produce an idea in almost any imaginable form. Their regular range covers medals, die-cast models, jewellery and ornamental plates. In this case Julie was asked to design two ornamental daggers.

FAR RIGHT: ***Crystal Dagger, 1998***
Oils, 20 x 15 in (51 x 38 cm)
Dagger design. The Franklin Mint.
Fantasy is a new area for The Franklin Mint so it was a doubly interesting assignment. For the theme, Julie imagined a tale in which the female and the dragon are tied by some bond of destiny which they act out in the companion piece. She and Boris also came up with some designs for pocket knives which have proved very popular.

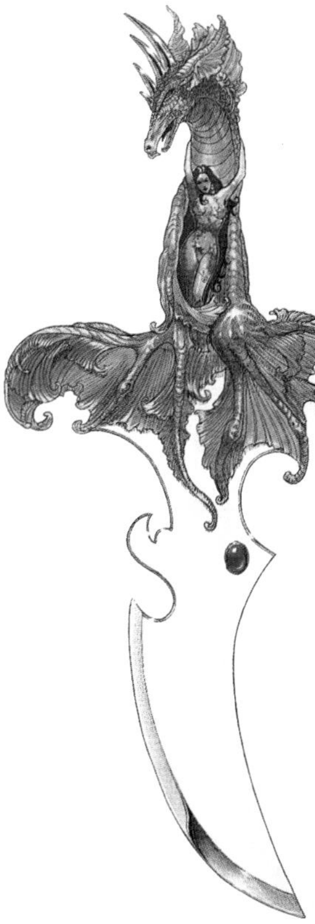

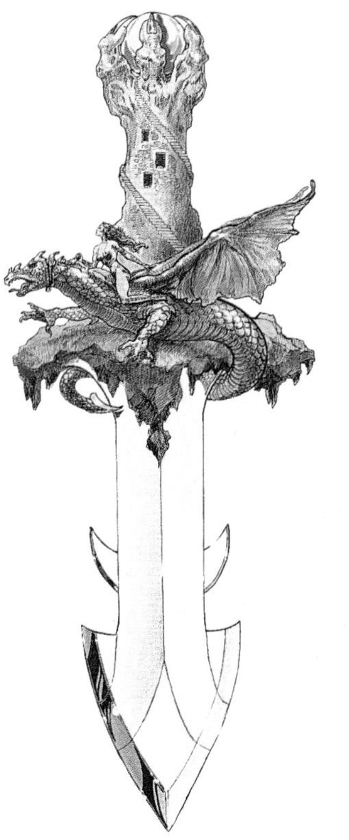

IN THE PAST FEW YEARS Julie's commissioned work has broadened out from the comic book superheroes for which she is famous. They remain the roots of her painting, because it is through them that she became a professional artist, but she is interested in experimenting with other styles, looking for new outlets, clients and so on.

This had long been her wish anyway, but finding the time to do anything about it was the problem. In the end, it only became possible because of a slump in comic book publishing and a demand for her talents. As with all genres, this happens as regularly as the turning

RIGHT: *The Winding Path, 1998*
Oils, 20 x 15 in (51 x 38 cm)
Book cover. Tor Books.
This illustrates a story about some kids who are staying in a hotel for a fantasy convention and find that it is not all talk. Julie's son, David, modelled for the centaur, her other son, Tony, posed for the young man embarking on the path and the one in the leather jacket is a friend of theirs. Julie herself posed for the female. For ten years now her sons have been appearing thinly disguised in her paintings. Being aspiring artists themselves helps when it comes to modelling because they know what Julie is looking for.

FAR RIGHT: *Afternoon Drink, 1997*
Oils, 20 x 15 in (51 x 38 cm)
Portfolio piece.
A sample to show that Julie is quite able to paint 'softer' dragons than those in her more 'heroic fantasy' pieces. There is a contrast here between the size and strength of the beast and its innocent, almost Bambi-like delicacy in sipping water.

of the seasons. Even knowing this, it was unsettling at first but then rather refreshing. Julie loves a challenge so she built up a portfolio of new ideas and, for a while, went knocking on New York publishers' doors just like any other aspiring illustrator. As their doors opened, so were new avenues for her artistic expression.

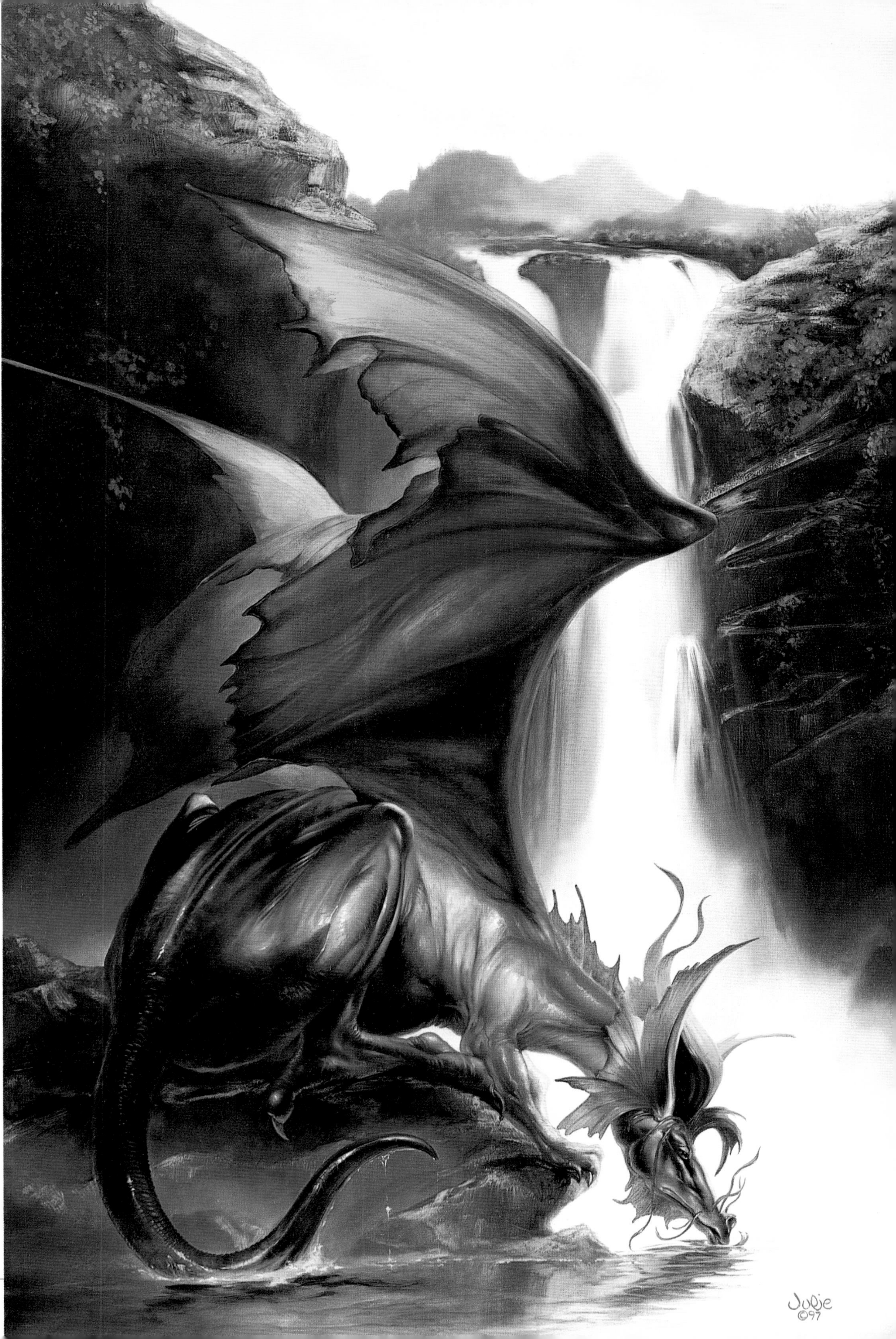
Julie
©97

Flowerchild, 1997
Computer-enhanced photomontage.
Portfolio piece.
An experiment suggested by a publisher
in view of the popularity of computer-
enhanced imagery. The main photographs
came from Julie's private collection. In the
event she really liked the effect so may try
her hand at it again, but she cannot really
see herself abandoning paint for this
medium. Ironically the overall effect she
was told to aim for was that of a
painting, but as it took almost as long,
she was left wondering why. One of the
ironies of being able to manipulate images
so fast and easily on the computer is that
you are left with a glut of choice. Instead
of adapting photographs to what you have
in mind, you are left with a dilemma
between several specific shots. Being able
to change colours at the touch of a button
is also great in theory, and an obvious
attraction for art directors, but in practice
it can complicate making decisions by
postponing them indefinitely.

Like most artists, Julie is never
completely satisfied with her finished
paintings. She can always see huge scope
for what could have been. In a painting,
decisions made along the way all go to
shape the end result, and unless there has
been some drastic misjudgement they add
up to something organic that has its own
self-contained logic. But if all colour
decisions are left open till the end, a lot of
time can then be wasted juggling the
options; and after all that someone else
can come along and effortlessly change it
all again in a moment. So, overall verdict
from Julie: a wonderful, new challenge. In
fact, she has already started a book of
photography that will include some more
of her computer fantasy art.

Boris is a recent convert to computers
after years of scepticism, his main interest
being their potential as tools for graphic
design. To Julie's amazement he actually
enjoys reading computer handbooks and
magazines and has become almost
independent of professional advice. A
sample of what he has learned can be found
on their Internet site, which Boris mostly
designed (http://www.borisjulie.com).

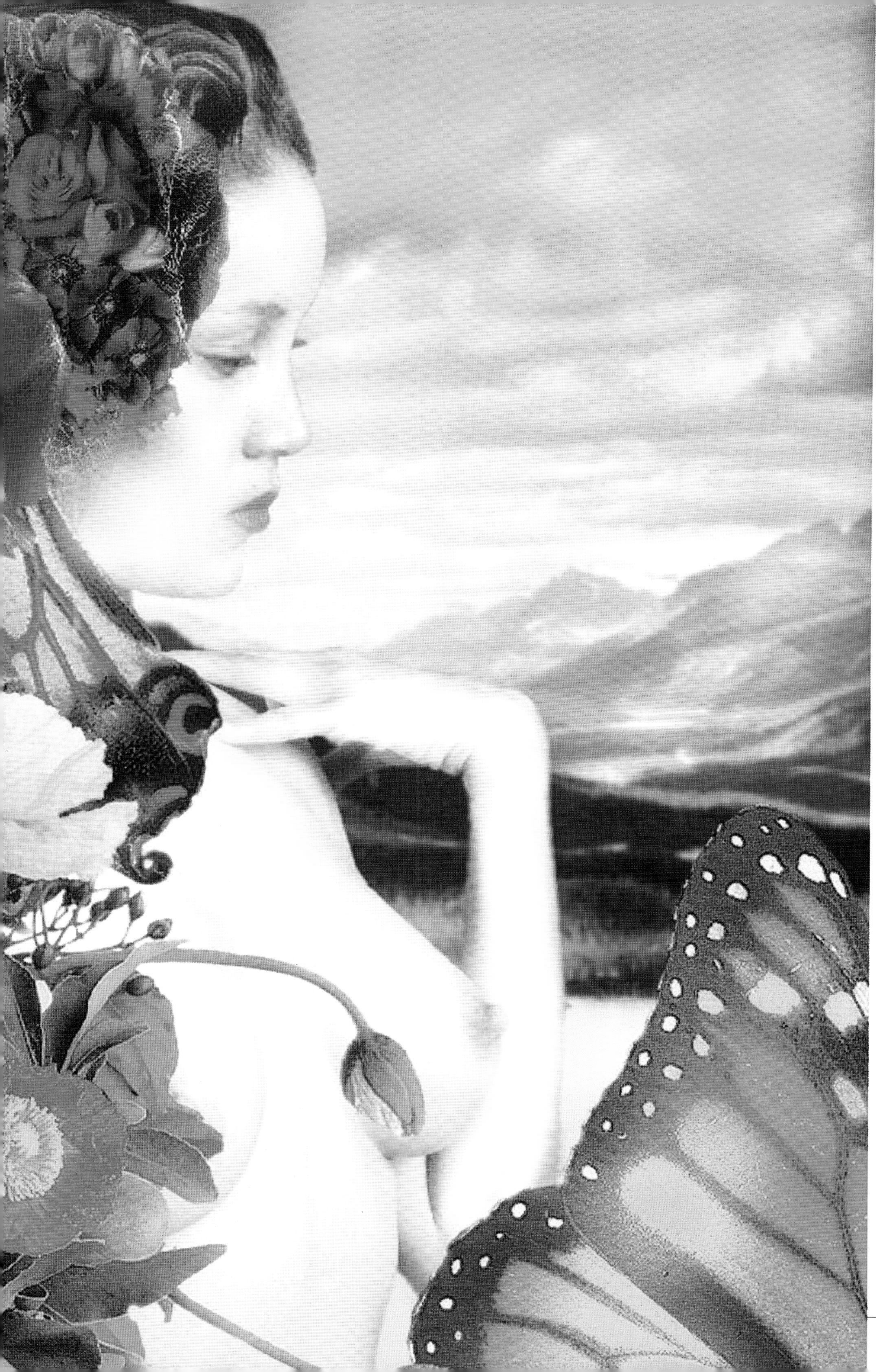

BELOW: *Romance/Still Life, 1997*
Oils, 20 x 15 in (51 x 38 cm)
Portfolio piece.
A sample for romantic book covers. The aim was to hint at a story purely through a still life, leaving the viewer to imagine how the lady in the photograph relates to the surrounding objects, what has happened to her and whether the portrait is current or loaded with nostalgia.

RIGHT: *Love on the Beach, 1997*
Oils, 30 x 20 in (76 x 51 cm)
Portfolio piece.
Another sample to test the possibility of doing romantic novel covers. It does not illustrate any particular story but is just the kind of scene Julie would ideally like to paint, beaches for her being naturally romantic places. The models were posed together. This is more natural than drawing figures separately and then trying to fit them together, but it has its own complications as it can be tricky focusing attention on more than one person at a time. The setting is derived from photographs of Hawaii with the ship added in the distance just to conjure the ghost of a background story.

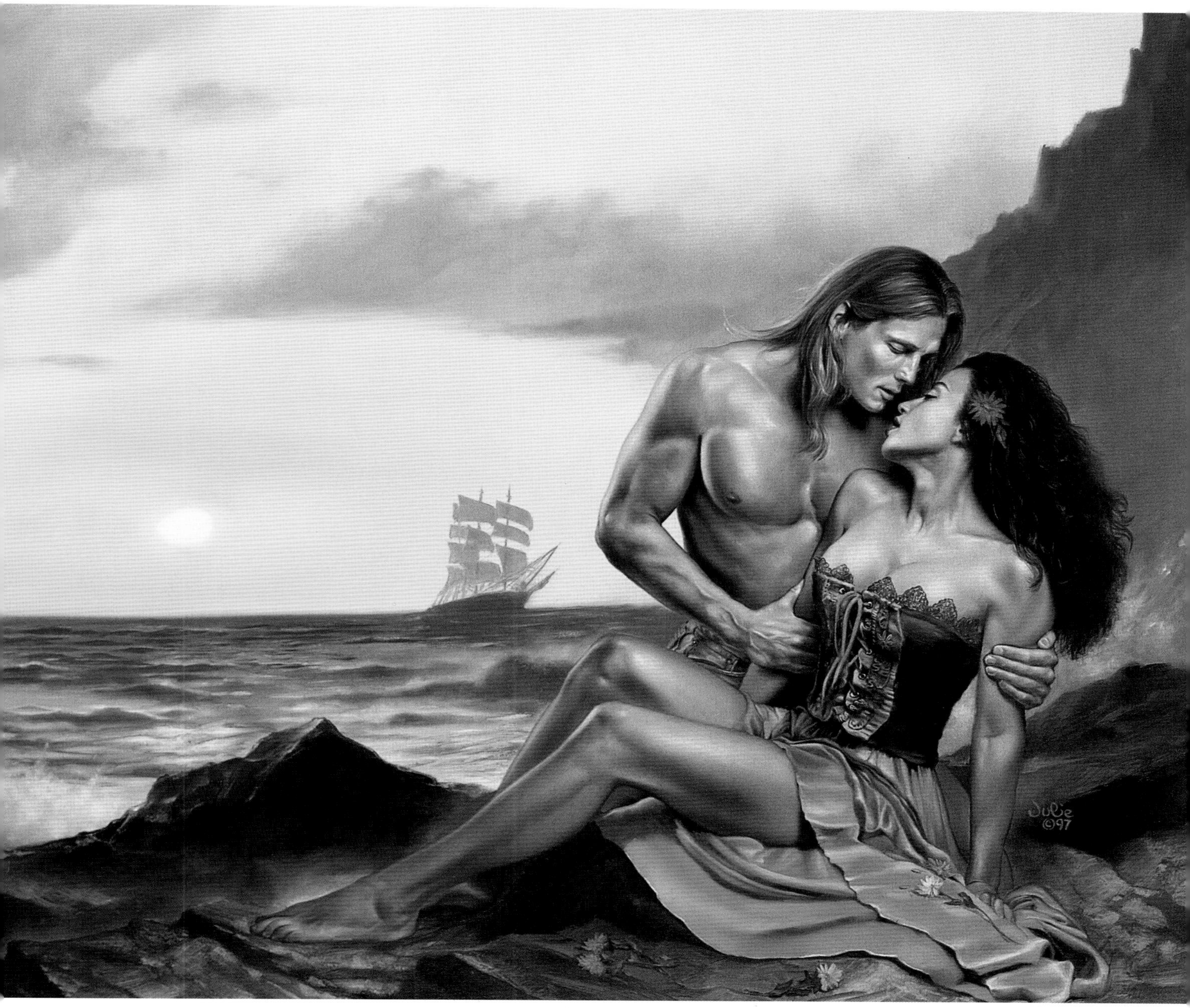
Julie
©97

Mystical fantasy and romance were two fields Julie had long wanted to explore, but it is less easy than outsiders imagine to move from one kind of illustration to another. Technique and success count for little unless you can show proof of being able to capture the feel of another genre. Which means doing samples such as those shown here. The pleasure of this is that while you are aiming to paint something within the conventions of a genre, there is a free choice of subject so you can aim for the ideal of what you would like to do.

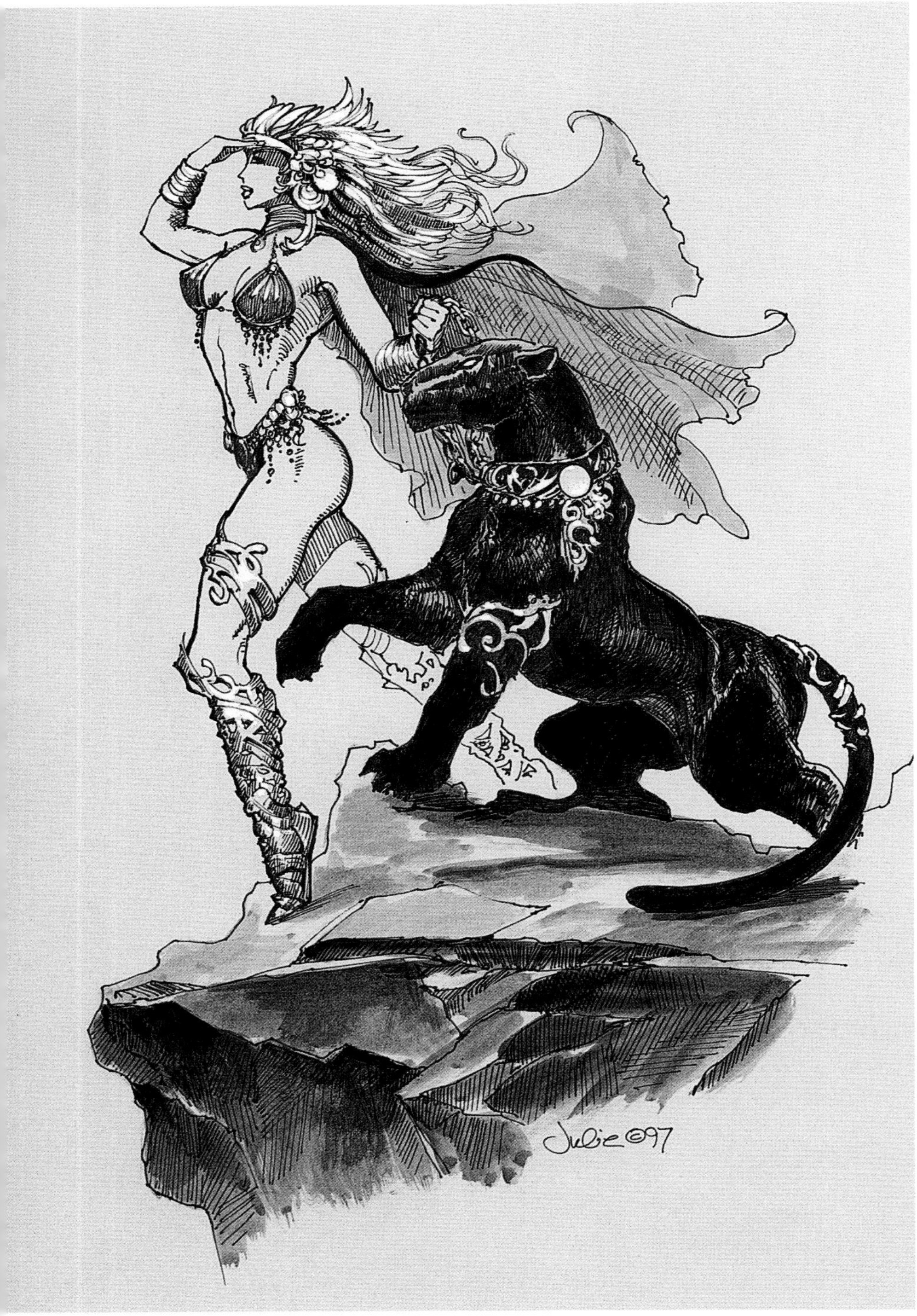
Julie ©97

LEFT: ***Black Panther (sketch), 1997***
This was one of several ideas for The Franklin Mint who wanted a set of collectors' plates with a fantasy theme. Julie particularly likes this design because it shows woman and beast in equal partnership.

OPPOSITE: ***Tiger Magic, 1998***
Oils. Diameter: 22 in (55 cm)
Ceramic plate design. The Franklin Mint. Julie's first published plate. One of the attractions of moving into new fields is the challenge of creating new products. Besides daggers and plates Julie has designed jewellery and sculptures for The Franklin Mint. She sees the company as a kind of artists' heaven after having visited their warehouse – a huge building crammed with every possible kind of sculpture and art.

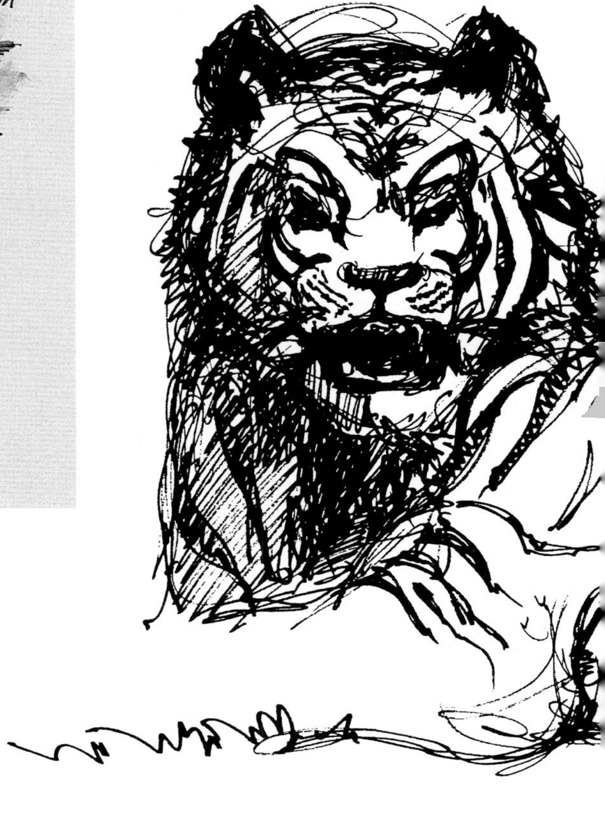

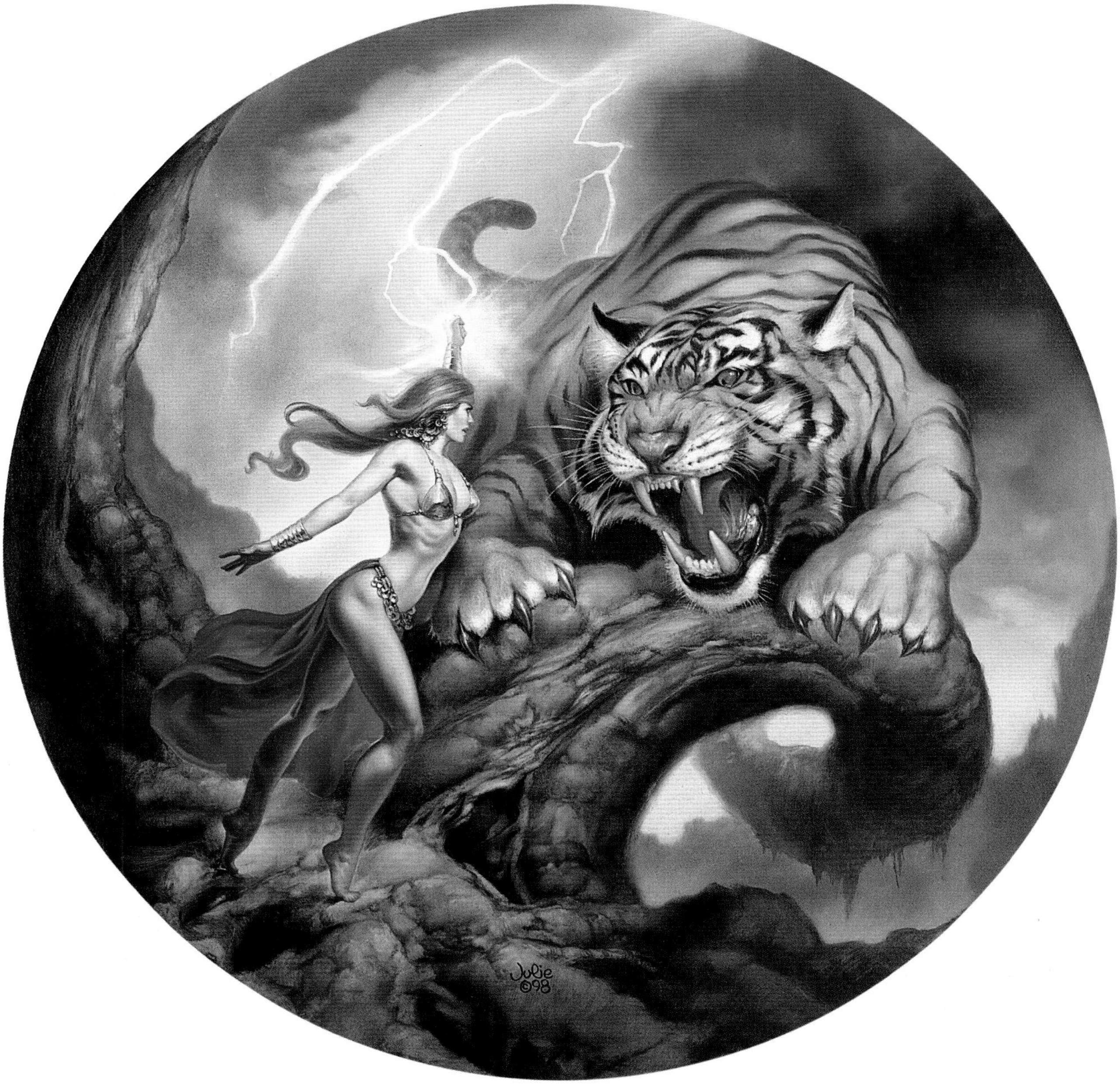

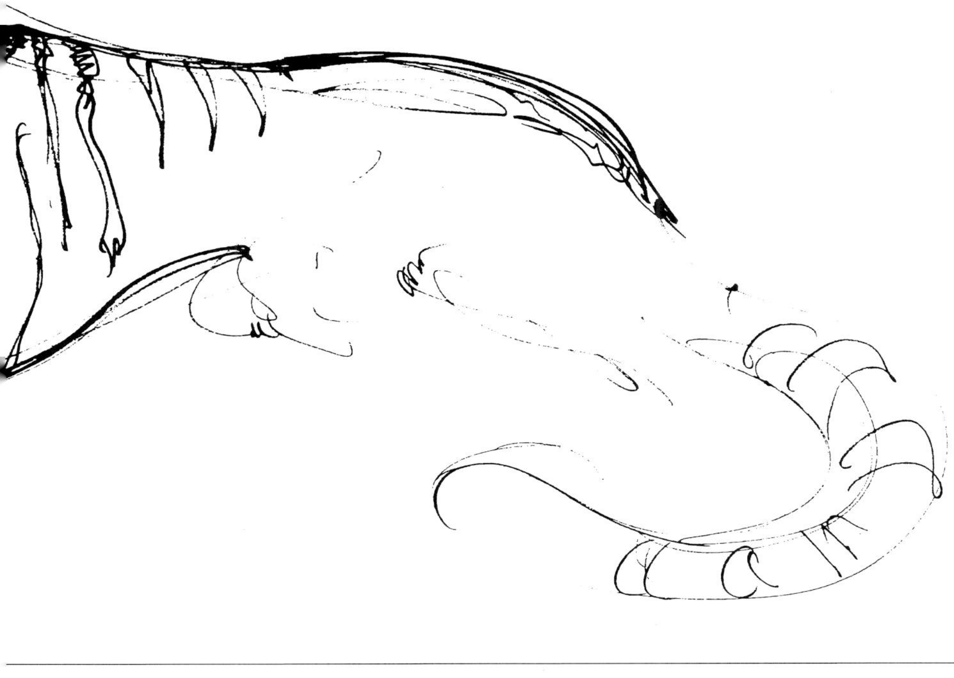

LEFT: *Tiger (sketch), 1997*
One of a set of drawings from a visit to Houston Zoo in Texas. Zoos are one of Julie's favourite places for live drawing but she finds it most productive going alone or with another artist because somehow it is impossible to concentrate on drawing when it is a social visit. Curiously it doesn't bother her at all having passers-by stop to comment or chat while she is working, which happens all the time.

Paradise, 1997
Oils, 30 x 20 in (76 x 51 cm)
Private commission.
This looks like two sisters but, in fact, both are portraits of the same model, who with her husband has commissioned several paintings from Julie and Boris. Such commissions are always a pleasure because, says Julie, you know they are going to be appreciated for years. The husband came up with the general scenario in this painting.

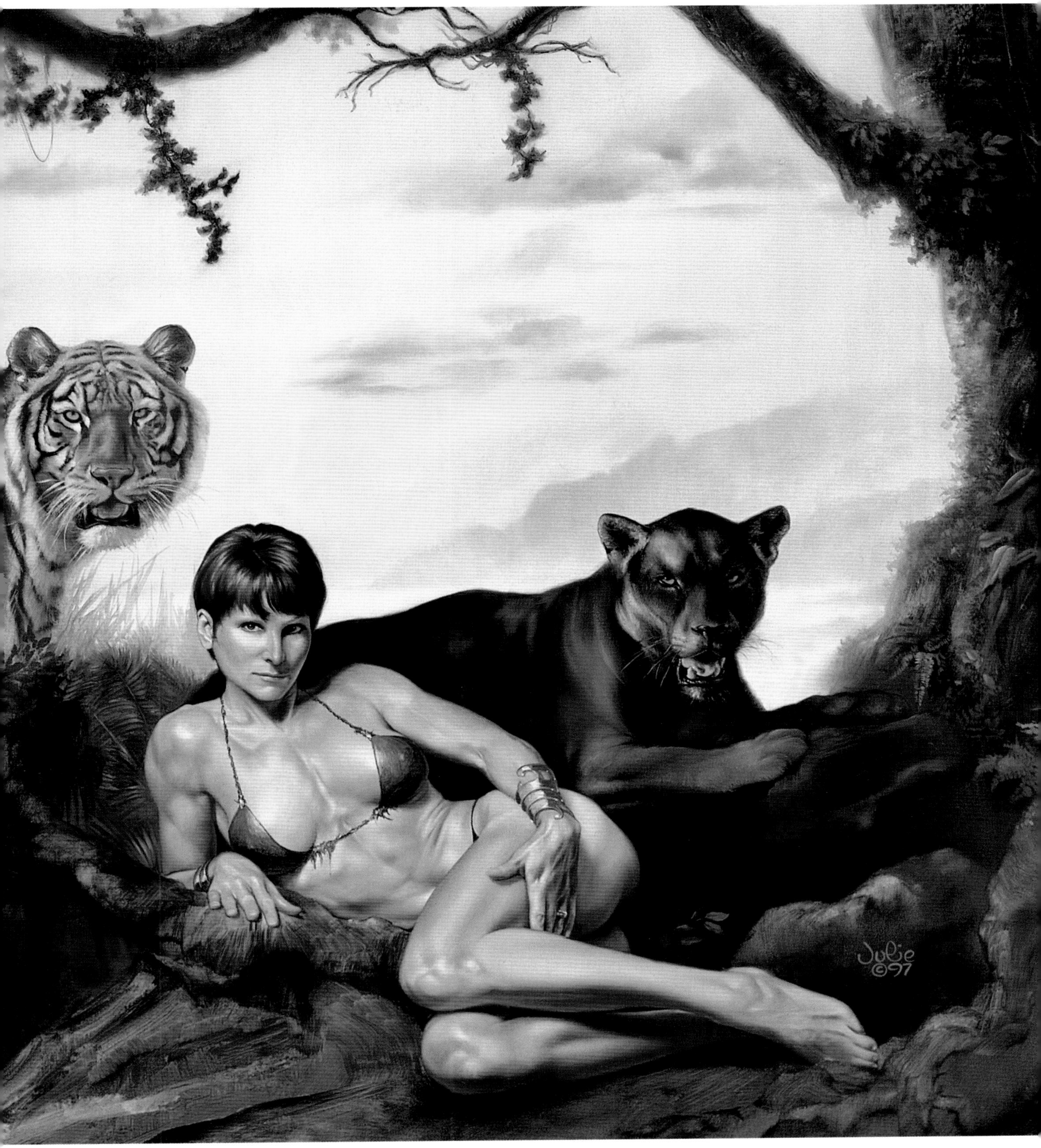
Julie
©97

RIGHT: *Cindy, 1995*
Oils, 20 x 15 in (51 x 38 cm)
Private commission.
With this portrait Julie enjoys thinking about how when the subject reaches the age of 95 she will be able to surprise her great-grandchildren by pointing to it and saying 'That's me!' The setting reflects Julie's own fond memories of the swampland where she grew up in south-east Texas. There are noticeably no bugs and snakes like those that infest the real swamps and spoil the romance, but otherwise the aim is to convey to the viewer what the swamps feel like. The staff Cindy is holding is a kind of standard like those of Roman legionaries, a badge of strength and assertion.

One of the interesting things Julie has learned about colour is that skin tone can be almost any colour and the viewer will see it as flesh tone in a strange light. If you want skin tone to look unusual it generally has to be contrasted with another figure nearby with more natural colouring. The lesson for aspiring artists is basically not to worry too much about flesh colours, but as a general guide, to obtain a tanned effect on skin one adds green and blue tones; for pink one adds oranges and reds.

FAR RIGHT: *Possibilities Bound, 1997*
Oils, 20 x 15 in (51 x 38 cm)
Portfolio piece.
A portrait of a particular mood and thoughts that were going through Julie's head at the time. The wings contain a universe of possibilities but the figure is chained to the rock. There is an impression that the chain is fragile enough to break if she tried hard enough, or that she could simply let go of it; but there is some strange reluctance, some link to the island that keeps her from trying.

One of the most common questions Julie gets asked at conventions is where she gets her ideas from? 'Ideas are the easy part, they are constantly coming through, even from the wallpaper in the bathroom sometimes. A lot of times I get ideas from looking at art books upside down. The brain registers the colours and shapes but puts its own interpretation on them.'

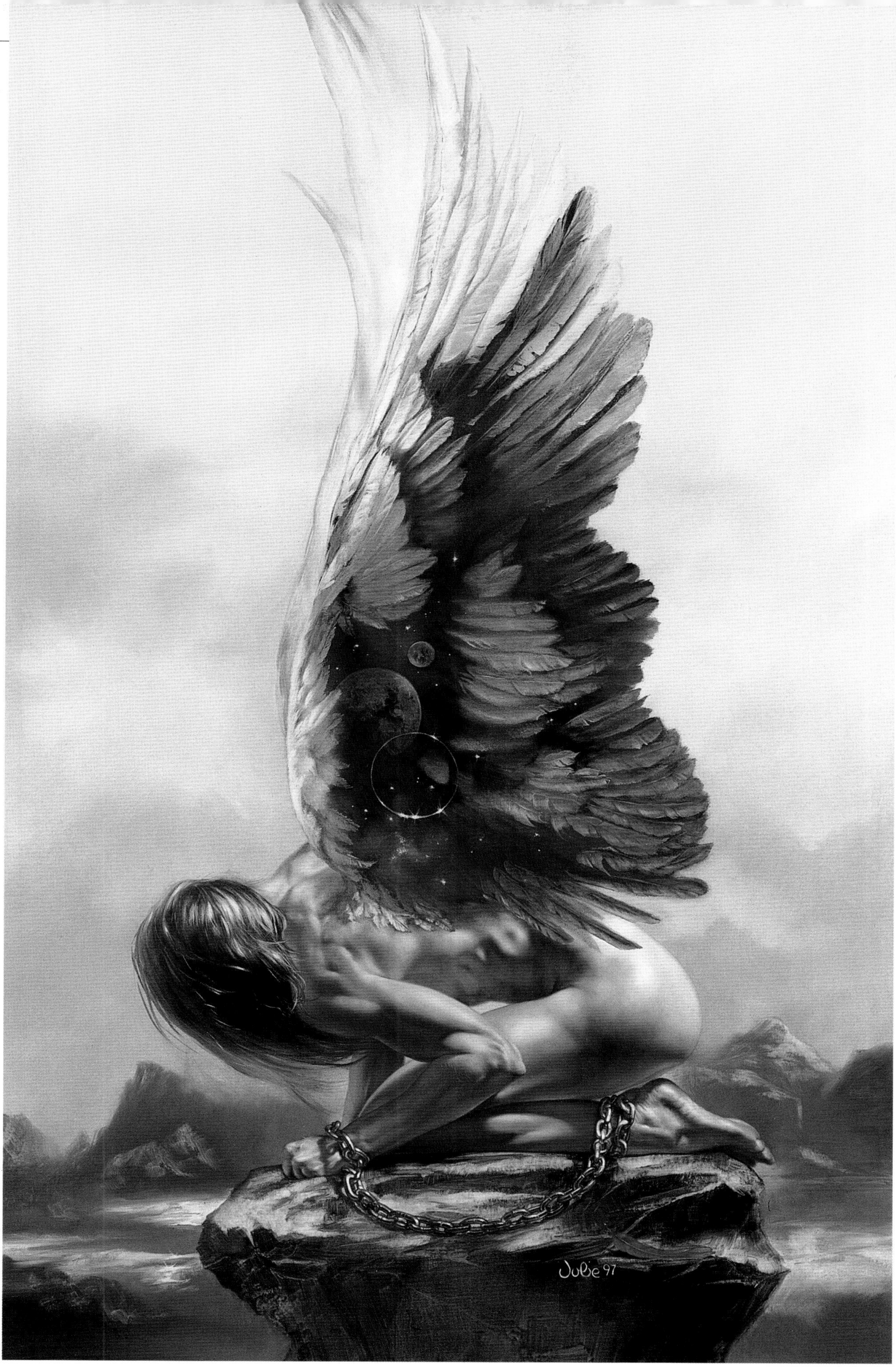
Julie 97

RIGHT: *Fountain in the Redwoods, 1998*
Oils, 20 x 15 in (51 x 38 cm)
Book cover. Penguin Books.
The Californian Redwood forests are another special place for Julie so it was a pleasure to be able to bring them into this commission. The elves and fairies in the tale are as much a mixture of innocence and evil as any other people; they have a dark side that is hinted at in the incongruity of the fey, beautiful statue and the skulls.

FAR RIGHT: *Figure study*
Graphite.

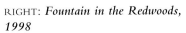

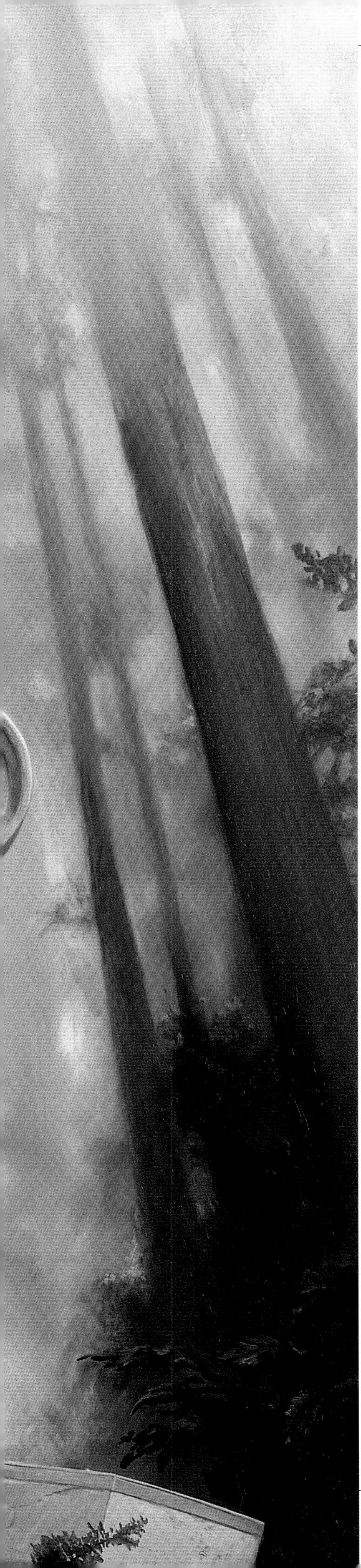

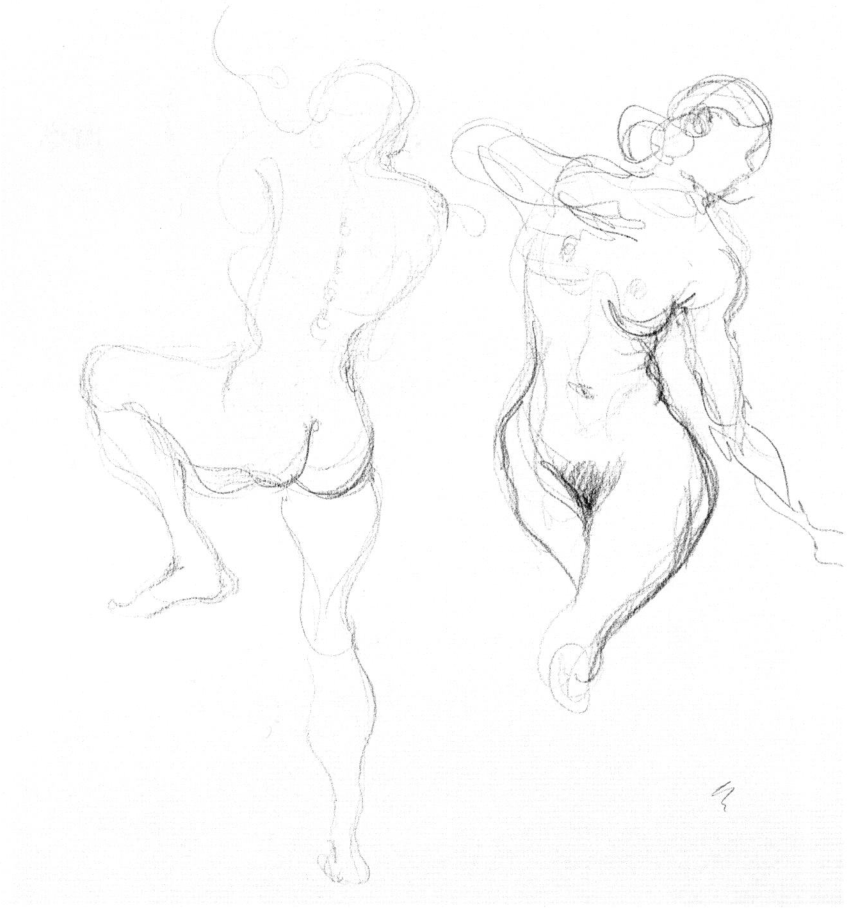

Julie: 'With ideas, the more you practise, the easier it gets to create and visualize. Now I find that I can completely visualize a picture in detail and move things around even before anything is down on paper. Ideas come from everywhere, even the things people say sometimes as you pass them in the street. When things are taken out of context they can take on a whole new meaning, so often it's best when you don't get the whole picture. It's like picking up the seed of an idea. Put into a creative mind it can expand into something unusual. Ideas are everywhere. I wish I could have twenty-five lifetimes to get them down somehow. Or maybe a thousand, and that would probably still not be enough.'

Julie: 'A lot of the struggle artists have with getting ideas comes from thinking of the limitations too soon, instead of just letting the ideas flow. It's best to think at the start that anything is possible for the time being.

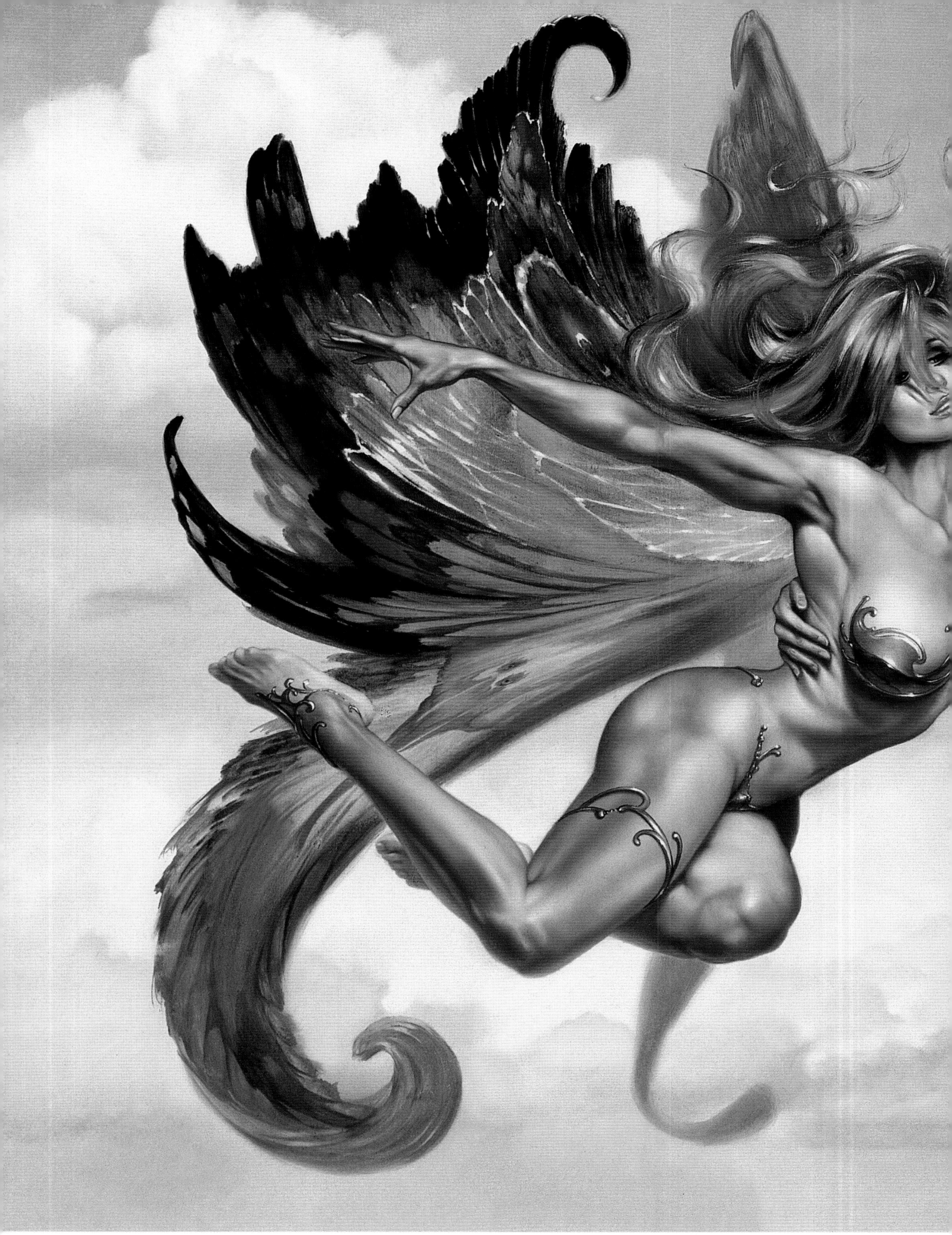

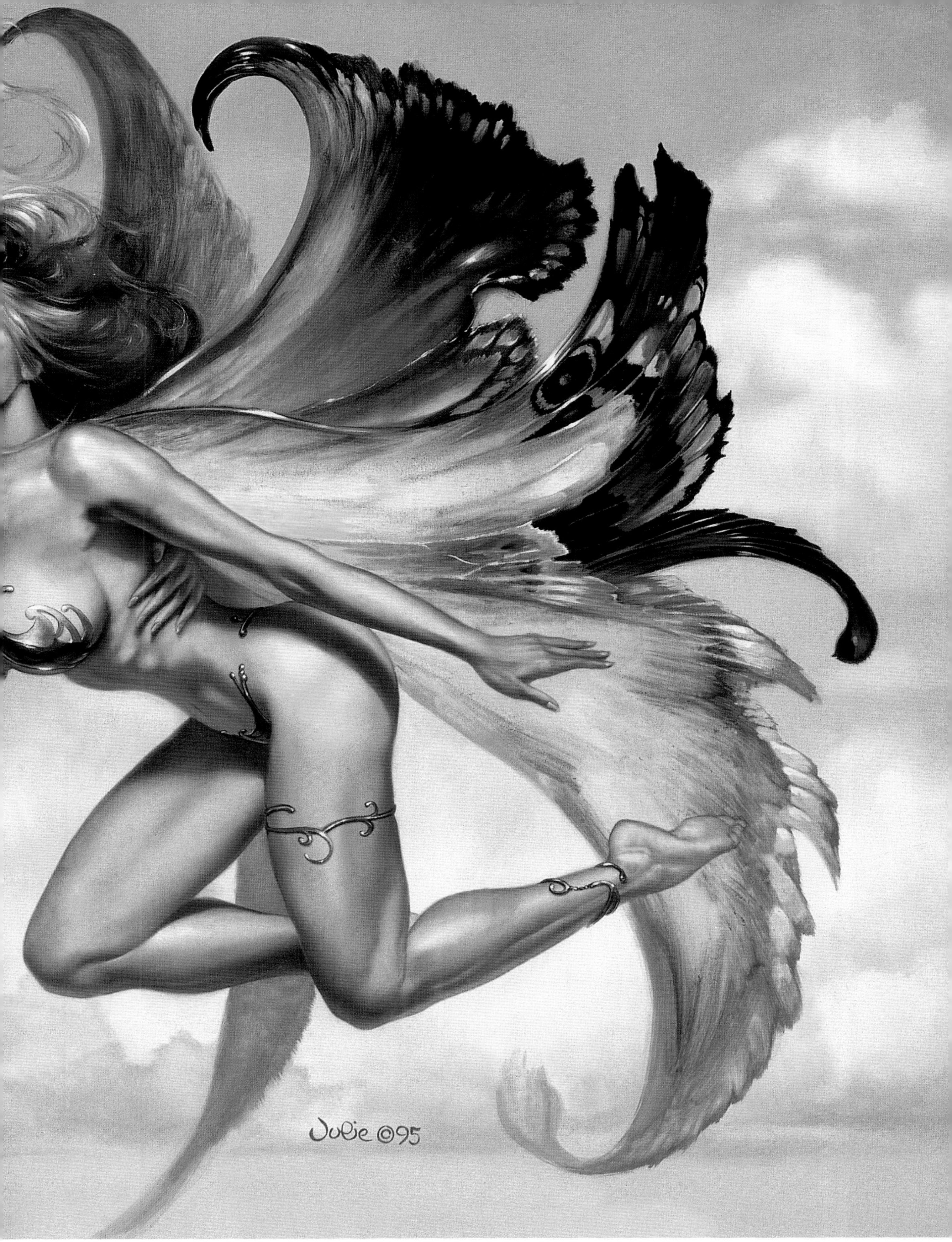
Julie ©95

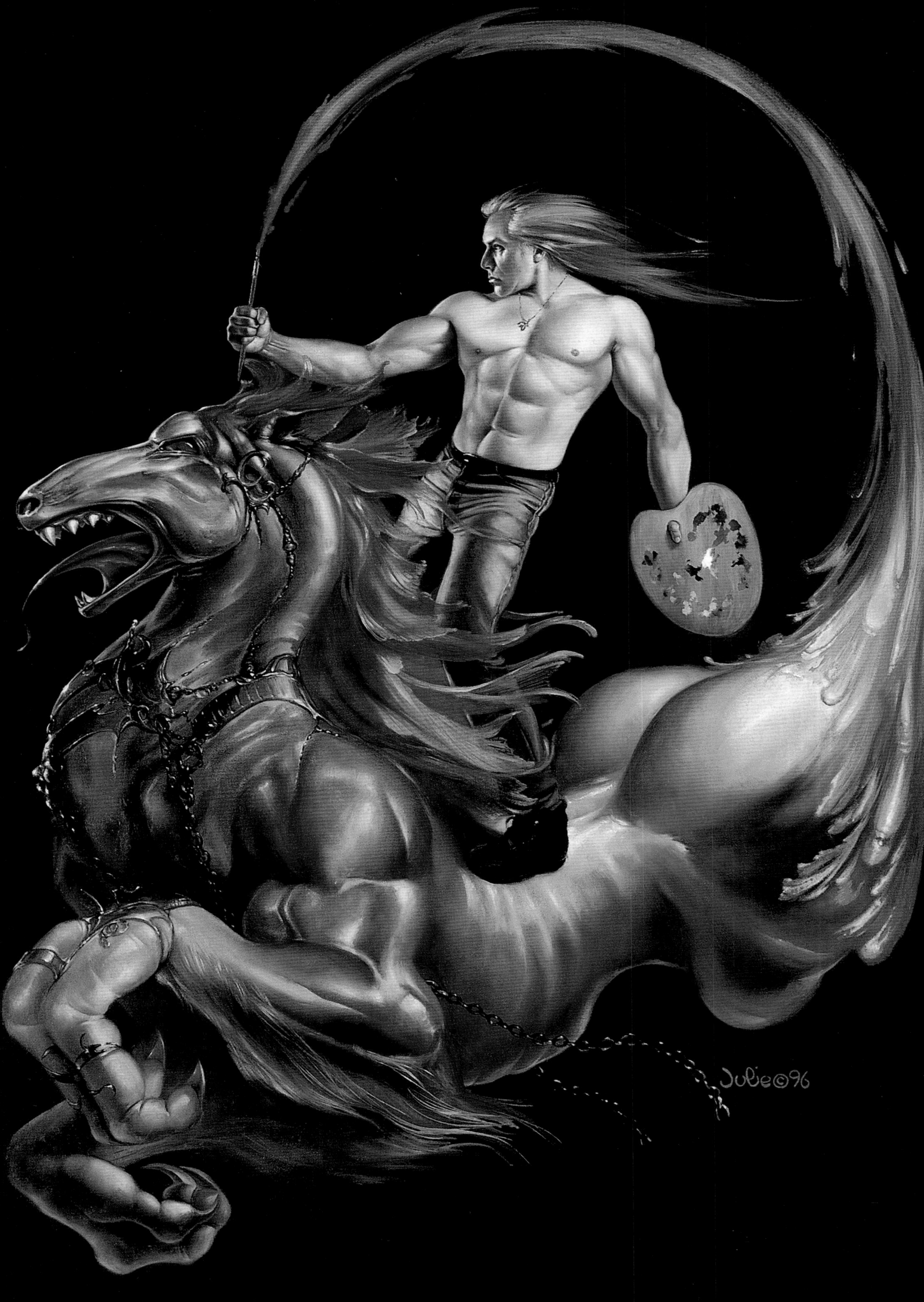
Julie©96

PREVIOUS PAGES: *Heavenly Twins, 1995*
Oils, 30 x 20 in (76 x 51 cm)
Calendar illustration. Topps Co.
The models are the famous Barbie Twins who commissioned the painting for a calendar and were very happy with the result. Almost everyone seems to like it, which has been encouraging because the gentle mood is so different from most of Julie's work.

ABOVE: *Figure study*
Black Conté crayon.

OPPOSITE: *Boris Bosforus, 1996*
Oils, 20 x 15 in (51 x 38 cm)
Portfolio piece.
Just for fun – a symbolic portrait of Boris Vallejo armed with the shield and sword of his profession and riding a steed of his own creation into the battlefields of heroic fantasy! The dragon-horse is trailing a broken chain to suggest that freedom demands an effort of will. Julie: 'Being an artist allows you a freedom to have this whole other world which you can bring into your life at any time.' In paint, daily trials and tribulations can be translated into the heroic ventures they often feel like but so rarely seem from the outside, except to others in the same position.

'You only put the limitations in much further down the line when it becomes necessary to think of what the picture is for. The great thing about working for The Franklin Mint [pages 45 and 52] is that they give you the feeling that anything is possible. For instance, with a sculpture I don't have to start by thinking "will this work?" I just look for an idea and then get practical at the end, maybe then toning it down so it is physically possible.'

The main impetus behind Julie's paintings is a love of physique but she is also fascinated by the invisible structures of the natural world on the instinctive and social levels, by how well for the most part they work and by the societies humans and animals have evolved in order to rub along together. Watching her children grow has been a special revelation but she draws less sharp distinctions between humans and animals than most people. Obviously there are differences but what she tends to notice more are the similarities.

For example, she and Boris have a pet rabbit that freely wanders their house, outside of the studio from which it has been banned after eating artwork. Rabbits are not generally famous for their communication skills and rarely make a sound, but Julie is amazed by how fluently their pet can convey what is on its mind. Mainly that is 'Feed me! Love me!' but it is surprising how many ways it can say this. Also the rabbit and Boris have a running competition for a particular chair, and Boris does not always win.

So for Julie, humans are animals first and whatever else they are second, and she enjoys emphasizing this whenever possible by giving the beasts in her pictures an equal dignity.

Art, says Julie, is a strange profession because often it is simply a matter of focusing people's attention on something which is there all along but

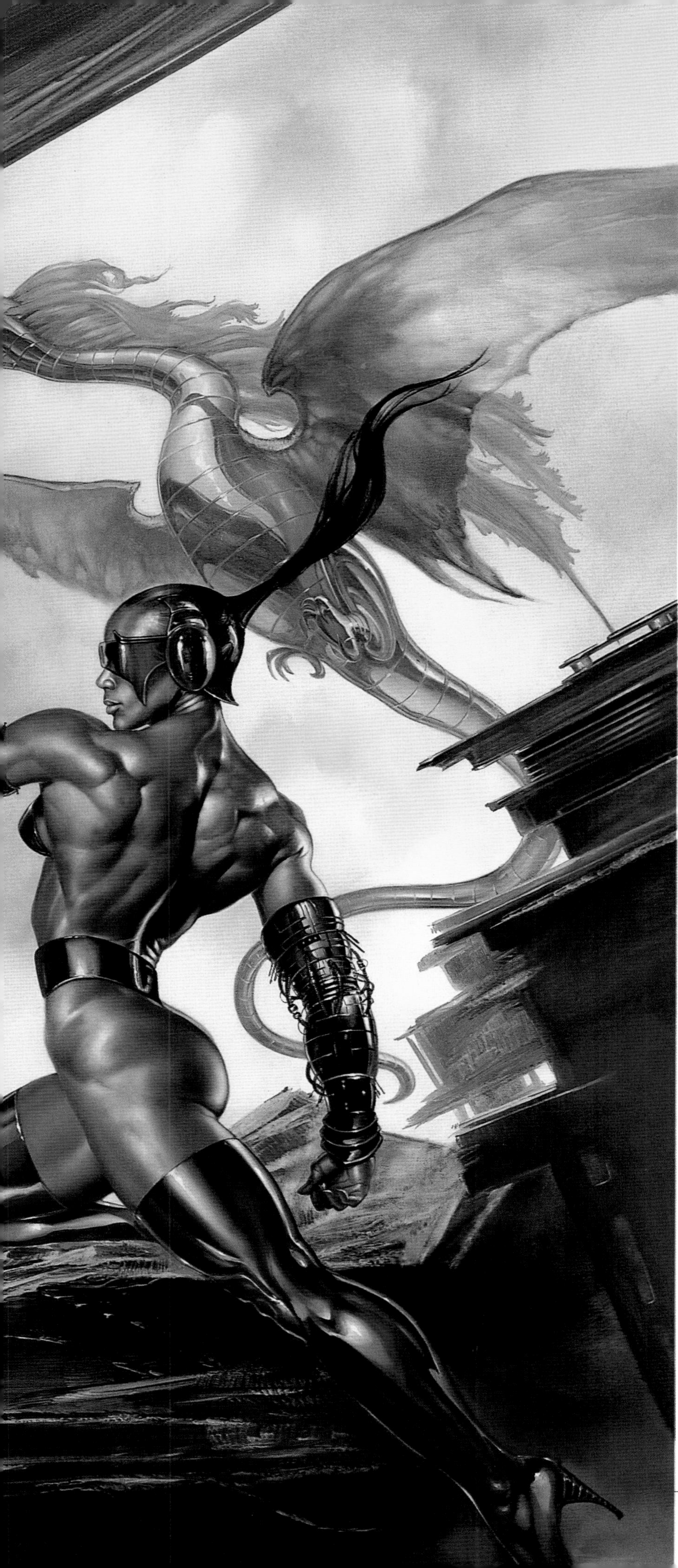

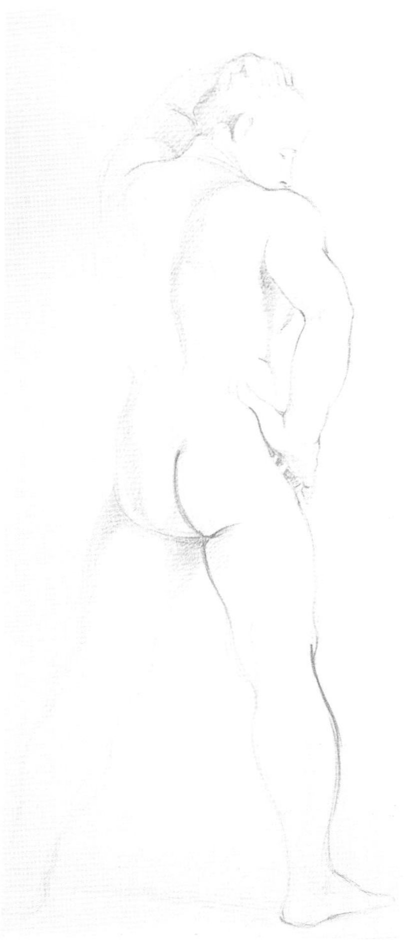

LEFT: ***Huntress, 1996***
Oils, 20 x 15 in (51 x 38 cm)
Portfolio piece.
The model was Lenda Murray who was Ms Olympia when she came for a photo session with Julie. They only did the one shoot but almost every picture has become the basis of a painting, including many of Julie's own favourites. 'Not only does she look fabulous,' says Julie, 'but she moves so gracefully she is positively regal.'

ABOVE: ***Figure study***
Coloured pencil.

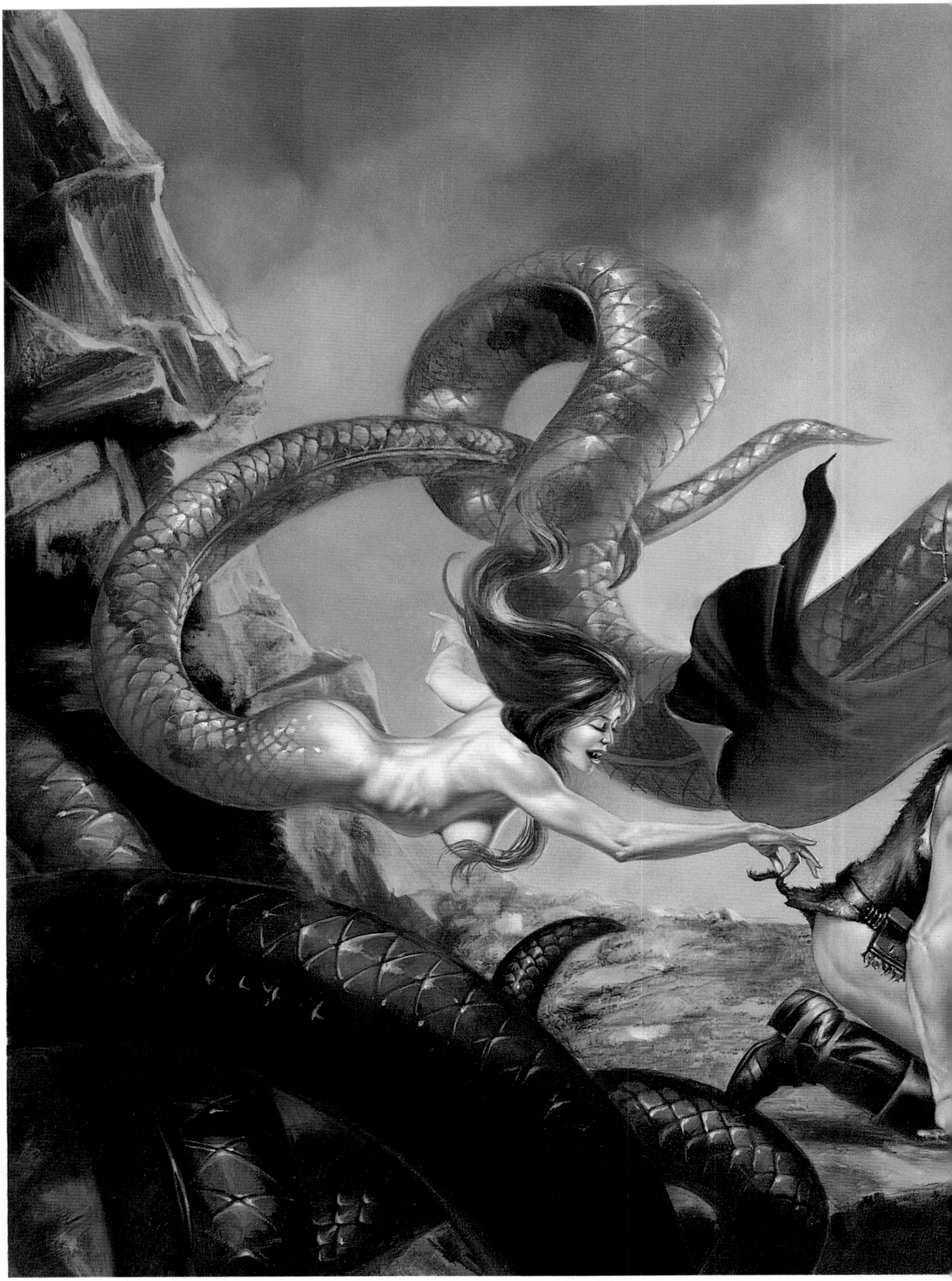

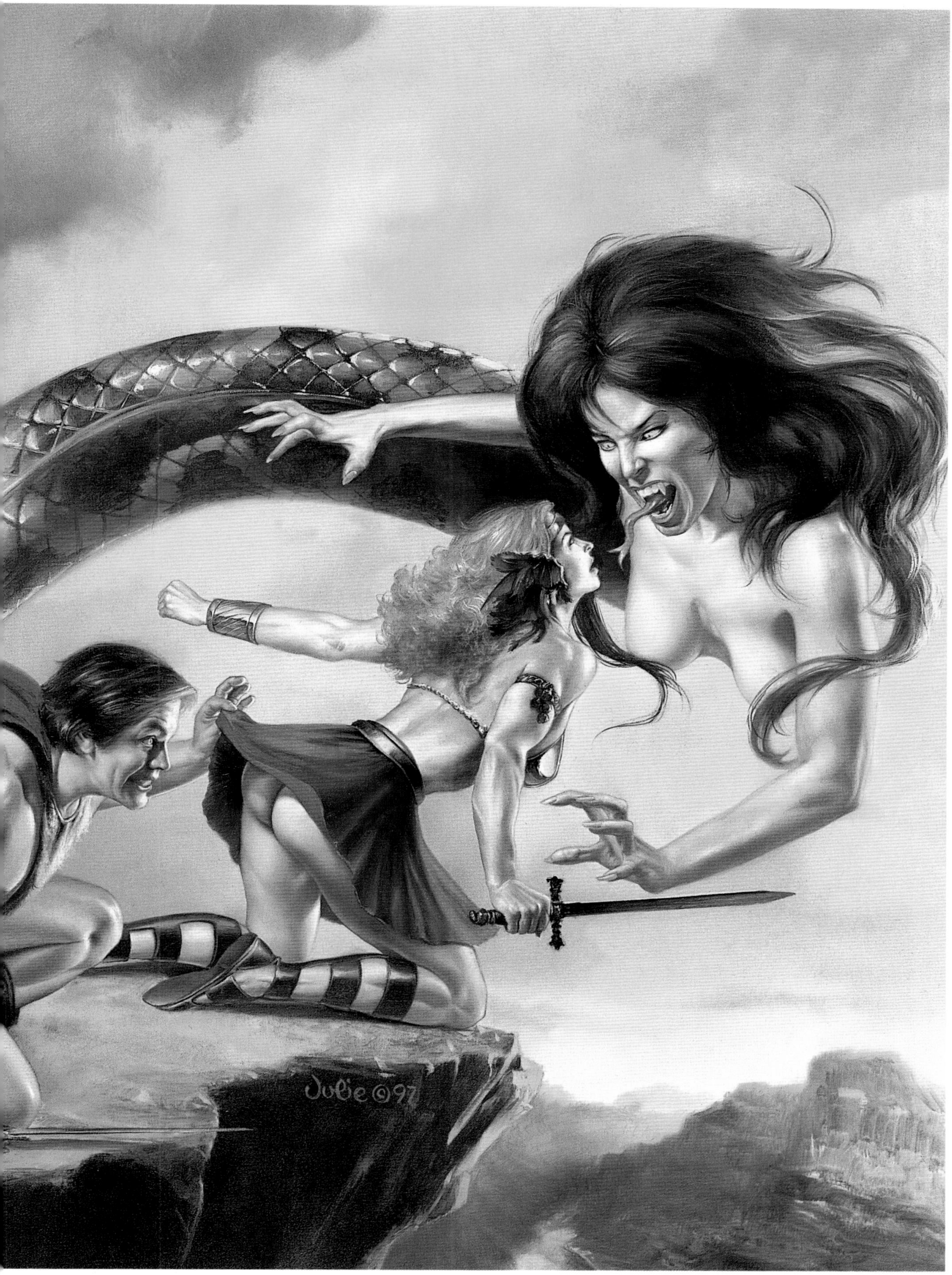
Julie ©97

PREVIOUS PAGES: ***Valley of the Snake Ladies, 1997***
Oils, 30 x 20 in (76 x 51 cm)
Portfolio piece.
This was commissioned by Penthouse Comix. They asked for something funny, so Julie came up with a little joke. The heroine is battling for her life with one of Lilith's daughters, but all the hero is interested in is lifting her skirt. The second snake-woman was added as an afterthought, a kind of second punch line because the picture was intended as a wraparound cover.

RIGHT: ***Bubble City, 1994***
Oils, 20 x 15 in (51 x 38 cm)
Trading card. SkyBox.
Julie's father is an architect and as a child she often went to his office and used the model-making tools there to create fantasy houses. There is much the same appeal in painting a picture like this, trying to imagine how these structures might work and how they would be divided internally. In a similar vein she and Boris have begun to get involved in film design – creating fantasy environments for movies which, with the power of computer graphics, has become an almost limitless field.

FAR RIGHT: ***Empress of a New World, 1995***
Oils, 20 x 15 in (51 x 38 cm)
Portfolio piece.
Julie enjoyed the blend of past and future in this painting, and the sense that this place is a crossroad of time and dimension. The empress is conjuring a new world into being by the power of pure thought, which is what Julie rather enjoys doing with her paintbrush.

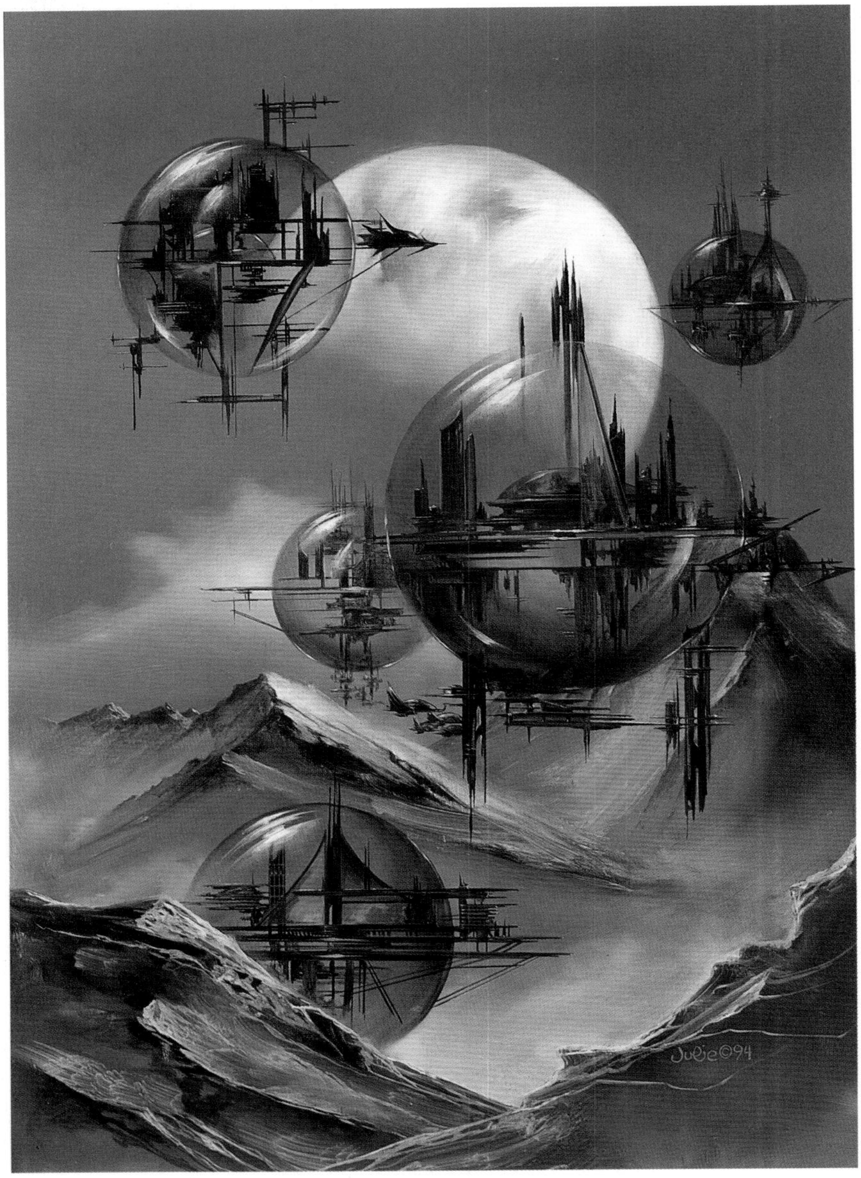
Julie©94

which they have just not noticed. Often the simple statement 'this is art' makes people pay attention and see things differently. For example, a family snapshot that barely gets attention may have some detail that can be blown up and placed in a fresh context which makes people say 'What a great portrait!' But it was there all along.

So much is often the result of framing things correctly, noticing what deserves to be noticed and drawing attention to it. Often just calling something 'art' makes viewers notice, appreciate and analyse the subject of a picture in a way they otherwise wouldn't.

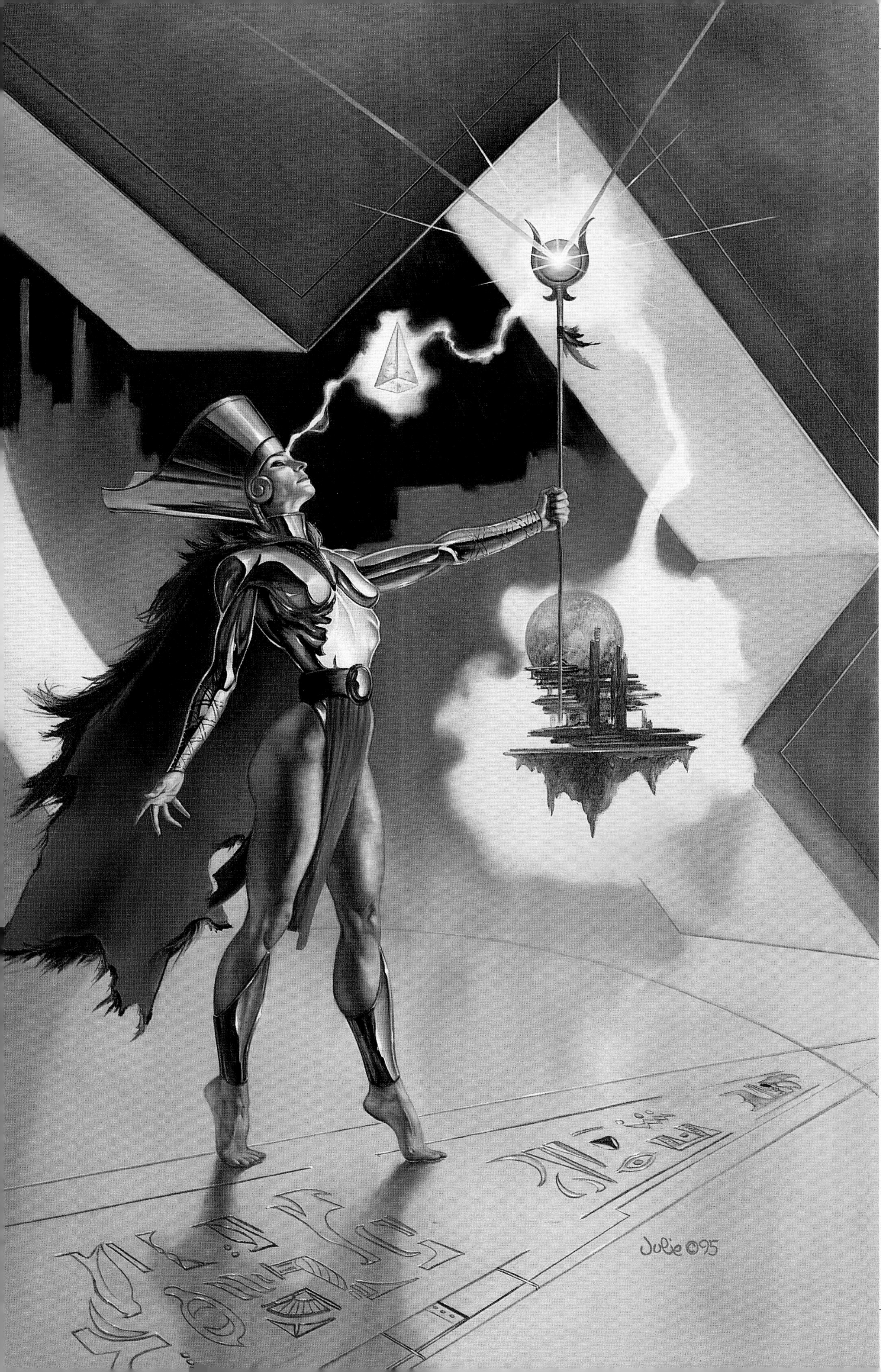
Julie ©95

This does not necessarily require great technical skill, but because of her own kind of work Julie appreciates good technique, even when it is only being used in a light-hearted way. One of her favourite artists is the nineteenth-century Adolphe-William Bouguereau whose poetry she feels is as much in his technique and use of light and colour as in his subject matter. 'When an artist has control of their technique it is like the wrapping on a present, it makes something that is beautiful or funny even more beautiful and funny still. Also good technique makes it more likely that people will stop and take notice of what you're trying to say.'

Other favourite artists include Alphonse Mucha, Gustav Klimt, Kay Nielson and almost everyone involved in Art Nouveau. These are mostly 'illustrative' artists but, in fact, she and Boris have a very broad range of taste and take every chance to investigate new galleries. Whenever their imaginations are feeling a little jaded or dry they go out to look for fresh art and generally end up rushing home charged with fresh ideas and motivation.

The happiest outcome is when a picture that is painted for pure pleasure then gets bought or published because that is perhaps the most objective form of approval. There is no longer any question of it having been self-indulgent.

Painting to Julie is principally about communication – conveying perceptions and moods to the viewer, pointing out to them what you find funny or beautiful or sexy, sharing what you feel about whatever subject is in hand.

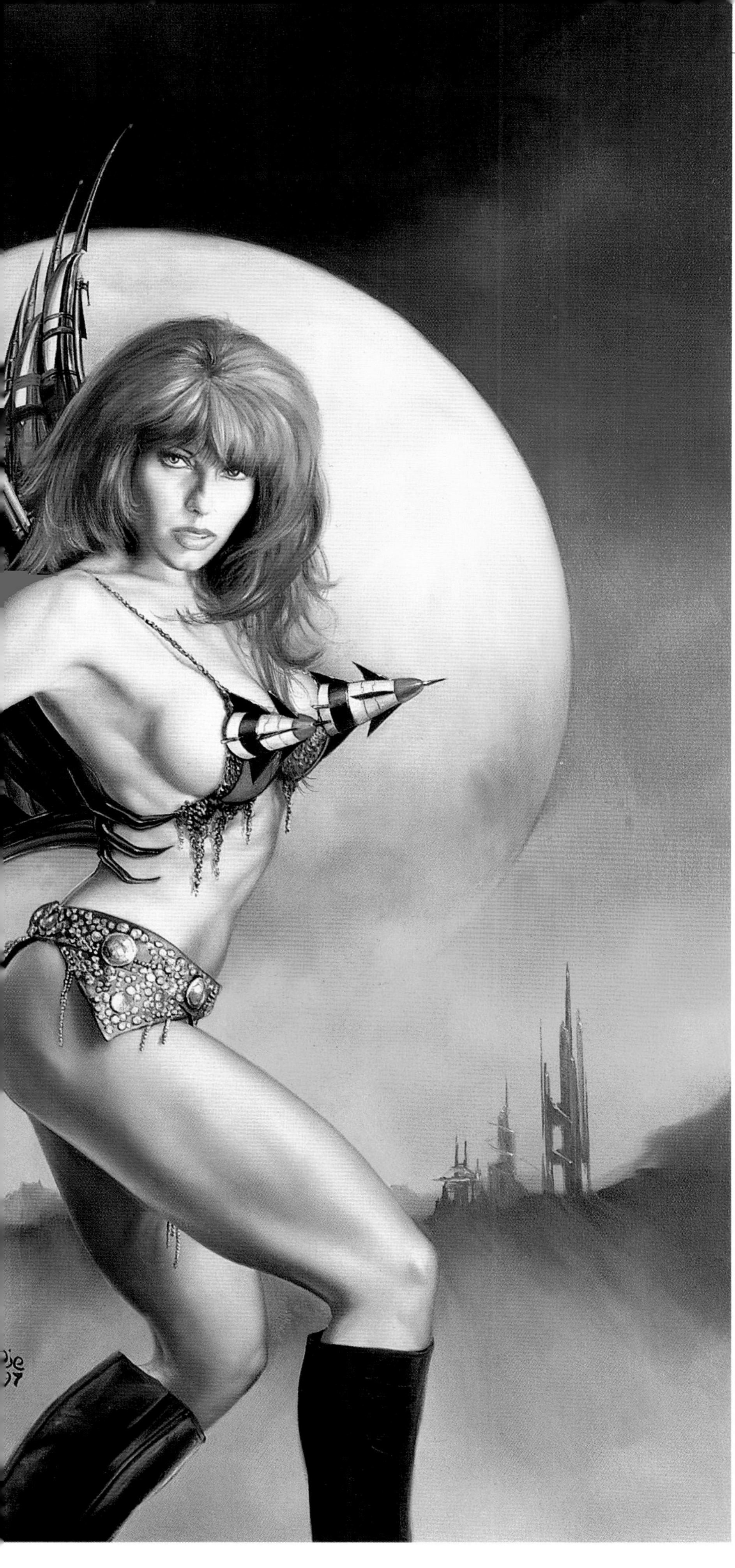

Torpedoes on Planet Pink, 1997
Oils, 20 x 15 in (51 x 38 cm)
Cover. Heavy Metal magazine.
Following the often tongue-in-cheek nature of the magazine, Julie's sense of humour once again came to the fore.

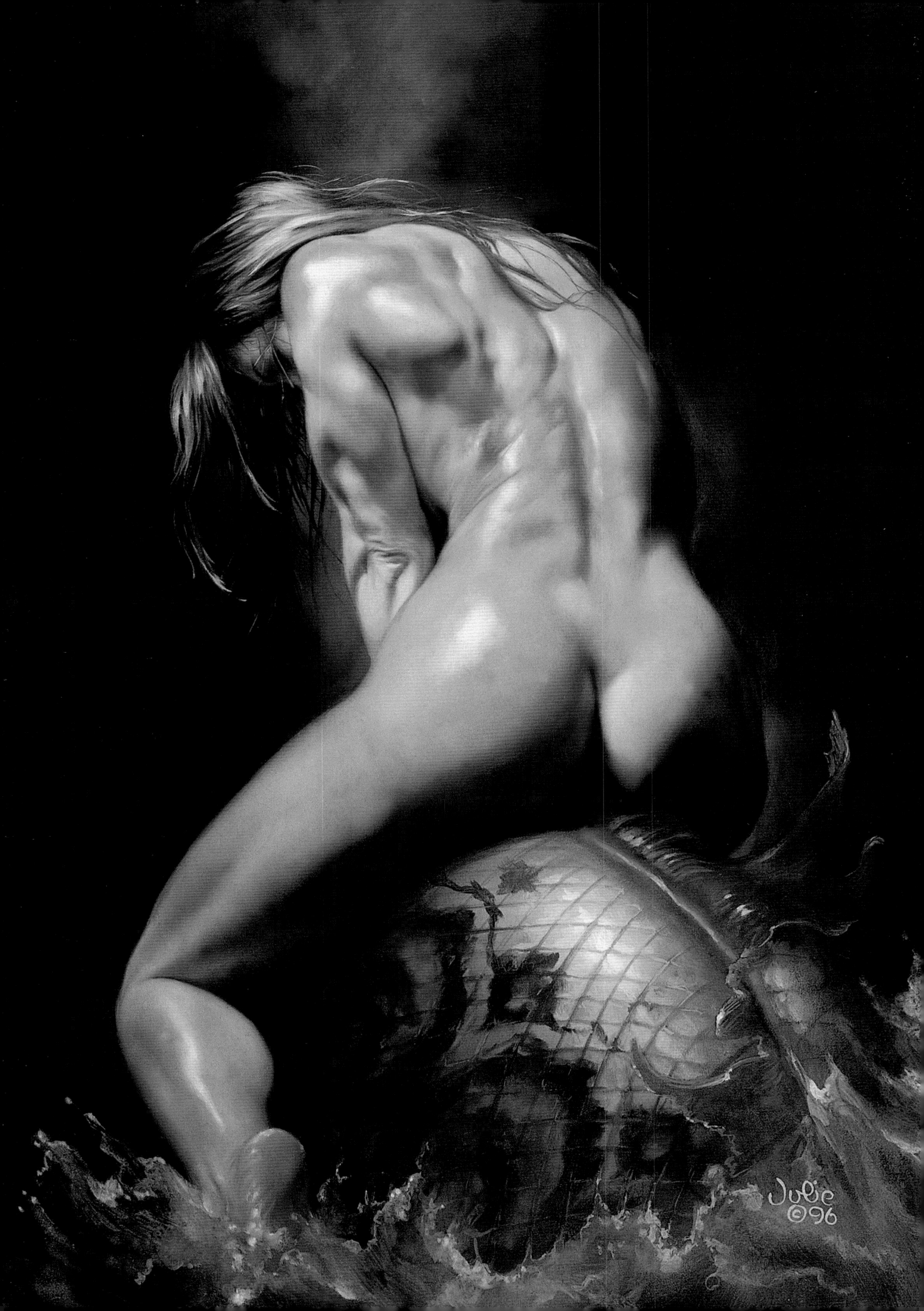
Julie
©96

OPPOSITE: *Wet, 1996*
Oils, 20 x 15 in (51 x 38 cm)
Portfolio piece.
One of several paintings for an erotic
art exhibition at the CFM Gallery in
SoHo, New York. The idea was to
convey a feeling of sensuality without
being too explicit.

BELOW: *Fish (sketch)*
Marker pen drawing.

Most of her paintings are commissions, or at least aimed at a particular audience, so their broad aim is defined from the outset. This takes something away from the creative process but there is still the challenge of capturing the mood and effect required by the art director. Julie: 'In some ways it's easier being given a framework like that, you know what you're shooting for. The hardest thing is when someone asks for a painting but says "just do what you want to do" or, even more challenging, "do something I will love," because you want to satisfy them but have no idea what kind of thing they're after. Then I try to get as many ideas from them as possible because it can save wasted sketches going back and forth for approval. The easiest thing of course, is when you are painting for yourself because then you can just follow the ideas that come.'

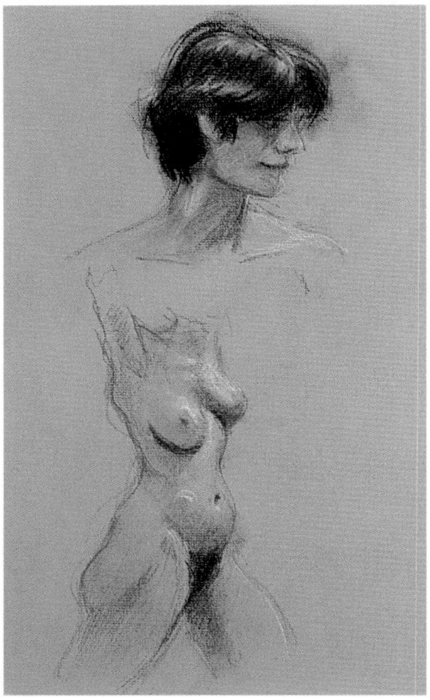

OPPOSITE: ***Albatross, 1998***
Oils, 20 x 15 in (51 x 38 cm)
Portfolio piece.
Another painting for the CFM exhibition. At some point Julie would like to do a book of purely symbolic pieces like this. The title hints at Coleridge's 'Rime of the Ancient Mariner', the point being that the albatrosses people carry around their necks come in many different forms.

RIGHT: ***Reflecting, 1996***
Oils, 20 x 15 in (51 x 38 cm)
Portfolio piece.
The idea here was to create something quietly sexy at the same time as playing with reflections. That one figure is a reflection is stressed by different skin tones and a slight fuzziness of the edges. The model was photographed in Julie's living room.

ABOVE: ***Figure study***
Pastels.

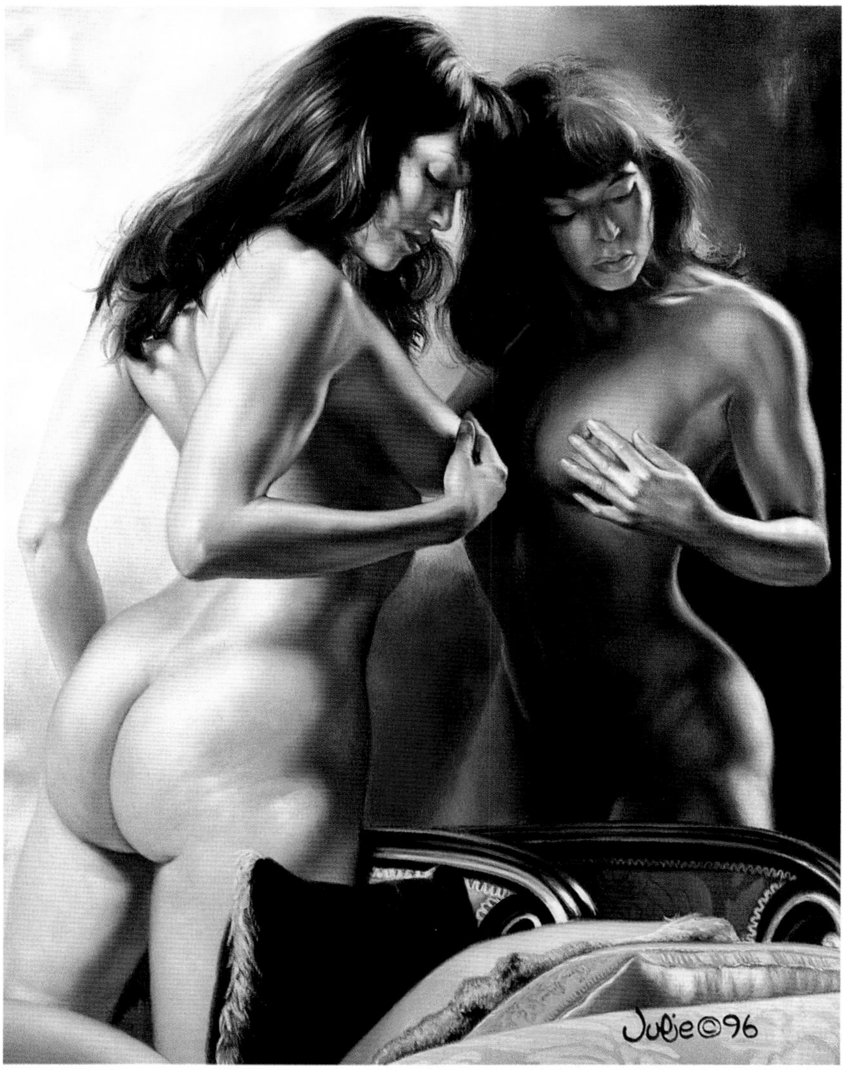
Julie©96

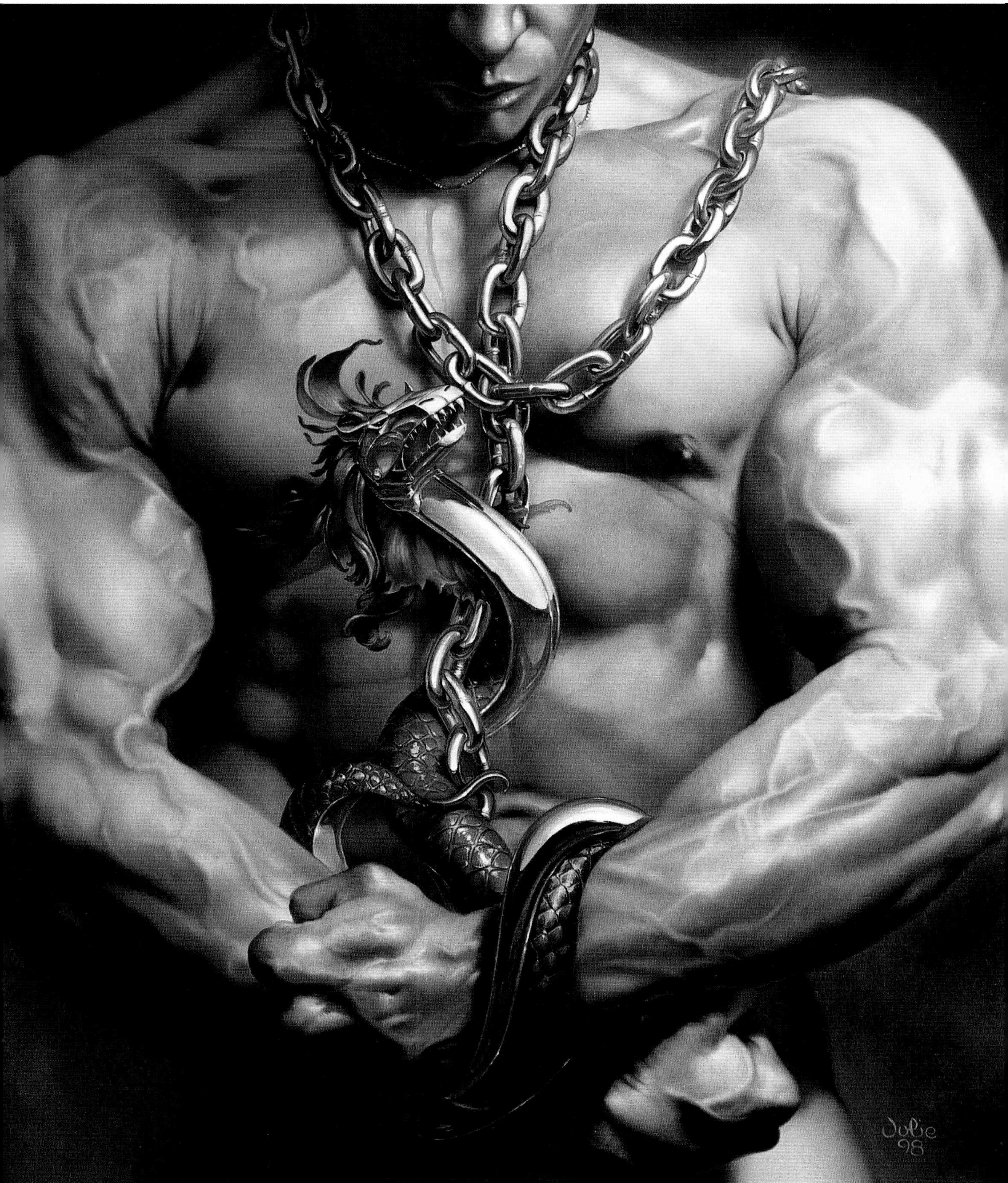
Julie
98

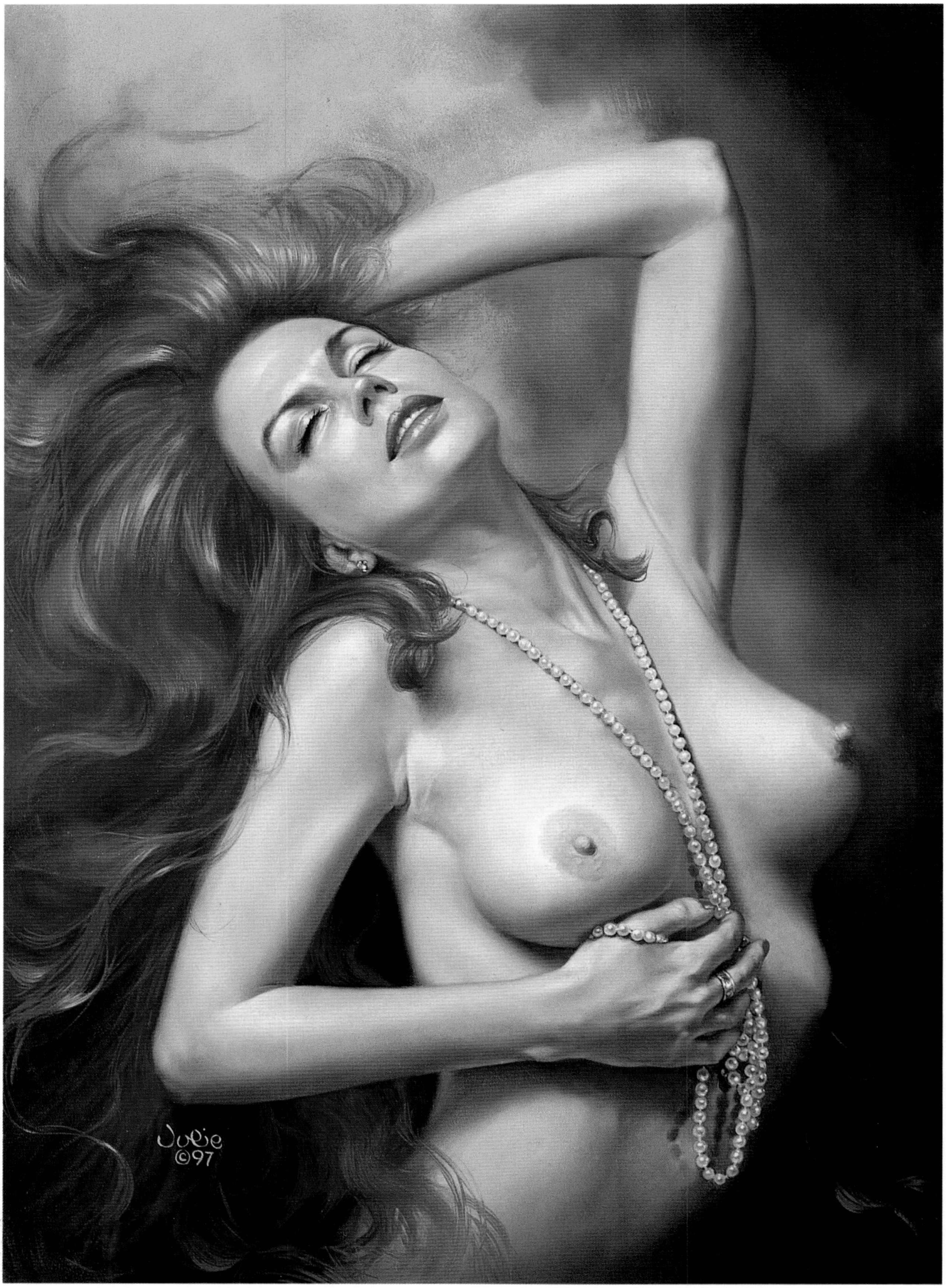
Julie
©97

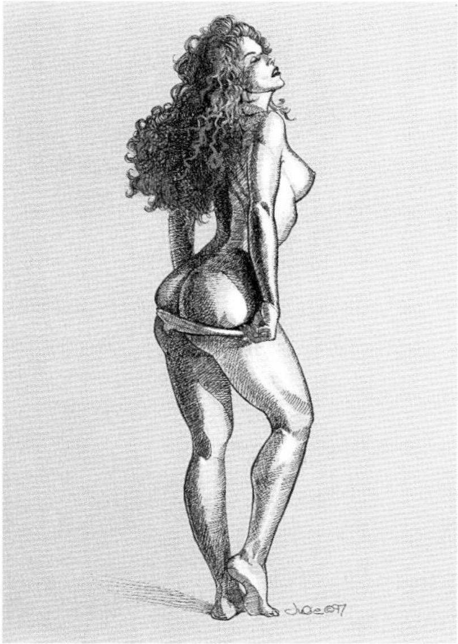

ABOVE: ***Panties (sketch), 1997***
On the eve of going to a show in Germany, Julie and Boris felt they needed more material to take along so they invited a model for some last minute sketches. This one attracted so much favourable attention Julie decided to expand it into a painting.

LEFT: ***Pearls, 1997***
Oils, 20 x 15 in (51 x 38 cm)
Editorial illustration. Penthouse Comix. This accompanied an article titled 'Sweet Chastity' and features a glamorous friend of Julie's who really loves pearls, jewellery and other aspects of the high life, so was a natural choice for the part.

RIGHT: ***The Alchemist, 1998***
Oils, 20 x 15 in (51 x 38 cm)
Portfolio piece.
The Art Nouveau border just suggested itself as painting began but there was no punch line until Julie thought that perhaps instead of panties, the female might be removing her outer skin or costume and thereby transmuting from base metal to gold, as in the alchemist's dream.

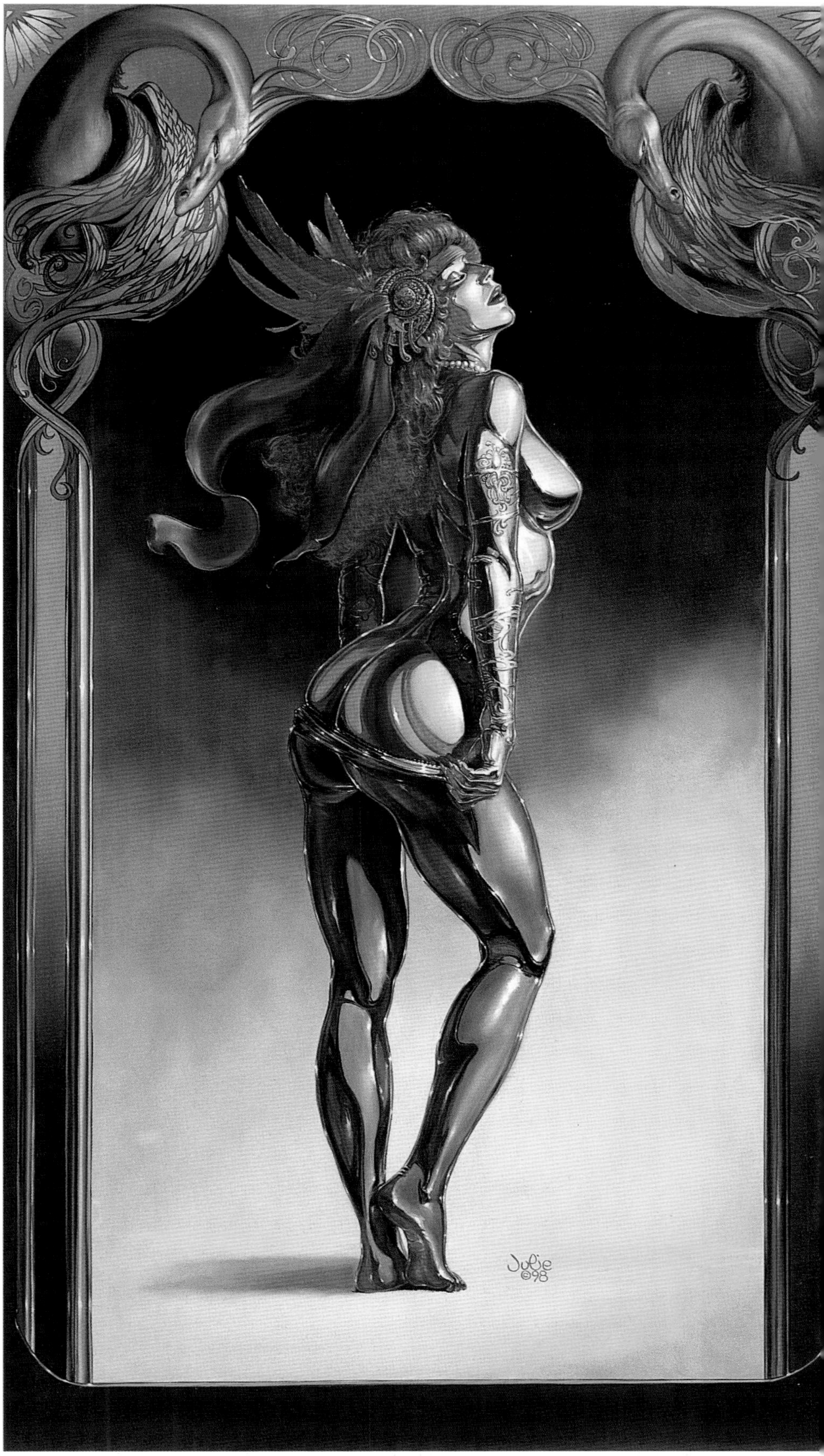

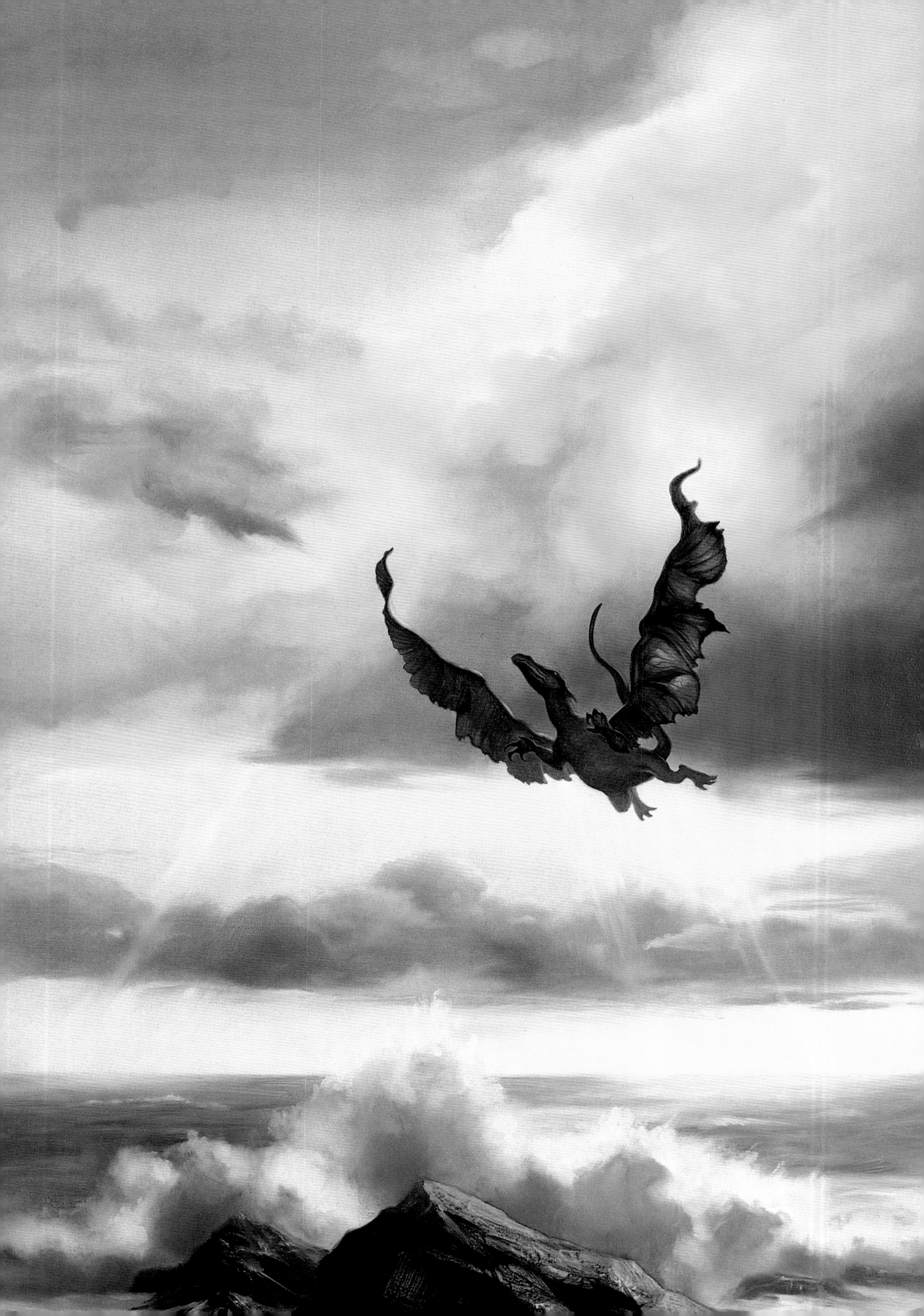

LEFT: *Happy Dragon Morning, 1998*
Oils, 20 x 15 in (51 x 38 cm)
Book cover. Tor Books.
*The picture title is simply the brief given
to Julie – the publishers wanted a happy
dragon in the morning sky over the
English coast. Never having visited
England, this required a little imagination
but it hit the right spot. When doing a
purely cheerful picture like this Julie finds
her own mood rises with it. Conversely a
dark picture can lead to sombre thoughts
no matter how beautiful it is.*

RIGHT: *Defenders of Paradise, 1998*
Oils, 15 x 20 in (38 x 51 cm)
Book cover. Tor Books.
*At first glance, this heroine looks like a
really strong character, then you realize
she is maybe not all that quick on the
uptake, although adorably cute. You also
have to admire her defiance – her chances
of inflicting even a pin-prick on the
invading hi-tech aliens seems remote, but
she means to give it her best shot. Her
robot companion looks perhaps a bit
brighter, though hardly the most
reassuring companion in a fight.*

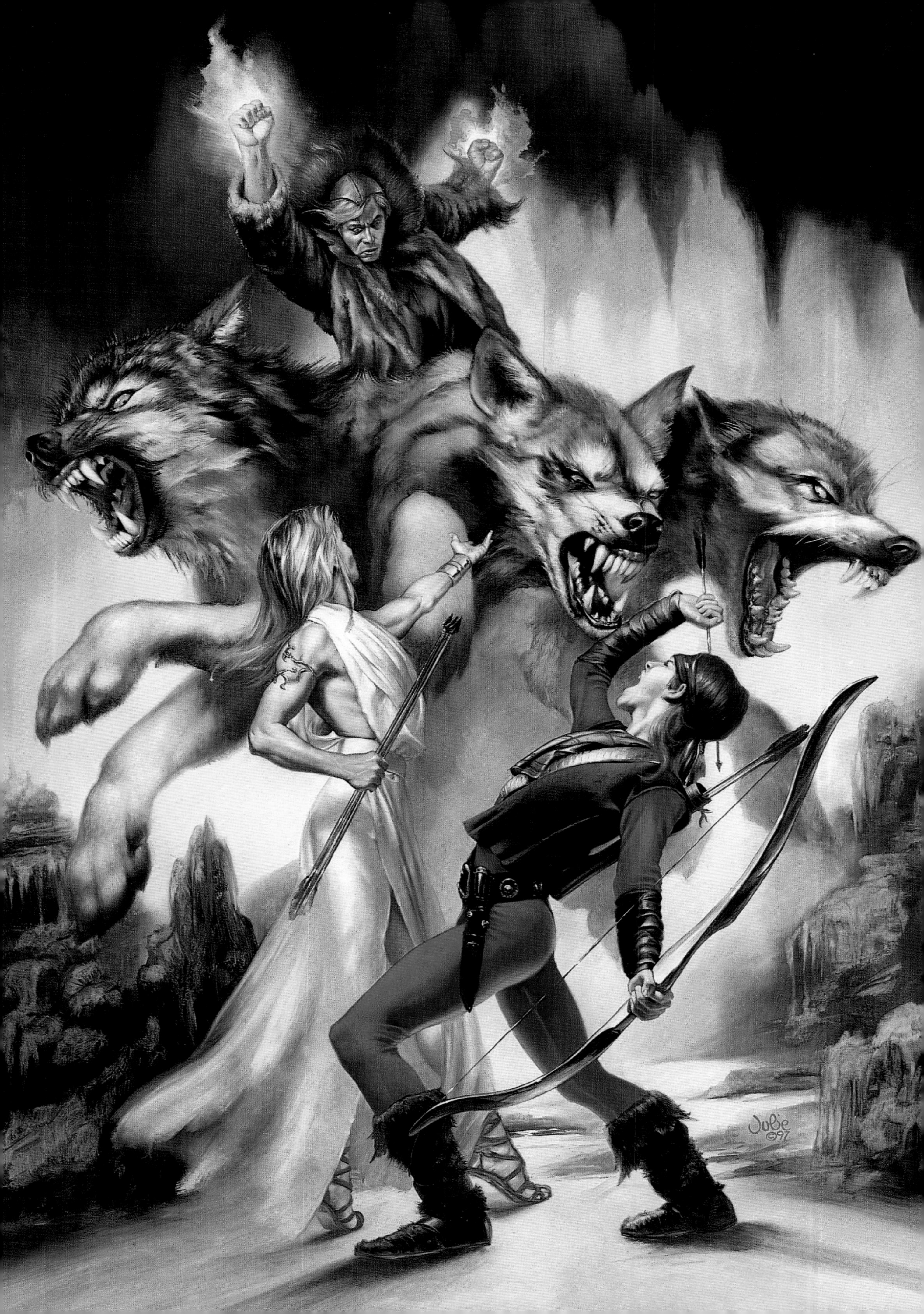
Julie
©97

3 WARRIORS

FAR LEFT: *Young Apollo, 1997*
Oils, 20 x 15 in (51 x 38 cm)
Book cover. Tor Books.
*Almost a family portrait. Julie's son
David modelled for Apollo, she is the lady
and Boris is riding Cerberus, the three-
headed hound from hell. She loves
combining real life and myth in this way
and believes that is partly the appeal of
fantasy. The setting and costumes may be
strange, but if the situation is familiar we
automatically make the connection. Young
Apollo is posing here like a rock star, but
then rock stars on stage pose like barbarian
gods and heroes. The same things happen
in movies, says Julie, where sometimes a
western is re-made as a science fiction
adventure. The setting might be different
but we unconsciously recognize the
familiar scenario.*

LEFT: *Young Apollo (sketch), 1997*

MANY OF JULIE'S comic book clients have recently bounced back into business. In an ideal world she would like a steady stream of such work as the foundation for exploring other fields, including straight landscapes and

RIGHT: ***Duel for a Rose, 1997***
Oils, 20 x 15 in (51 x 38 cm)
Book cover. Tor Books.
This was the first of three covers Julie did for Zorro novels. The model was a friend from her gym who was perfect for the part both in looks and temperament. This is important because character shows through in so many subliminal ways that simple looks are often not enough. Even as a child she always loved Zorro, beginning with the TV series, so, as with other favourite characters, it was a pleasure for her to be able to put that early love into action. The rose in the foreground was added as an afterthought but, as often happens with such tiny details, it throws the rest of the painting into perspective and immediately conjures the ghost of a story, hinting at the cause of the duel which is undoubtedly a female. The background is taken from Julie's library of photographs taken in Arizona and New Mexico, places she visits as often as possible.

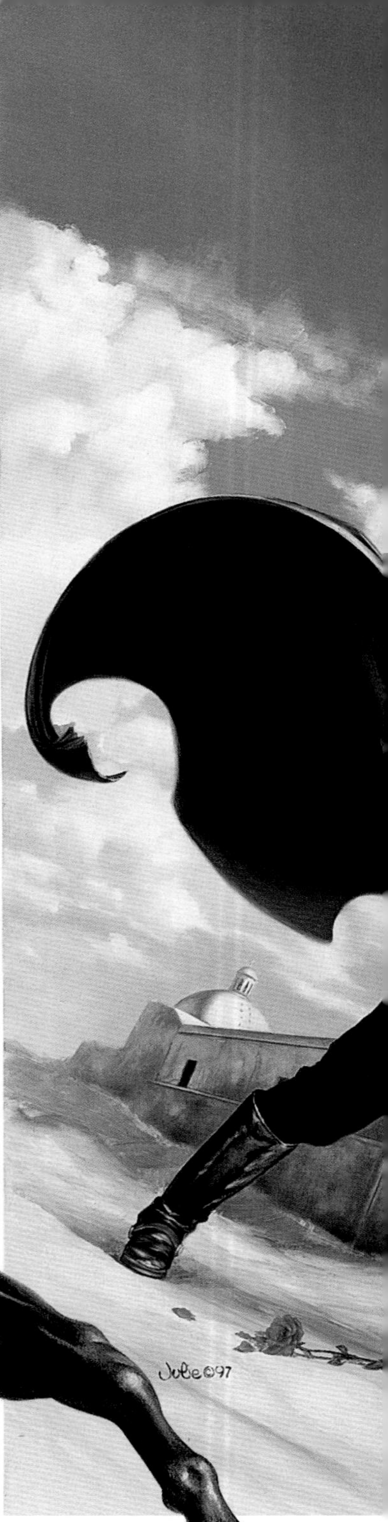
Julie©97

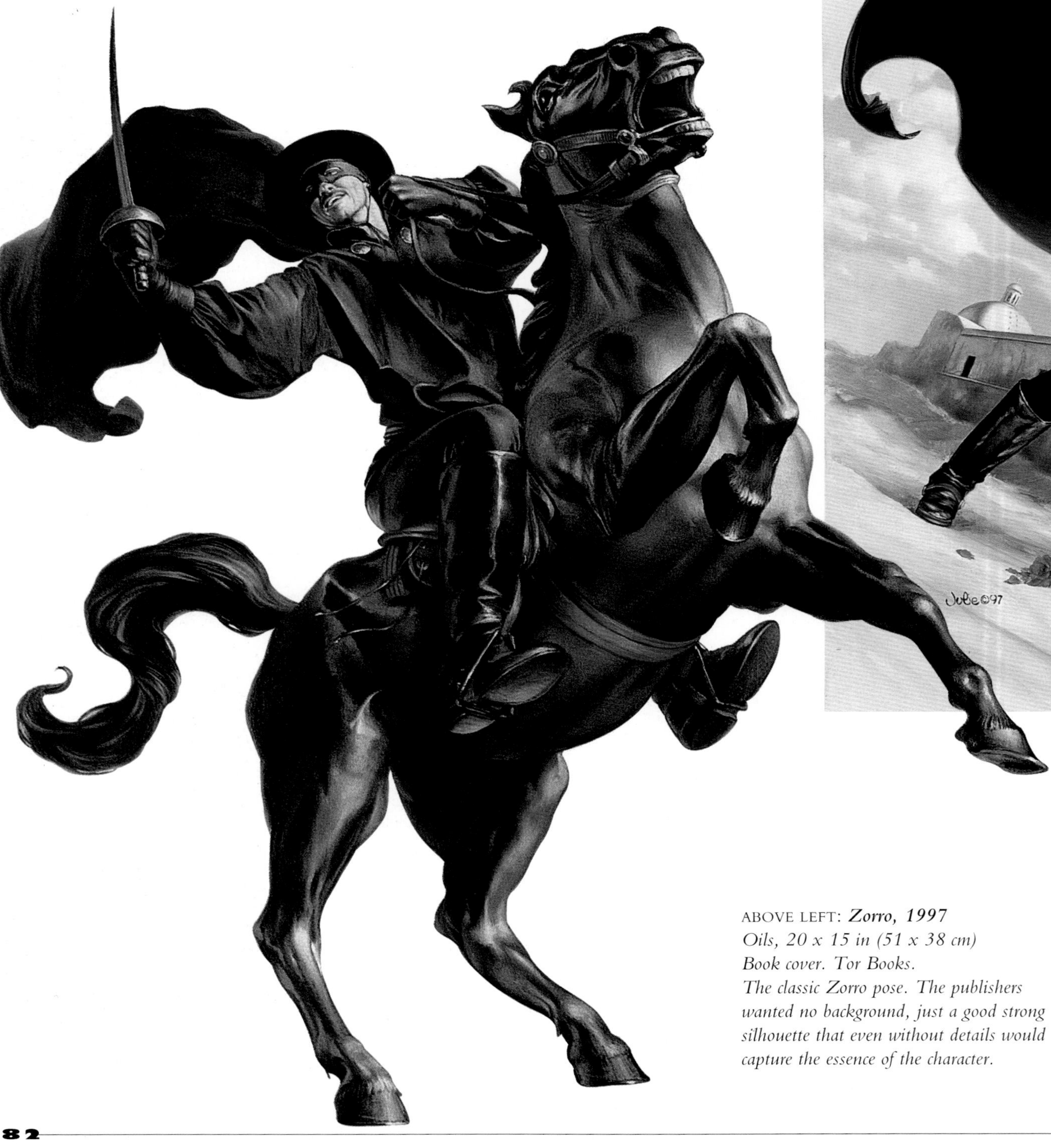

ABOVE LEFT: ***Zorro, 1997***
Oils, 20 x 15 in (51 x 38 cm)
Book cover. Tor Books.
The classic Zorro pose. The publishers wanted no background, just a good strong silhouette that even without details would capture the essence of the character.

figure studies. Somewhere in between come the book cover designs, often for novels derived from comics, which form the bulk of this chapter. Their mood is very similar to comics, but generally more attention is paid to the characters' settings, which is often a great excuse for landscape painting.

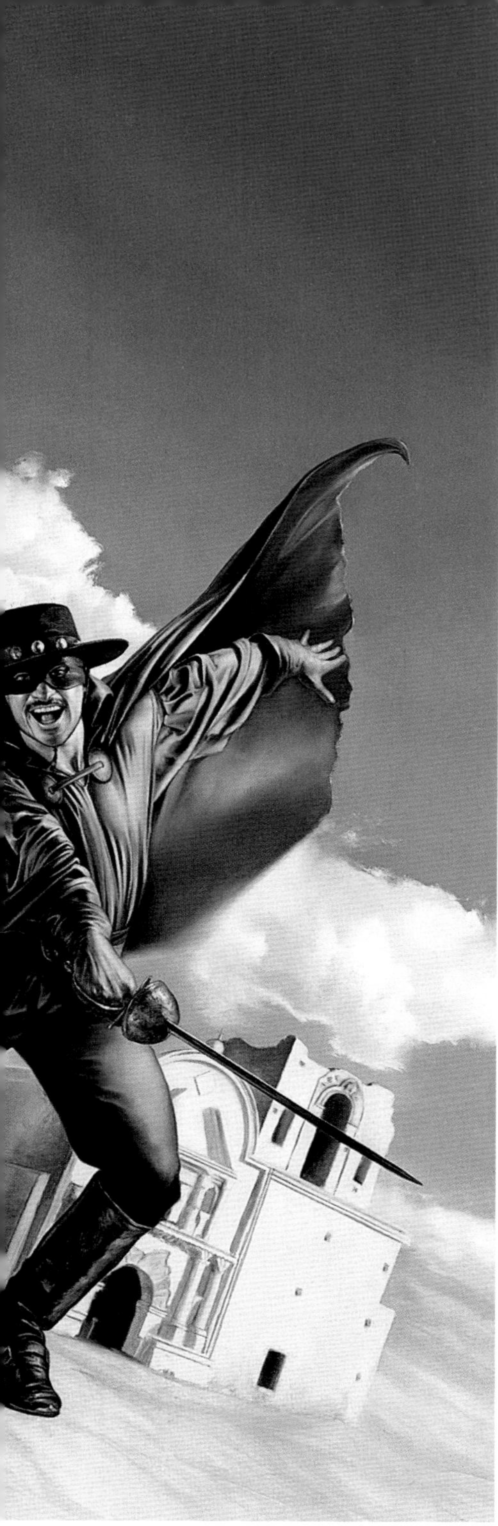

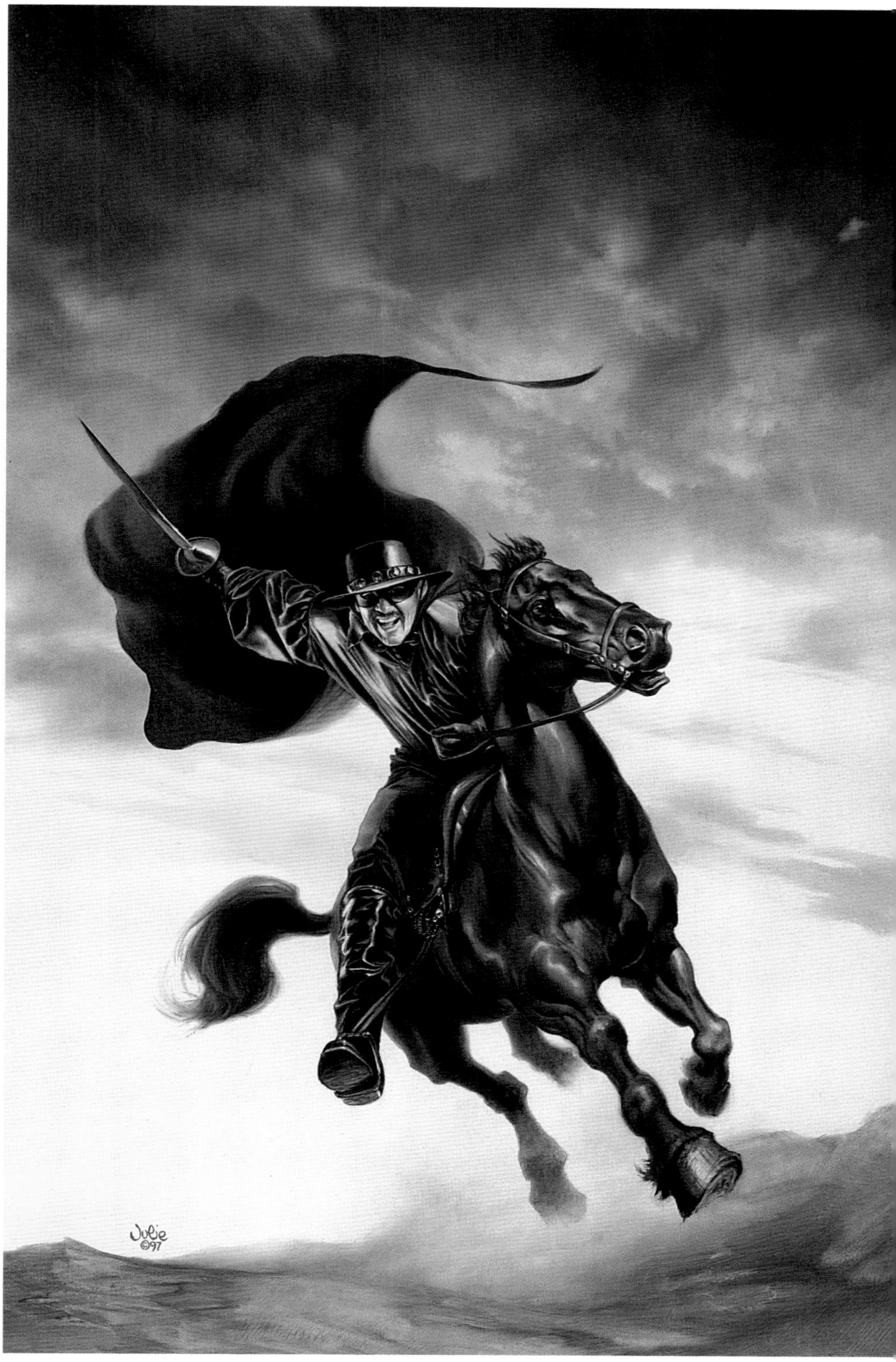

RIGHT: ***Into the Sunset, 1997***
Oils, 20 x 15 in (51 x 38 cm)
Book cover. Tor Books.
What Julie likes about the Zorro character besides his theatrical flair is that he is a real romantic and has a great sense of humour. He has a good time no matter how desperate his adventures, which makes the viewer or reader feel good too.

RIGHT: ***Soldier of Tomorrow, 1996***
Oils, 20 x 15 in (51 x 38 cm)
Portfolio piece.
When she began fantasy painting, Julie found she had a natural talent for shiny metal, and in particular shiny metal figures like this. For a time it became almost a trademark as she explored the paradox and contrast between warm flesh and cold metal.

This figure began as an early exercise which then sat in a closet for four or five years until just for fun Julie decided to finish it off with all the expertize she had acquired in the meantime. The contrast is less extreme than usual because although the warrior has a human face there is no warmth in it. It is the face of an android or cyborg devoid of feeling. The character was loosely inspired by one in the Turrican video game.

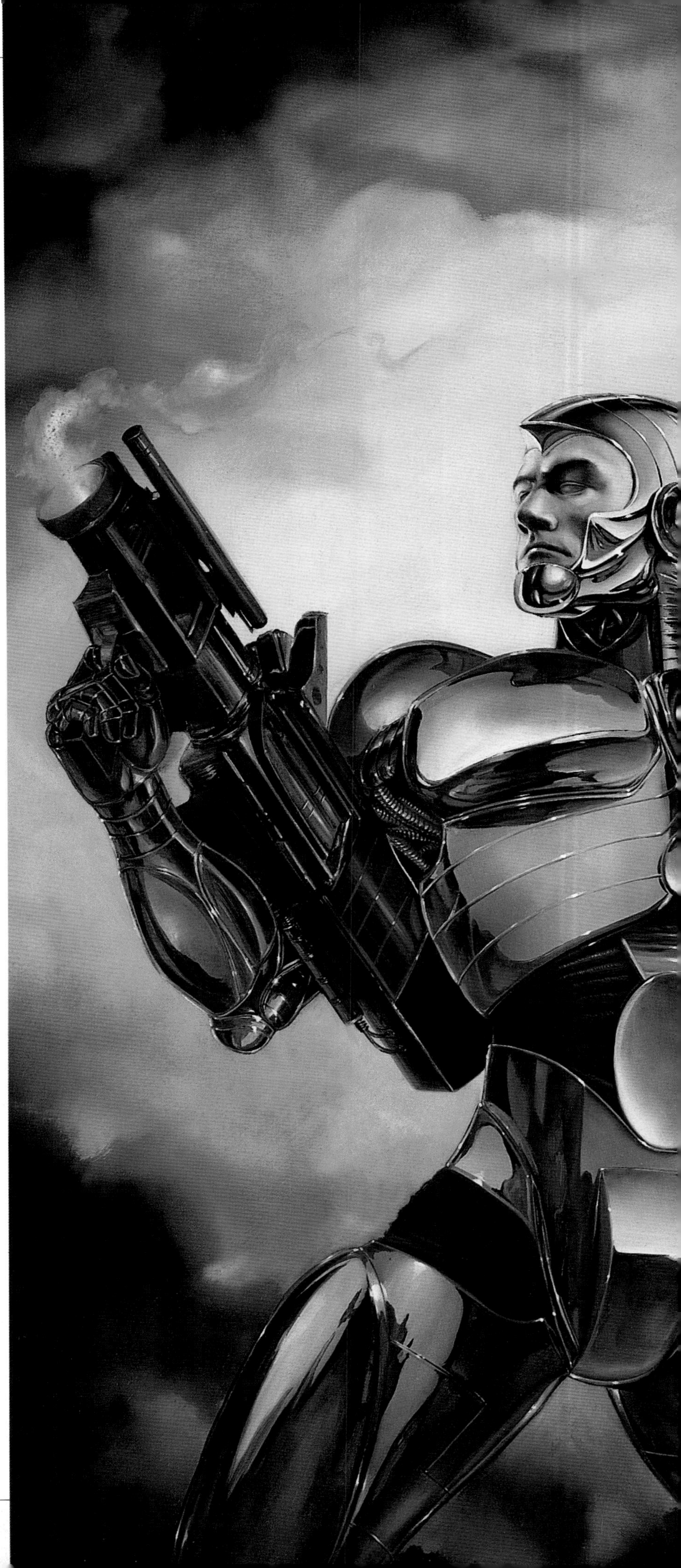

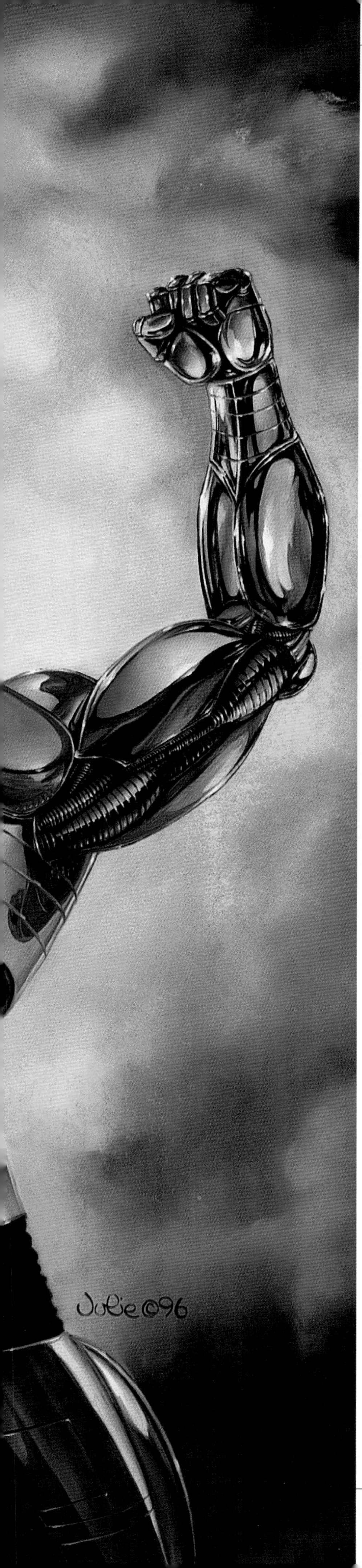
Julie©96

The battlefield is the natural home of heroic fantasy art, but only because of the visual drama and not because the artist would relish such situations in real life. Julie's heroes and heroines are never caught in moments of defeat. The violence is play-acting, a visual metaphor, and in practice it is a lot of fun acting out the parts for the photographs on which these paintings are usually based. Family and friends all join in.

BELOW: ***Elektra 1995***
Oils, 15 x 20 in (38 x 51 cm)
Trading card. Fleer Publishing Co.
TM & © 1999 Marvel Characters, Inc. All rights reserved.
The contrast here is between the dreary background with its mist and melting snow and the warm, red-costumed heroine; like the sun breaking through winter. As it happened, that was exactly the view from Julie's window the day she was working, so she just painted what she saw. The model was Marla Duncan, a famous fitness model.

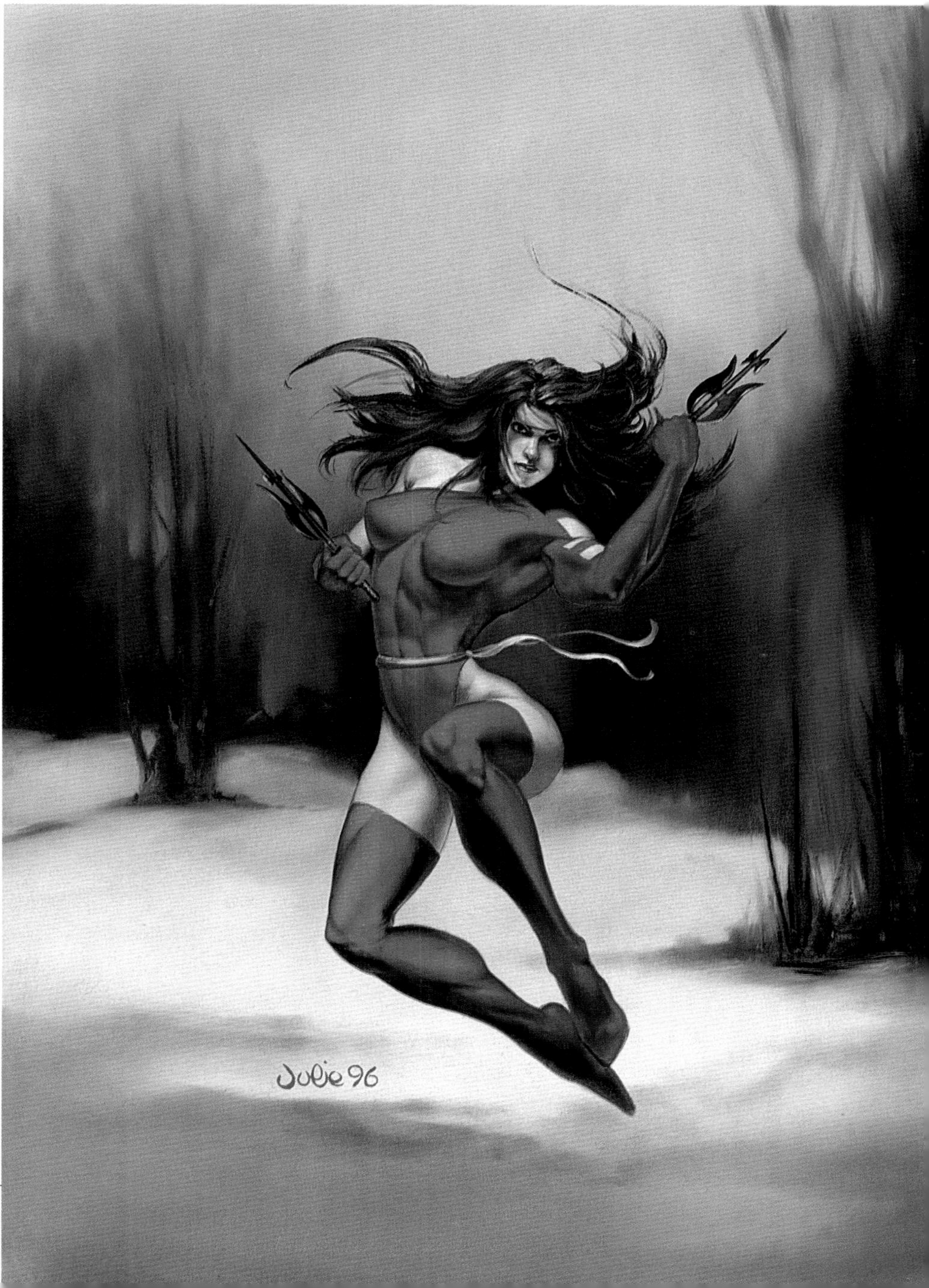
Julie 96

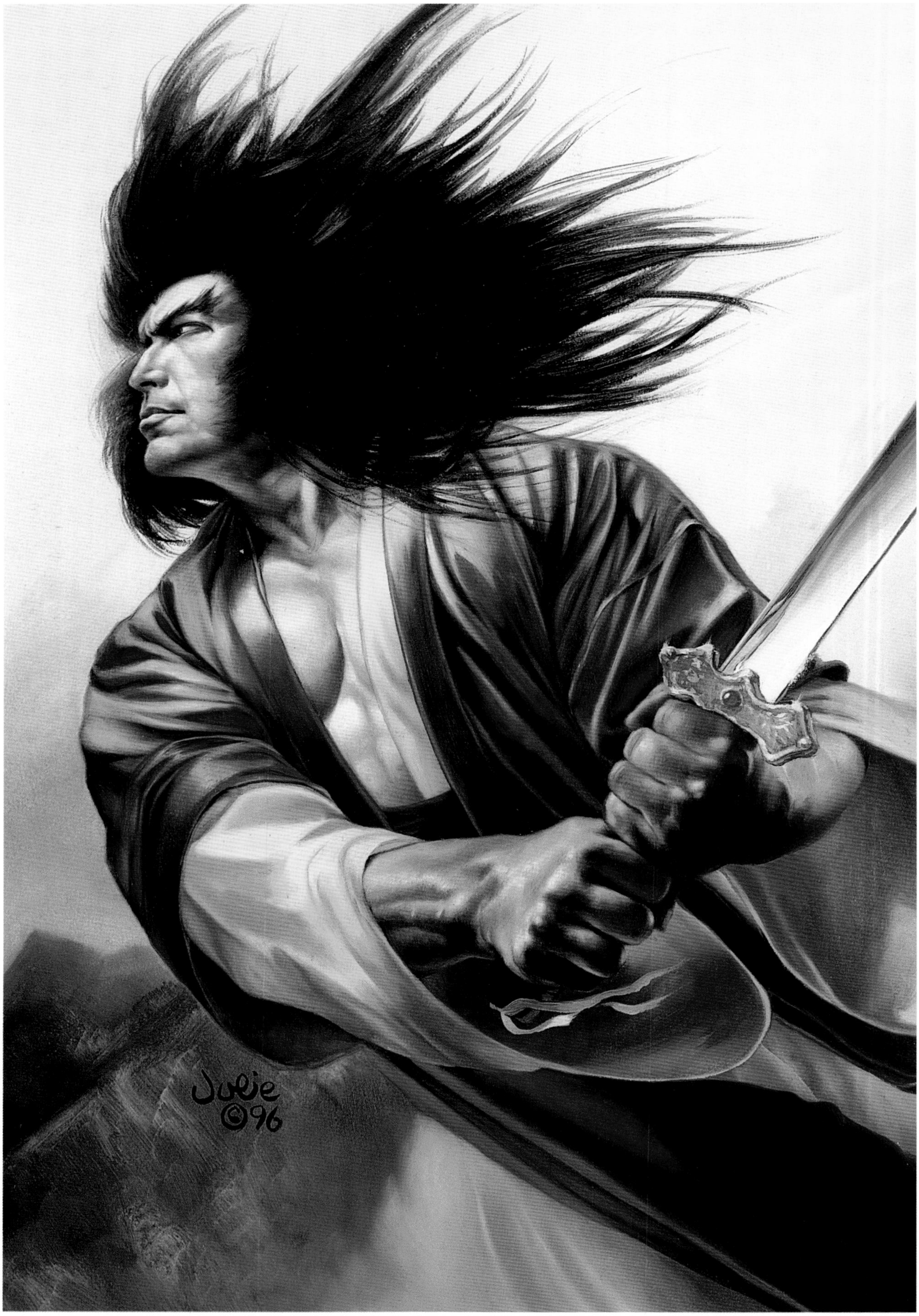
Julie
©96

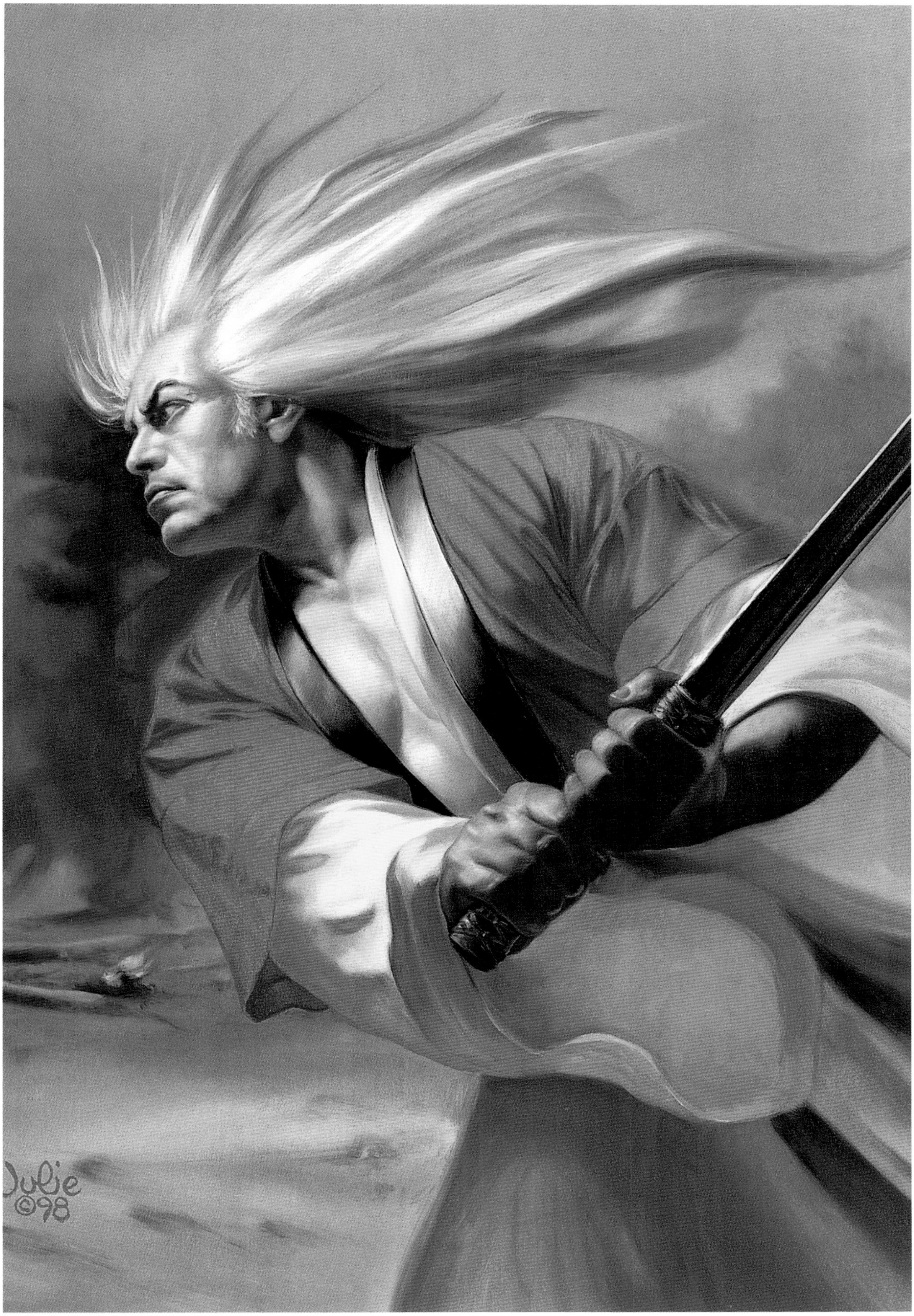
Julie
©98

PAGE 86: *Logan, 1996*
Oils, 20 x 15 in (51 x 38 cm)
Trading card. Fleer Publishing Co.
TM & © 1999 Marvel Characters, Inc.
All rights reserved.
*This was the first of Julie's cards in this
series of Marvel characters. The character
is Wolverine out of his usual costume and
indulging in his off-duty passion for the
martial arts and Japanese culture. The
model was Boris Vallejo who appears in
almost all Julie's pictures of Wolverine.
The colours (though not the mood) were
inspired by a painting by Adolphe-
William Bouguereau, one of her
favourite artists.*

PAGE 87: *Samurai, 1998*
Oils, 20 x 15 in (51 x 38 cm)
Portfolio piece.
*Julie was so pleased with her Logan
painting that she did a second version to
frame and hang on her wall. Starting
from the same premise she made it more
personal. This is a picture of dedication —
the warrior practising his art alone and
despite the desperate wintry waste of his
environment, the bleakness of which is
only accentuated by the spark of a camp
fire in the distance. His only enemies are
the bitter wind and the standards of
perfection he has set himself.*

RIGHT: *Bitch, 1996*
Oils, 20 x 15 in (51 x 38 cm)
Calendar illustration.
*The lady is Julie Strain, a professional
model who has appeared in Penthouse
and is married to the owner of Heavy
Metal magazine. For a calendar she
commissioned pictures by twelve different
artists including Julie and Boris and here
wanted to appear as a tough cookie —
super-sexy but liable to rip your head off
at the slightest provocation. In this
scenario she was obviously fully dressed at
the start of the action but, far from being
fazed by having her clothes blown away,
she has picked up her stilettos and is
relishing the prospect of revenge. The
background was suggested by an
exploding car in a movie Julie watched
at the time.*

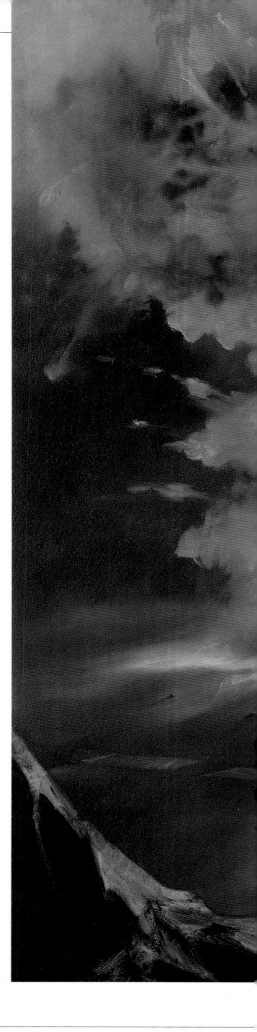

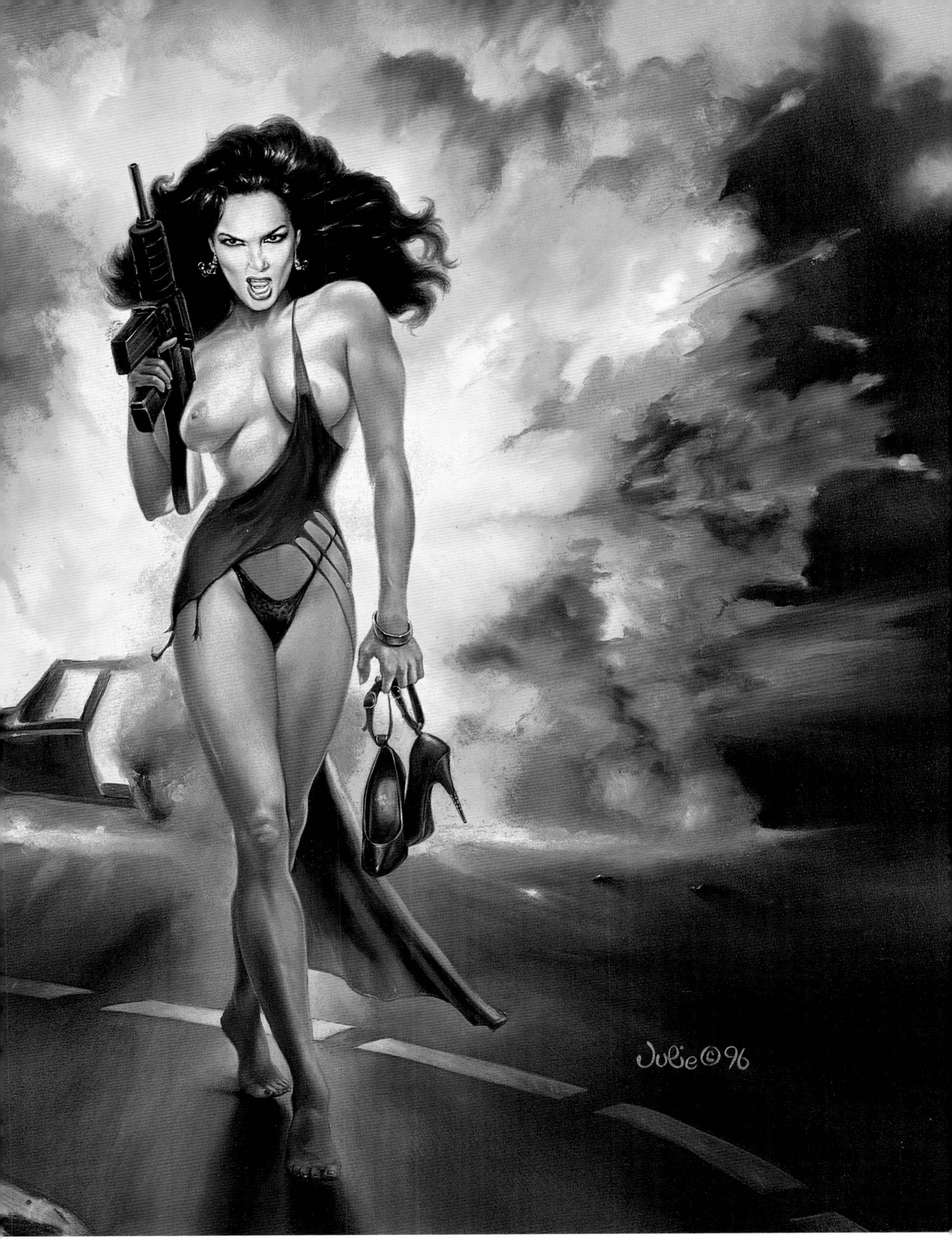
Julie©96

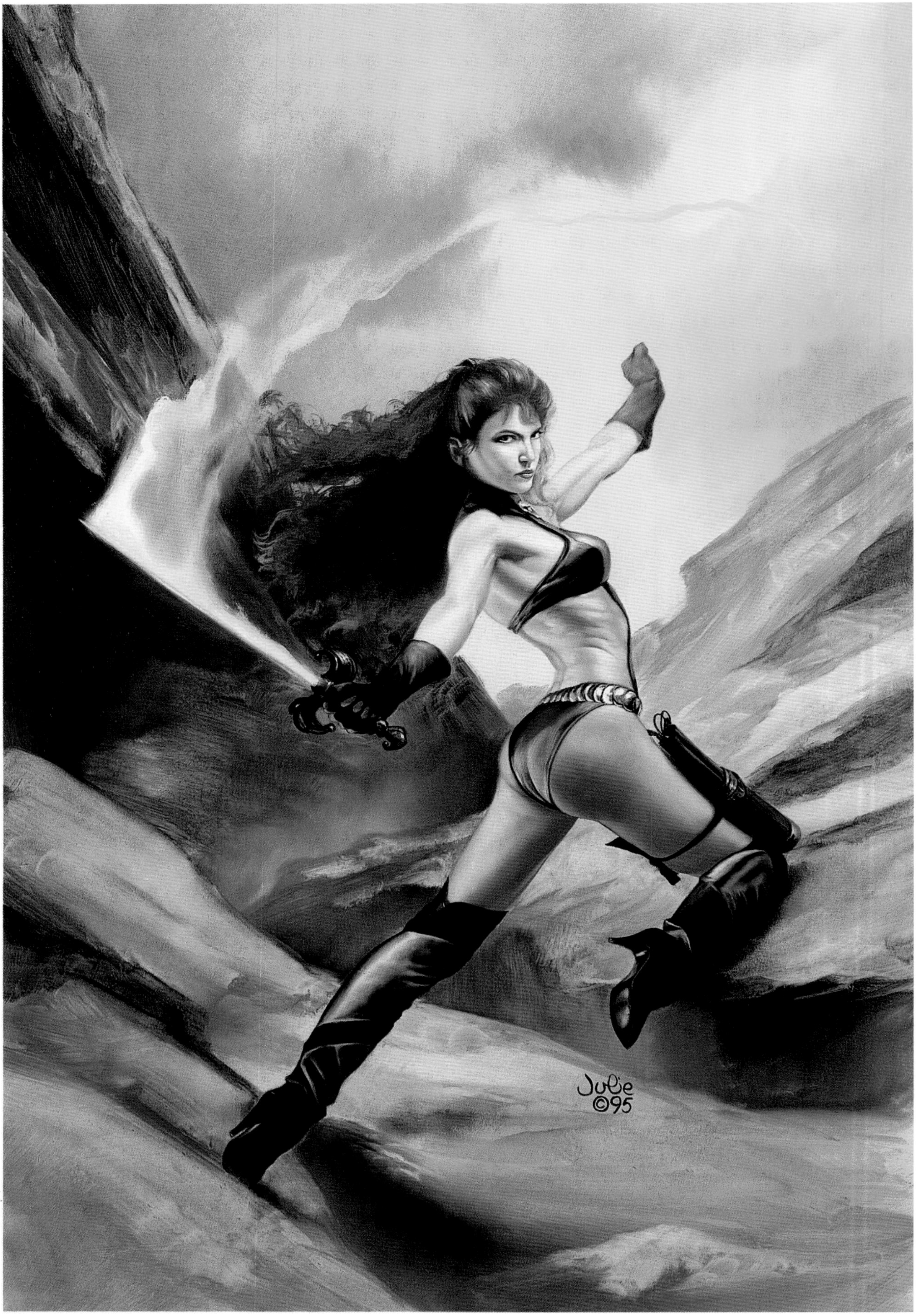
Julie
©95

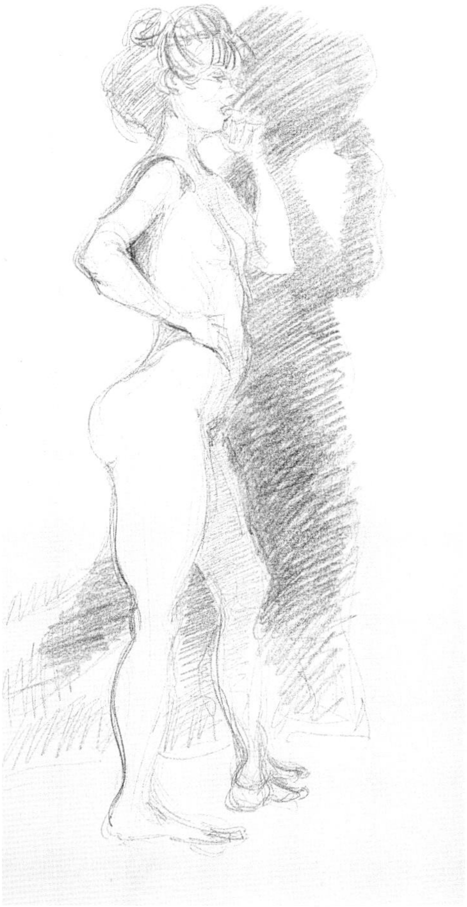

Julie is a fervent believer of studying the traditional methods of whatever kind of art one is aiming at. As it happens, she is by nature very good at teaching herself, but in any art form, she says, you can only go so far without the basic building blocks that have been hammered out over generations. For example, in her youth she learned the guitar informally from a friend and it sounded 'pretty enough'. But when, twenty years later, she wanted to play a classical piece she found that she had no idea of how to come to grips with it. So now she is starting to learn how to play the guitar again from scratch,

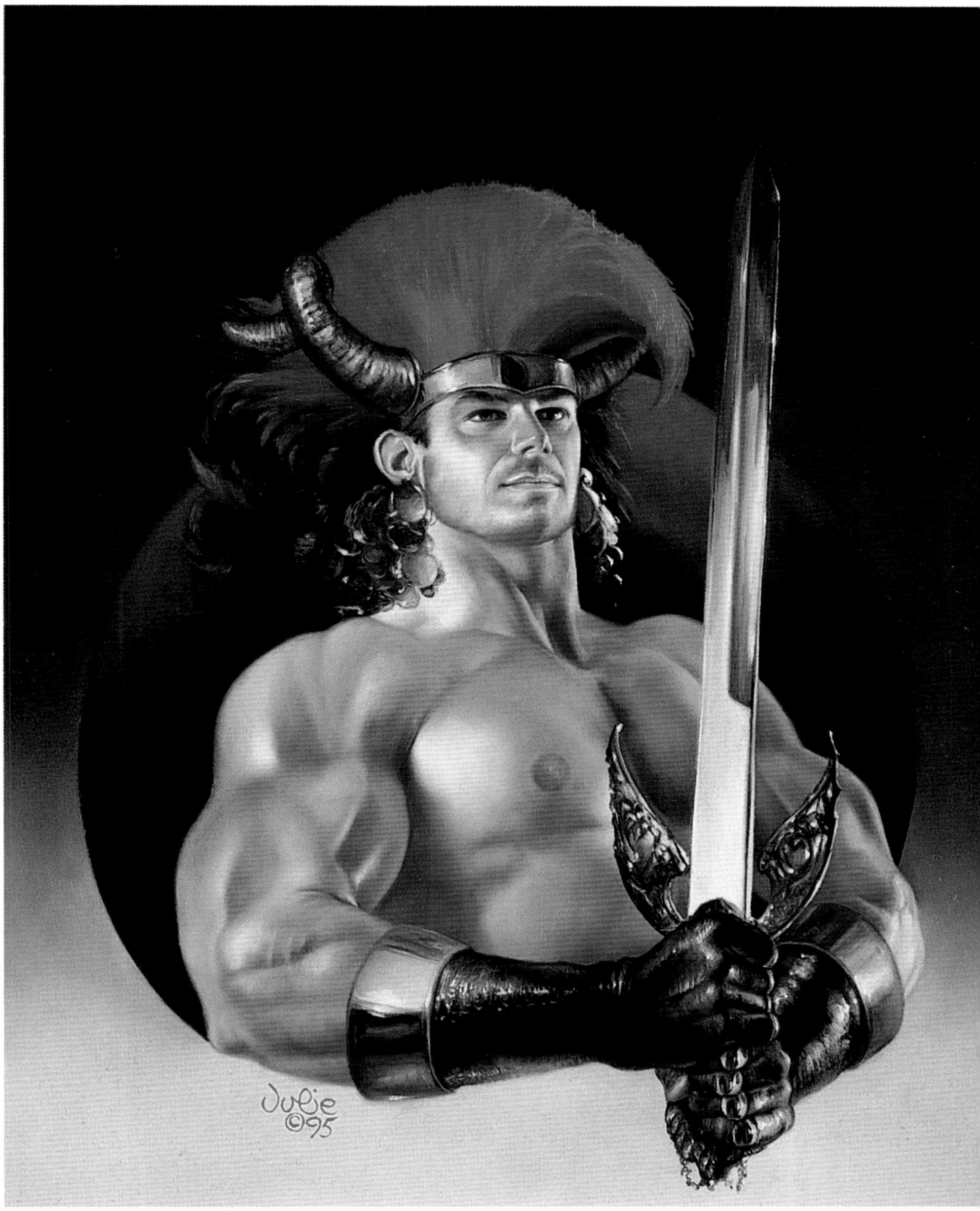
Julie
©95

ABOVE: ***Figure study***
Graphite.

LEFT: ***Brinke of Destruction, 1995***
Oils, 20 x 15 in (51 x 38 cm)
Comic book cover. Chaos! Comics.
Brinke Stevens is a model, actress and writer. In movies she has featured as heroine, vampire and victim, and is quite a cult figure among horror film enthusiasts. In the comic books she writes she is her own superhero with a grit very much like she displays in everyday life. Julie and Boris have both painted covers for her and always enjoy working with her.

RIGHT: ***Warrior of Truth, 1995***
Oils, 20 x 15 in (51 x 38 cm)
Trading Card. Comic Images.
This model, Kerry Palko, is a friend from Julie's local gym who has posed for many of her superhero paintings. One Christmas he asked if she could do something more personal and portrait-like that he could give to his mother at Christmas. The result happened also to fit a commission so all parties benefited.

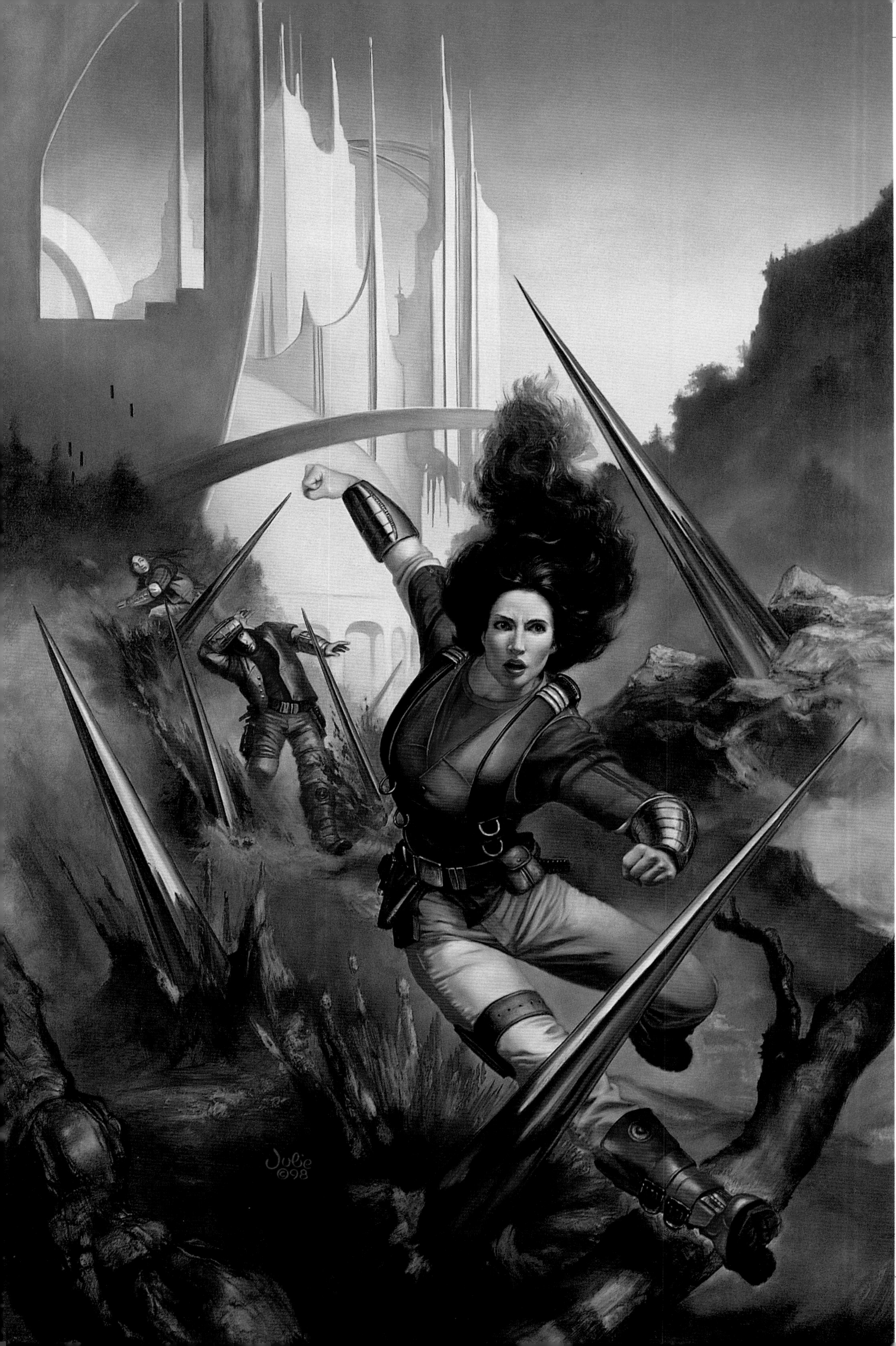
Julie
©98

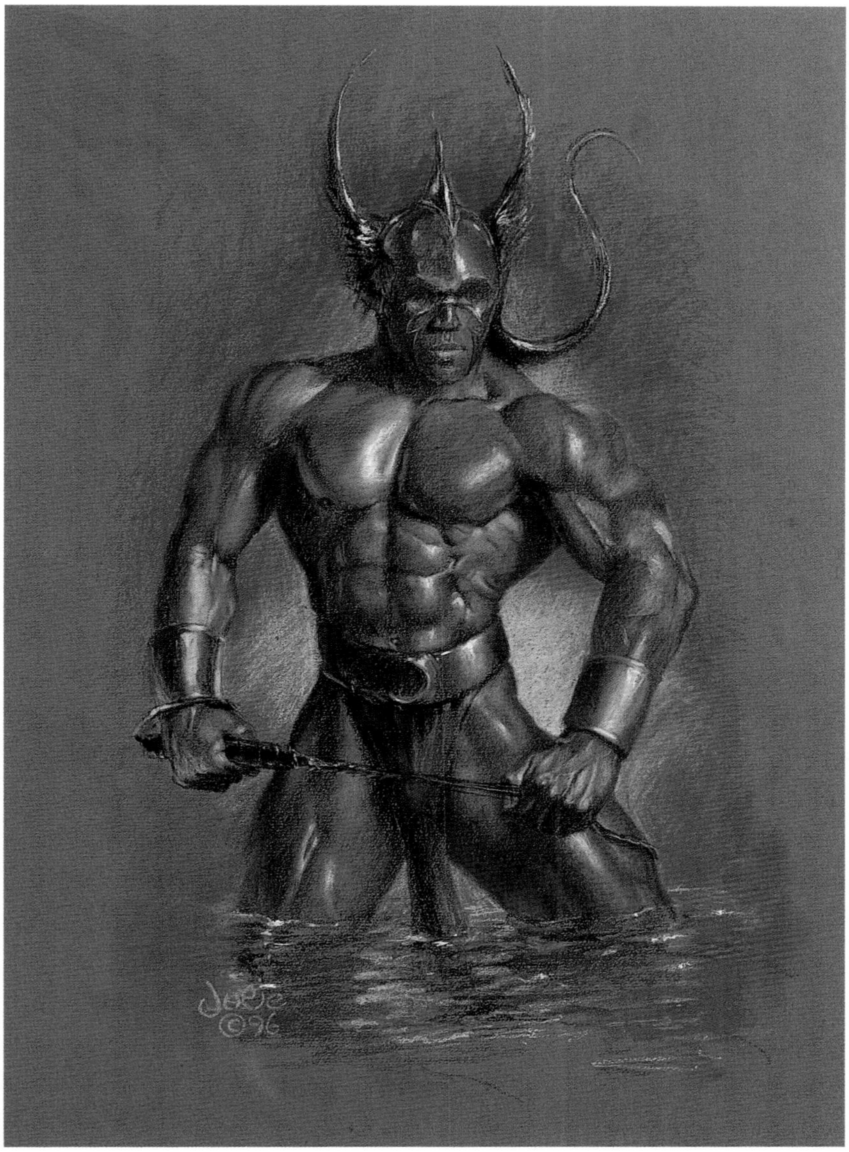

beginning with learning the names of all the notes instead of just playing them by ear.

Similarly, when learning to speak Spanish, Julie was content for a while to accumulate words, enjoying their strangeness and often likeness to those in other tongues, but she then took herself to a formal teacher to learn the basics of grammar and sentence construction.

The same applies to painting. At school Julie had a talent for art and experimented with drawing, acrylics and watercolours, but without any real structure or discipline and mostly working from pure imagination.

FAR LEFT: ***Obstacle Course. 1998***
Oils, 20 x 15 in (51 x 38 cm)
Book cover. Tor Books.
Given the chance, Julie enjoys reading the books she is to illustrate but often has only time for a few chapters relevant to the scenes suggested by the art director. Occasionally, as here, she receives only a brief outline and has to hope her imagination chimes with the author's.

Creating cities in paintings reminds Julie of building models as a child in her father's architectural practice. Here she ended up painting this picture in his office, having taken it along with her on a visit. There was a particular satisfaction in this, being able to work on a professional painting there instead of just playing. 'But I could never be an architect – I really hate all that careful measuring and perfect symmetry.' A deliberate contrast has been drawn between the serene city and violent foreground. It is no training exercise being shown. The spikes springing out of the ground are meant to impale the fugitives.

LEFT: ***Barbarian,*** 1996
Pastels, 20 x 15 in (51 x 38 cm)
Portfolio piece.
Pastels are one of Julie's favourite media. She loves handling them and simply looking at them in the box, so it is often hard to leave an art shop without buying more. Because pastel drawings generally look less 'finished' than oil paintings, people assume they are quicker but this is rarely so. Paint brushes can cover large areas quickly whereas with pastels it is a painstaking and slow process. Using toned paper helps bring out contrasts, but achieving a paint-like finish still takes a long time and is not what Julie is after anyway.

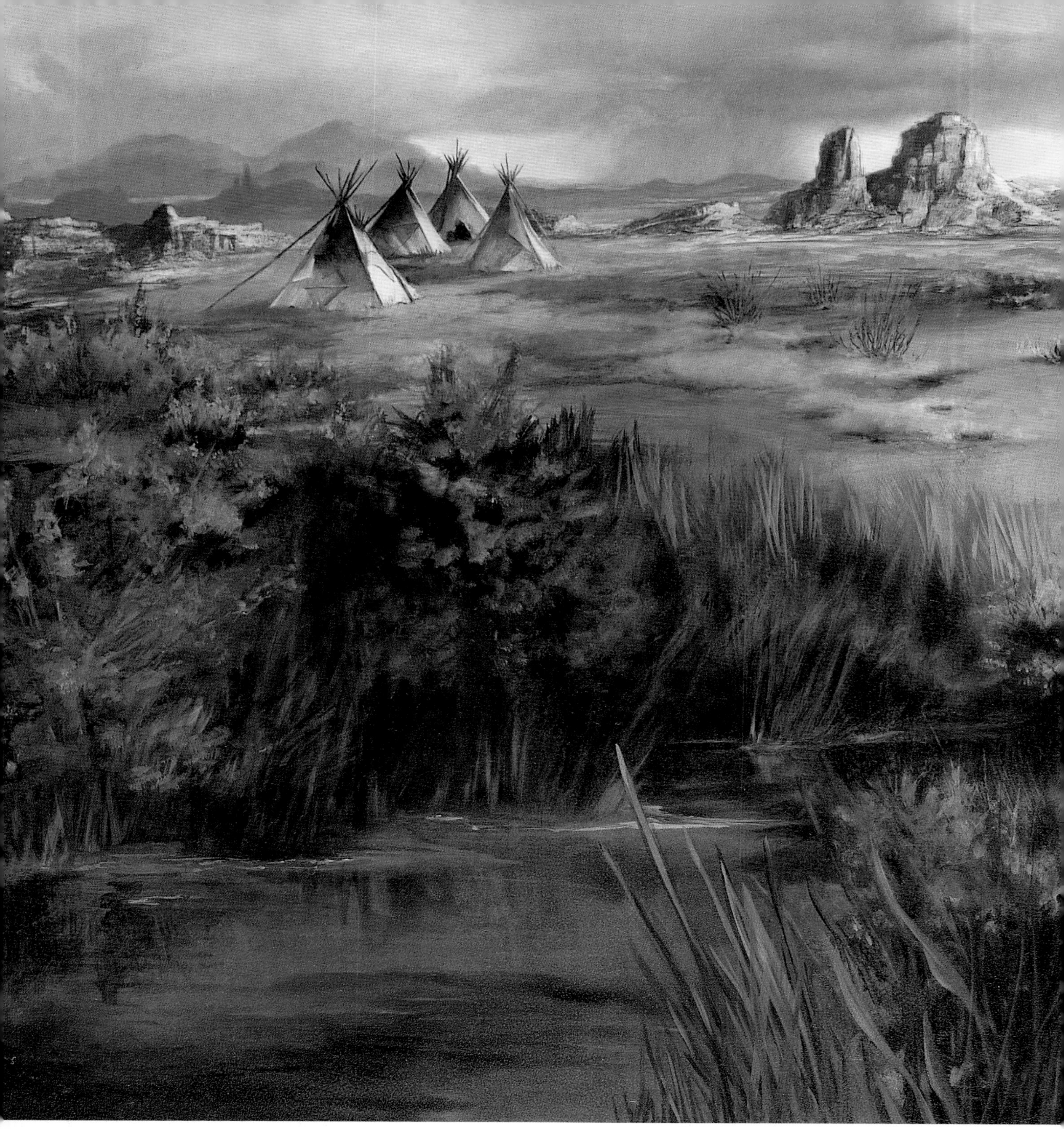

When she later met Boris Vallejo and showed him some samples (this was before any romantic involvement), he saw talent in them but had two suggestions – that she learn to use reference material which would add strength and credibility to her pictures, and that she applied more attention and patience. As it happened she was ready to hear this so she

Storm Approaching, 1997
Oils, 20 x 15 in (51 x 38 cm)
Portfolio piece.
A sample painted with the aim of testing the romantic fiction market. Most romance novels feature a couple in deep embrace on the cover, but some just have a single handsome man, as in this painting. Besides the commercial possibilities, this was also a good excuse to try something different, and lightly explore the theme of native Americans.

said OK, she would do exactly as he said. She learned to tackle each piece as if it was the only one she would ever have the chance to do in her life, putting everything she had into it and pushing the limits of her art farther than she had ever imagined possible. Also for the first time she tried painting with oils.

LEFT: *The Expedition, 1997*
Oils, 20 x 15 in (51 x 38 cm)
Book cover. Tor Books.
Featuring Boris as a Dr Livingstone-type
explorer on some distant planet with alien
porters and a strange moon or twin planet
in the sky. The model for his human
companion is a friend who is a chef at a
local restaurant. Putting the men in 20th-
century safari suits was a deliberate play
with the concept of throwing together the
familiar and strange.

RIGHT: *Defender of the Prairie, 1997*
Oils, 20 x 15 in (51 x 38 cm)
Book cover. Tor Books.
Often realism can be enhanced by
deliberately borrowing familiar effects from
other media. When Julie experimented on
a computer with 'Flowerchild' (pages 48–
49) it was suggested that she try to make
the result look like a painting. Here she
did the reverse by imitating the effect of
scorching sunlight on a camera lens. This
was accentuated by bleaching the sky.

The results were startling, as shown by her early oil portraits of Boris and her two sons on page 109. Then very soon after this she began to be commissioned professionally on a scale many illustrators only ever dream about; and not only being commissioned, but also painting

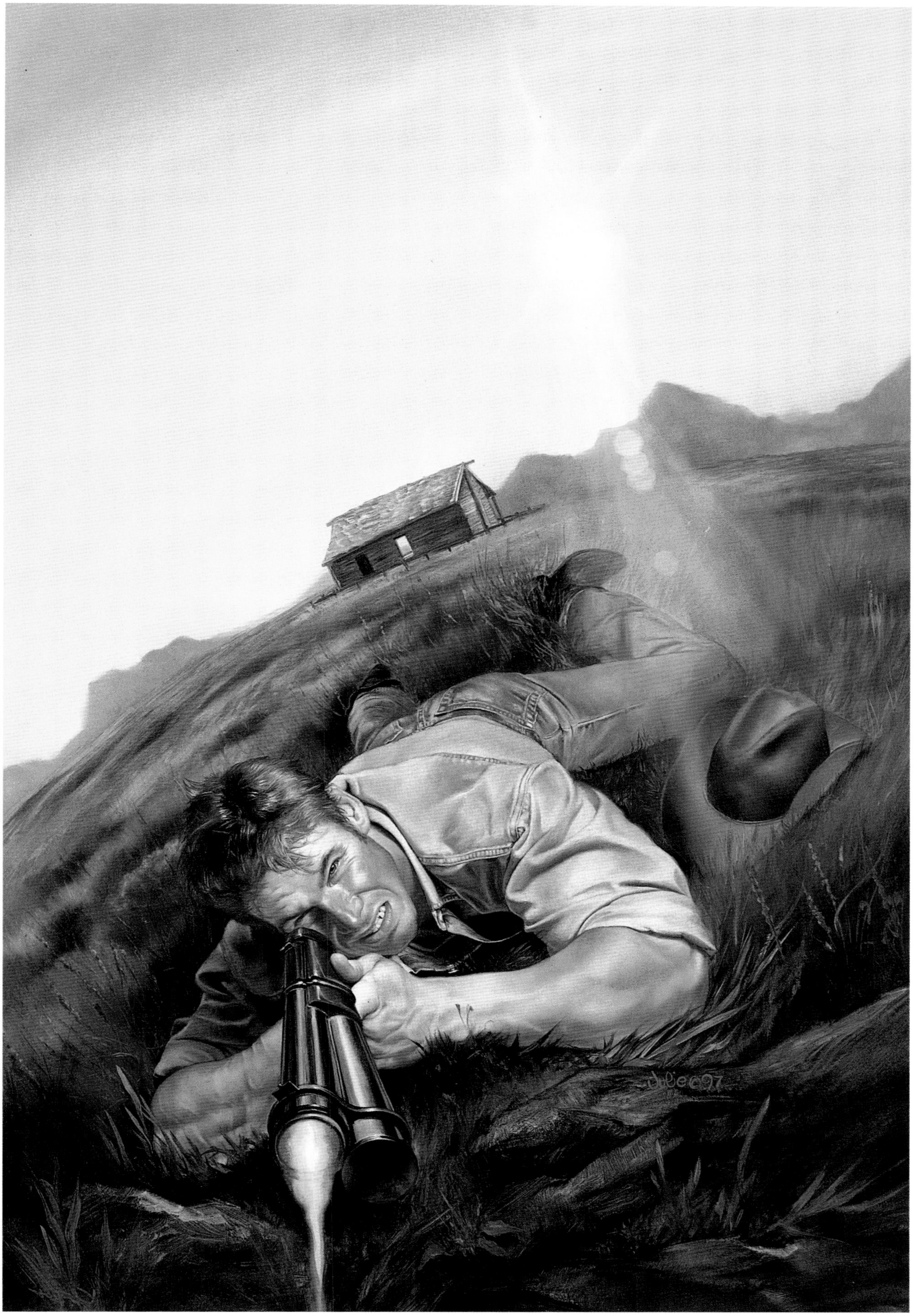

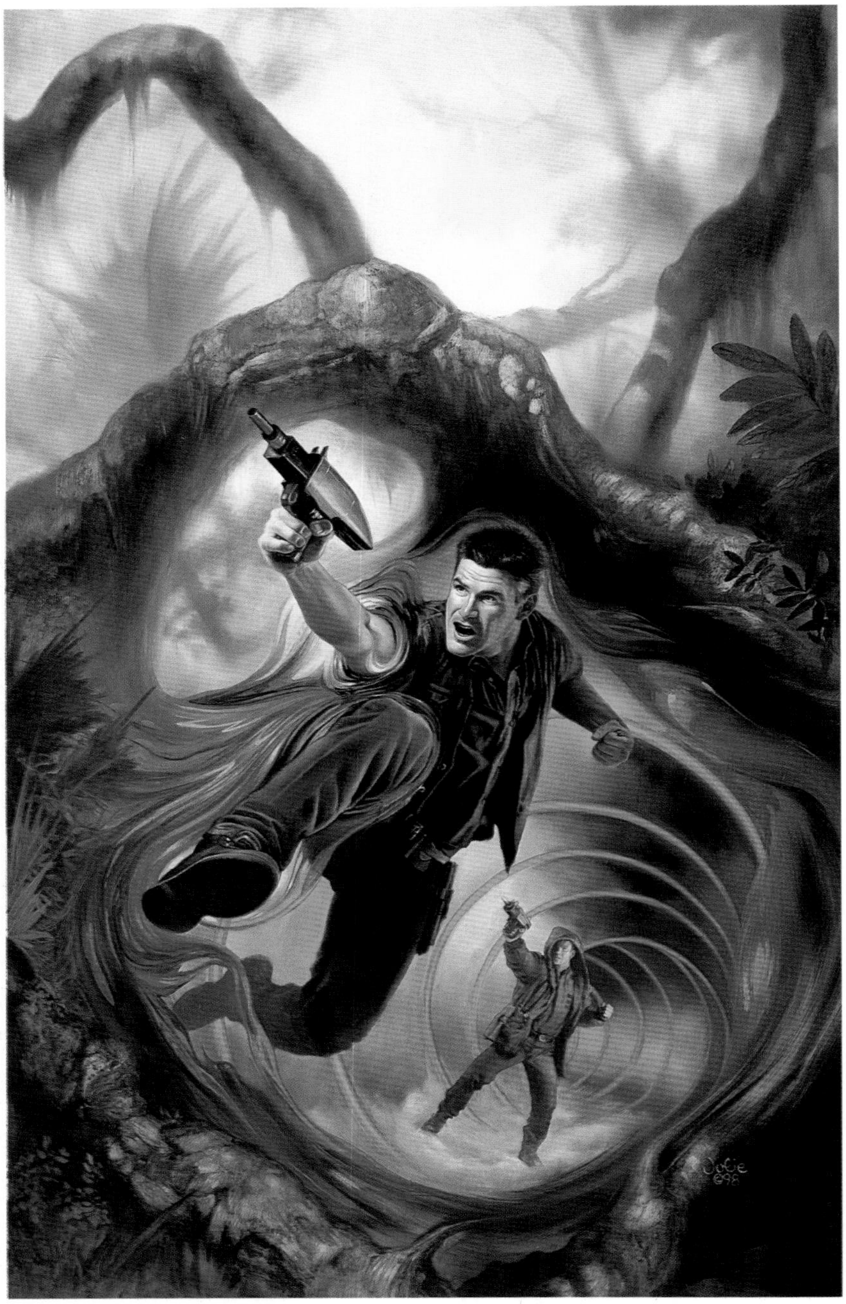

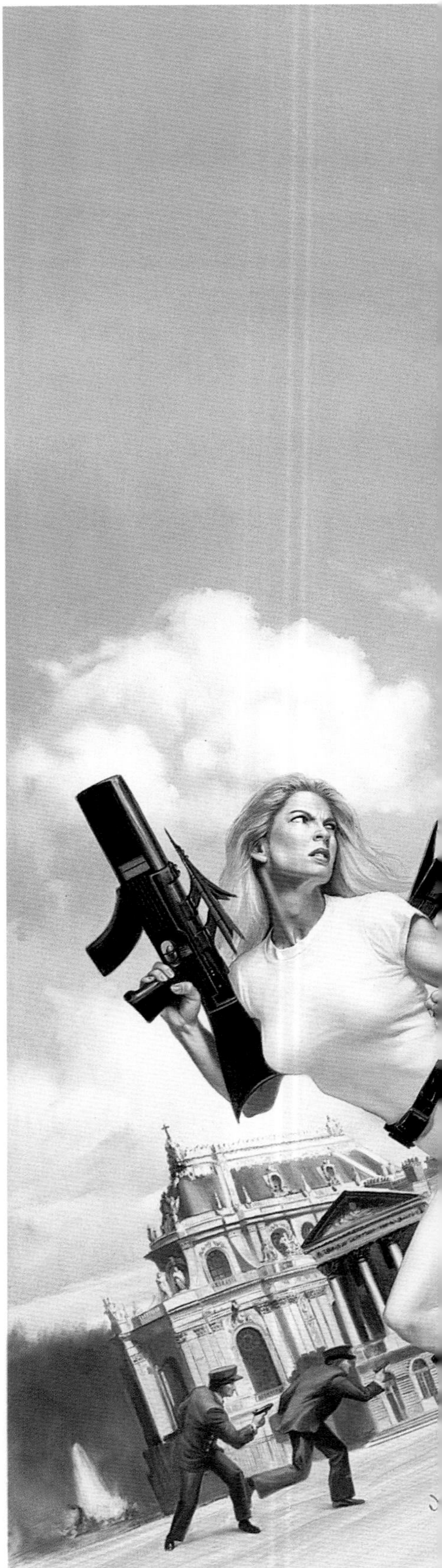

ABOVE: ***Chased From The Arctic, 1998***
Oils, 20 x 15 in (51 x 38 cm)
Book cover. Ballantine.
The first of three covers for novels based on the movie Time Cop *starring Jean-Claude Van Damme. As the movie title suggests, the stories are based on time travel which happens to be one of Julie's favourite kinds of fantasy because of the contrasts possible between past, present and future.*

RIGHT: ***Time Warp at Versailles, 1998***
Oils, 20 x 15 in (51 x 38 cm)
Book cover. Ballantine.
The intricate architecture of Versailles was a perfect base for the special effect of the time-travel wormhole. Julie makes use of the horizon to melt the building, sky and characters, which clarifies the message to the viewer that this is, indeed, an unnatural phenomenon.

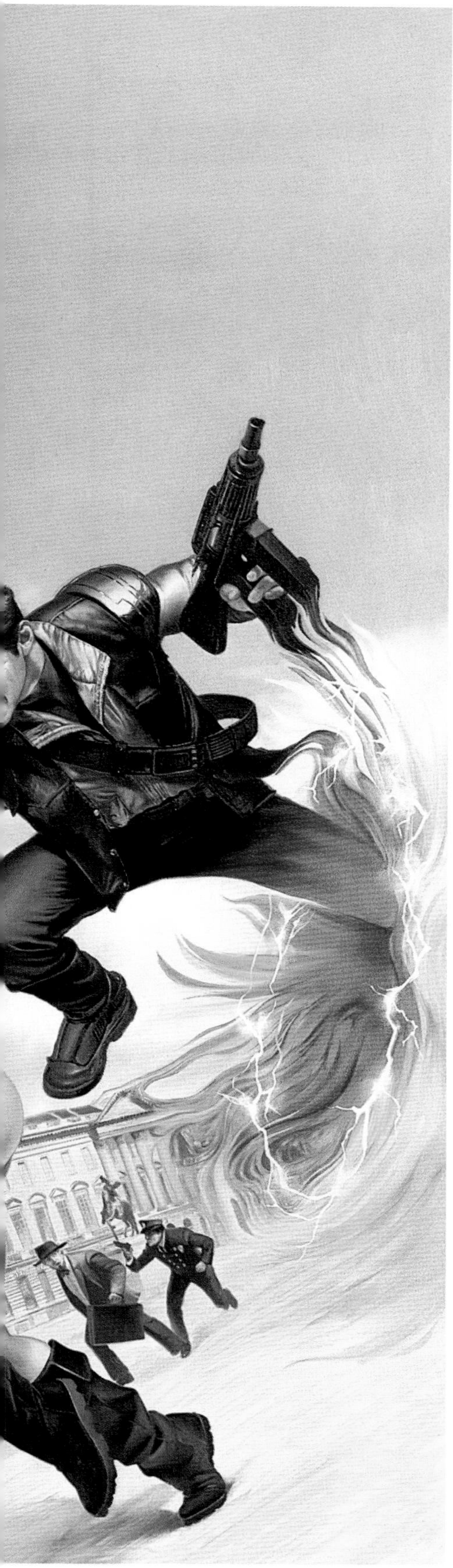

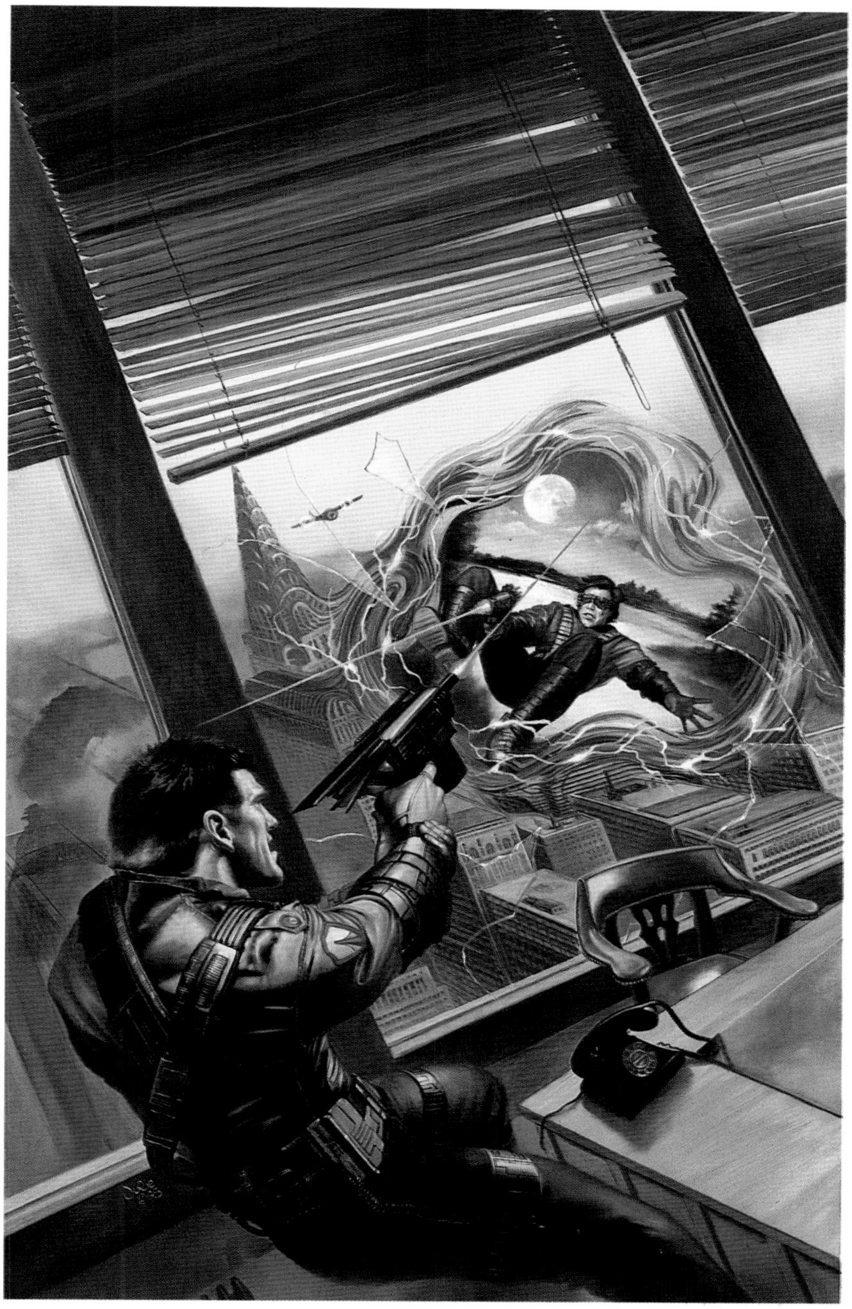

ABOVE: ***New York City: 1940-2040, 1998***
Oils, 20 x 15 in (51 x 38 cm)
Book cover. Ballantine.
To contrast the past and future elements of the scene Julie used different palette tones for each, drawing on the effects used in movies to suggest past and future. The two are linked by the exchange of gunfire.

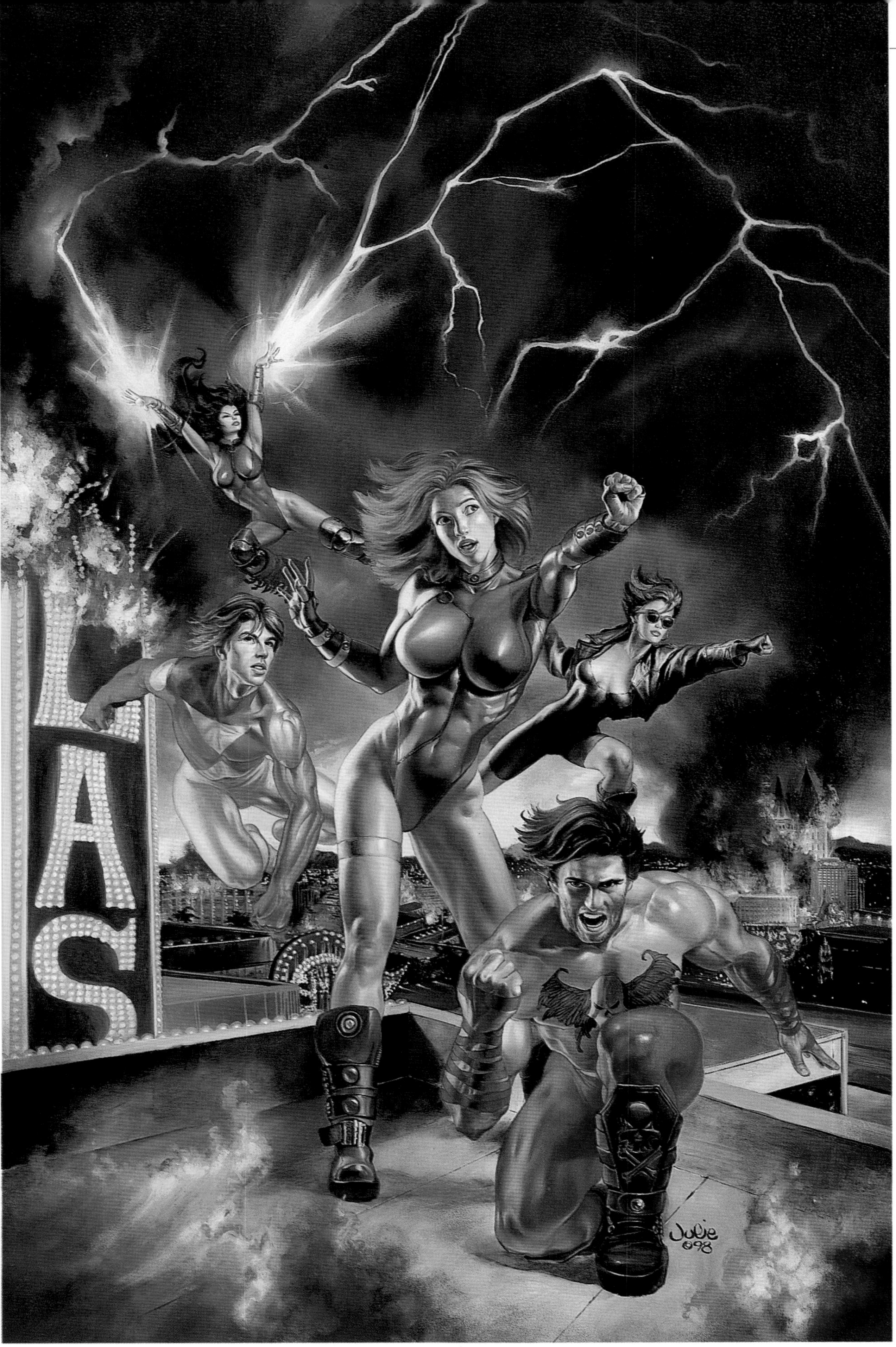
LAS
Julie
©98

LEFT: *Warriors of Las Vegas, 1998*
Oils, 20 x 15 in (51 x 38 cm)
Book cover design. Byron Preiss
Multimedia.
Gen ^{13} is ® and © Aegis Entertainment,
Inc., dba WildStorm Productions, 1998.
All rights reserved.
In this story Las Vegas has become the
gateway to hell in a very literal sense and
the Gen ^{13} team of superheroes has come
to sort things out. It is far more obvious
in the finished painting than in the sketch
that this is Las Vegas rather than
anywhere else.

ABOVE RIGHT: *Warriors of Las Vegas*
(sketch)

BELOW RIGHT: *Angel's Bike, 1998*
Pencil and pastel, 20 x 15 in
(51 x 38 cm)
Sculpture design. The Franklin Mint.
Although she loves the visual aspect of
motorbikes, Julie has not the faintest
interest in riding them personally as she
considers them far too dangerous.

Dragon Battle, 1994
Oils, 30 x 20 in (76 x 51 cm)
Video game cover. Nintendo.
The chance to paint dragons comes along
less often than Julie would like as she has
a great fondness for the magical beasts.
The main aim of this picture was to show
all the characters from the game together in
one scene.

with a confidence, strength and verve they might also weep over, appearing to burst fully-fledged onto the fantasy scene like Athena from Zeus' head. She gives all the credit for this to Boris' tuition, but he has a different tale to tell.

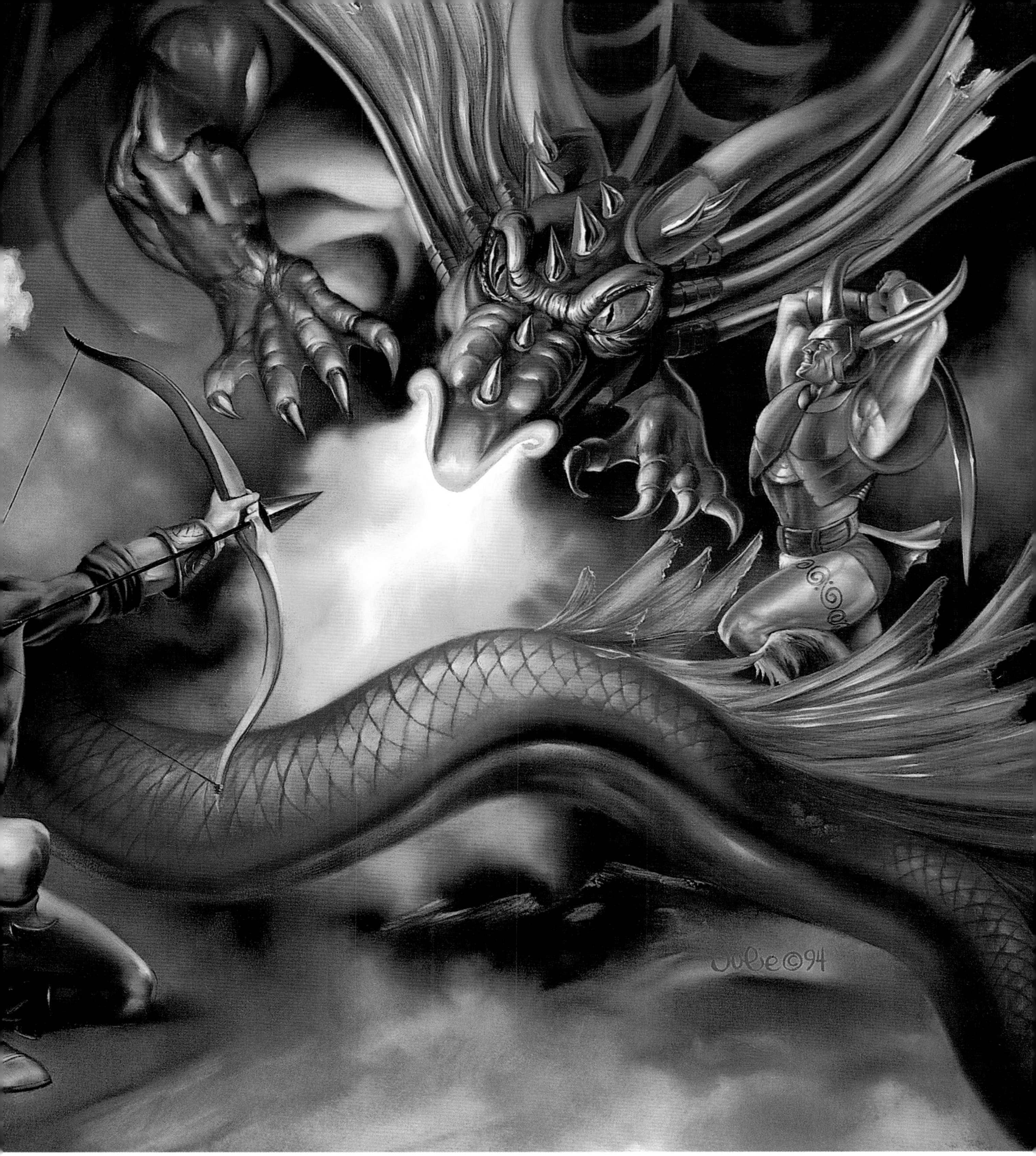
Julie©94

'I didn't really teach her,' says Boris. '99 per cent of it was that Julie sat, watched and absorbed what I did. Every now and then, especially in the first year, I demonstrated how some things were done, but that was all. One thing people comment on is how similar our styles are. Of course

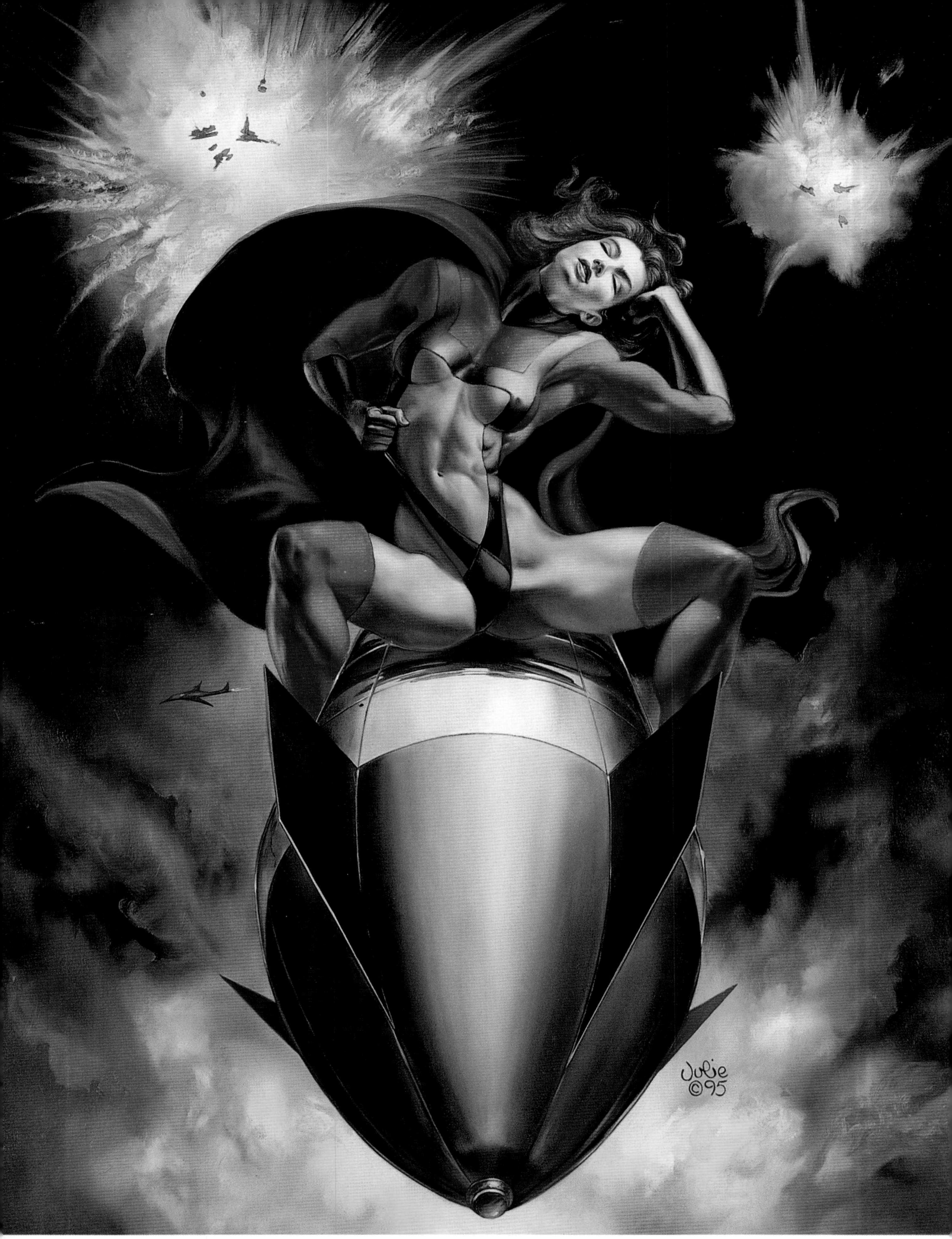
Julie
©95

OPPOSITE: ***The Bomb 1995***
Oils, 15 x 20 in (38 x 51 cm)
Cover. Penthouse Comix.
The idea here is that the female is so engrossed in her own sexuality that she fails to notice what is happening (and about to happen) around her. The publishers wanted to parody a similar scene in the film Dr Strangelove *in which Slim Pickens rides 'the bomb' to glory.*

this is because Julie learned a lot of technique from watching me, but also it is because our temperaments are so similar. We have an enormous kinship in art, life and general experiences. We see the world and relationships in the same way, so it turns out our approach to painting is similar.'

Did he realize when he first saw Julie's work that she would take to painting as fast and successfully as she has? 'Actually no, I have to

RIGHT: ***The Watchtower, 1998***
Oils, 20 x 15 in (51 x 38 cm)
Book cover. Ballantine.
The main character is a composite from three different models, one of whom was Boris. 'He turned out awfully handsome!' Julie says.

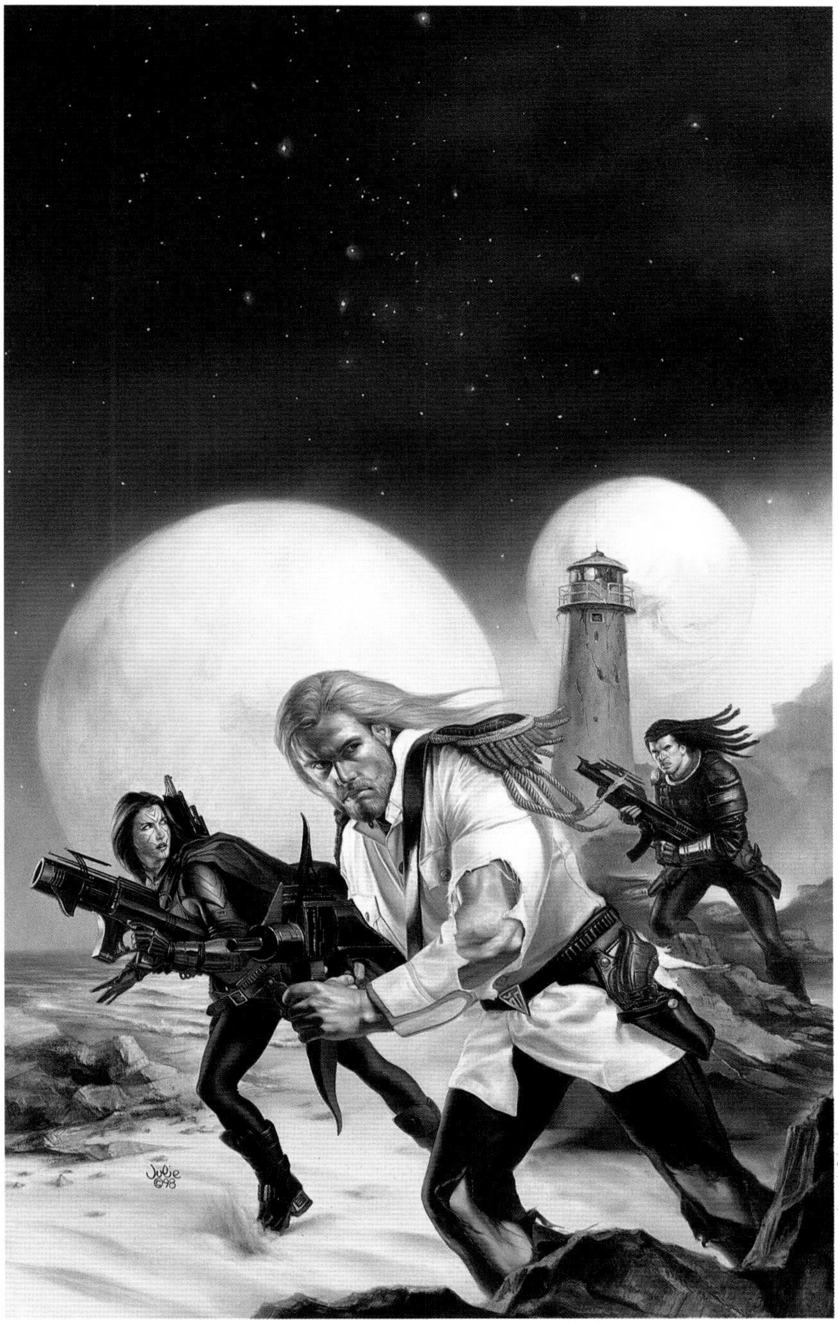
Julie
©98

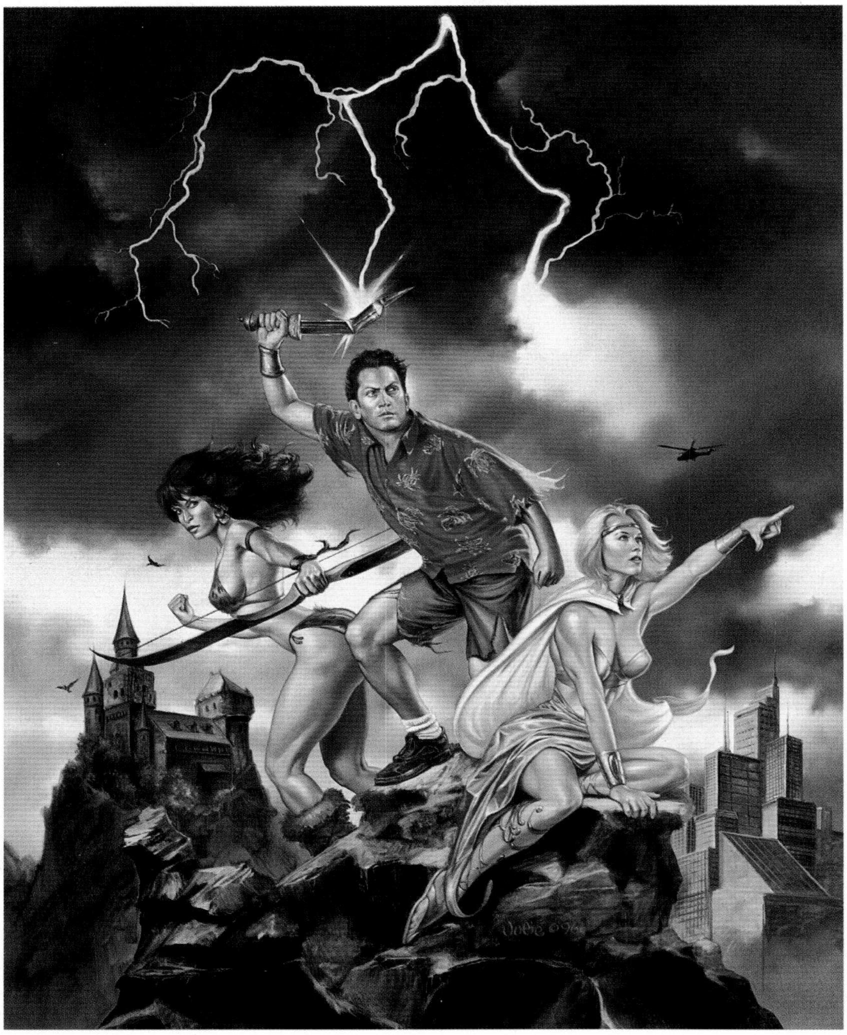

LEFT: ***Hero, 1996***
Oils, 15 x 20 in (38 x 51 cm)
Computer game cover.
Rob Schneider features as the hero in this game, but it is all a bit tongue-in-cheek because really he is far less able to defend his female companions than they are to save him. Since the actor was not able to come to Julie's studio for a photo session, the next best thing was to send a sketch to California, so that a photographer could shoot her reference pictures using her sketch as a guide for the pose and the light sources.

RIGHT: ***Seinfeld Wars, 1998***
Oils, 15 x 20 in (38 x 51 cm)
Editorial illustration. TV Guide *magazine.*
This kind of painting, almost a cartoon in oils, is a line of illustration Julie has always enjoyed and hopes to pursue in future with other magazines. Because of the tight deadlines involved with a weekly publication such as TV Guide, *there is a lot of time pressure, but she says that this is as much a good thing as it is a bad. It gets the adrenaline going. This impression of Jerry Seinfeld and friends in 'Star Wars' mode was painted for a special edition of the magazine to mark the much-heralded last episode of America's favourite comedy show.*

confess that I didn't. Of course I could see she had a talent that was not developed to its full potential, but really I didn't know how far she could take it. You have to realize that in my career I see hundreds of talented artists. Some are better than average but they still do not have what it takes to reach the top professional level. They remain "talented amateurs". So Julie was a surprise. I could see she was intelligent and talented, but not how much. I have to say, and not just because she is my wife, that she is probably the most extraordinarily gifted and mentally tireless person I have met.'

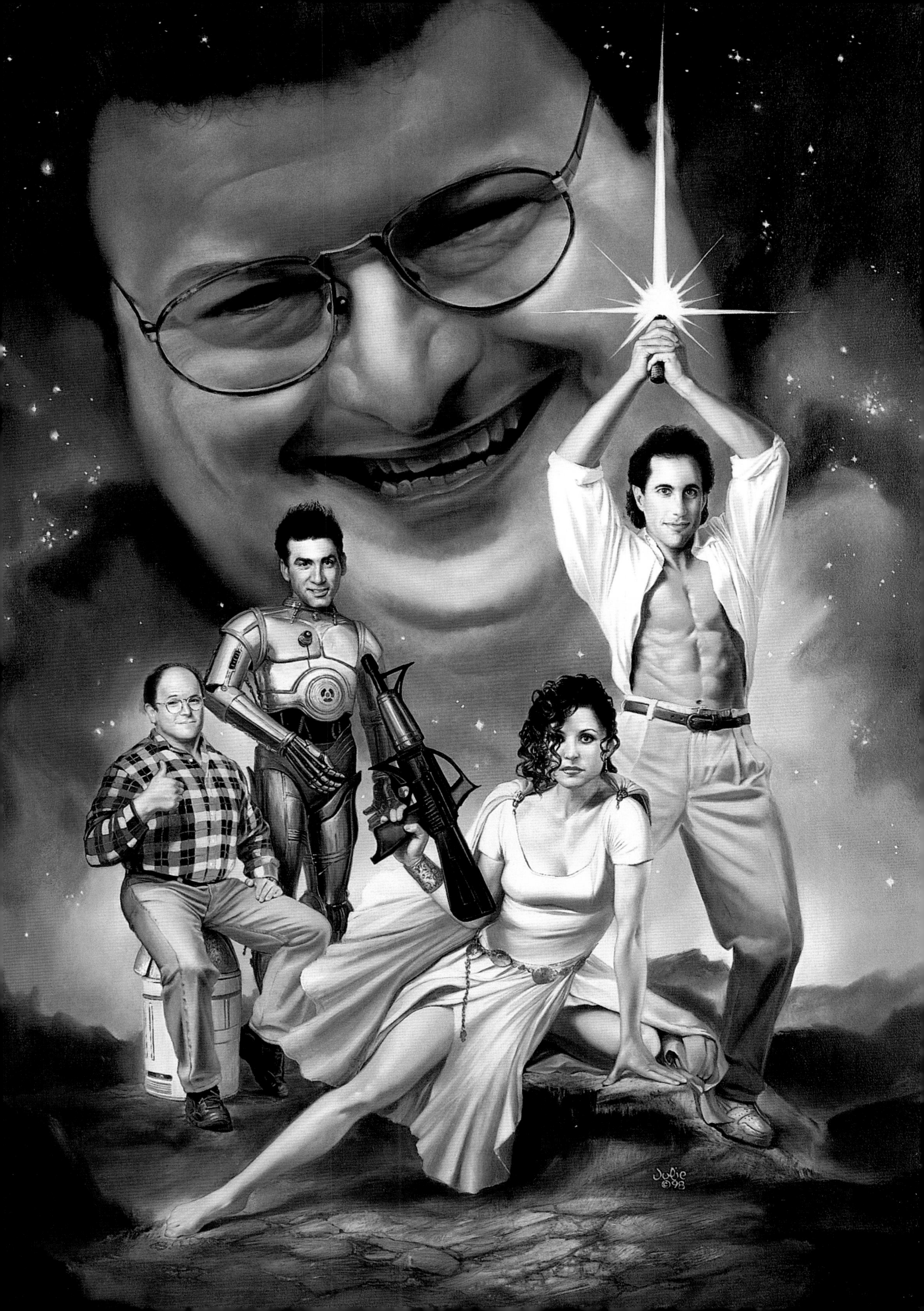
Julie ©93

4 PRIVATE GALLERY

Sedona, 1996
Oils, 20 x 20 in (51 x 51 cm)
Portfolio piece.
This is one of Julie's favourite places, a
little way north of Phoenix, Arizona.
It is famous for its magical atmosphere
of peace, stillness and beauty, and attracts
many visitors.

DRAWING AND PAINTING are things Julie does almost constantly. She nearly always has art materials with her in case something catches her eye or imagination, and often these things appear later in her published work. Often she just does them for the love of it, as in the pictures shown here, the excuse being that she is honing her technique for the future.

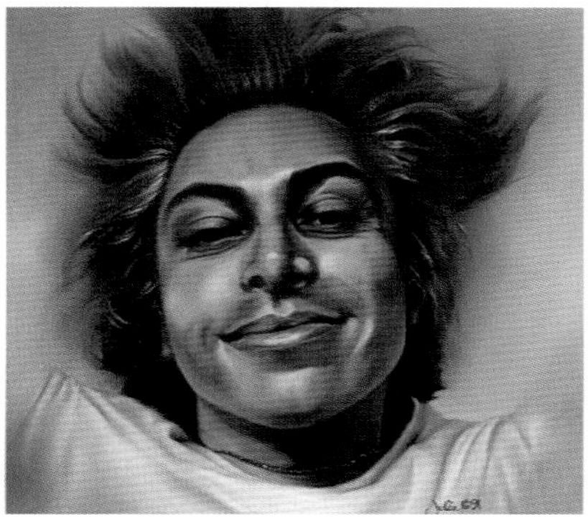

Boris, 1991
Oils, 20 x 20 in (51 x 51 cm)
Portfolio piece.
One of Julie's first oil paintings.

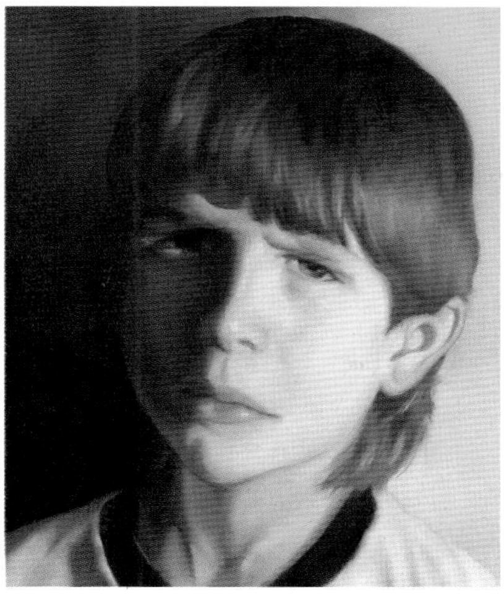

David, 1991
Oils, 15 x 20 in (38 x 51 cm)
Portfolio piece.
The faintly hostile look on both Julie's sons' faces was something she deliberately aimed for as a change from doing the obvious family portrait. With the younger one, David, the effect was achieved by having him pose when he was not in the mood and then asking him to squint into the sun. Both portraits (above and above right) were painted before Julie began illustrating professionally.

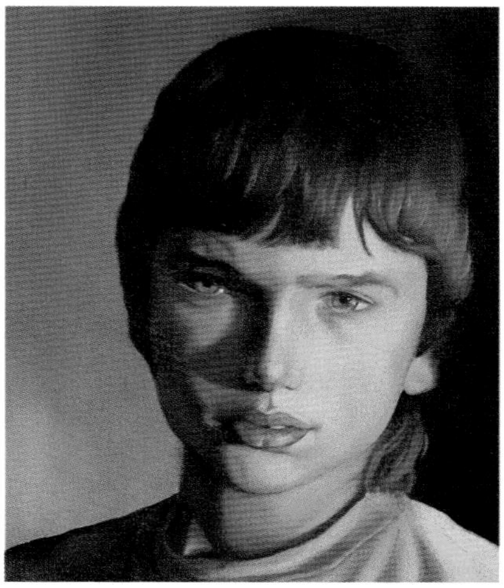

Tony, 1991
Oils, 15 x 20 in (38 x 51 cm)
Portfolio piece.

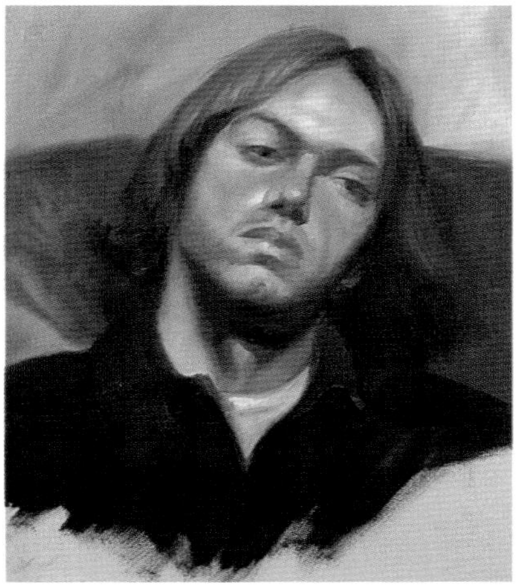

Untitled
Oils, 15 x 20 in (38 x 51 cm)
Portfolio piece.

Crystal Beach, Texas, 1997
Oils, 15 x 20 in (38 x 51 cm)
Portfolio piece.
Another magical place – a beach close to where Julie grew up.

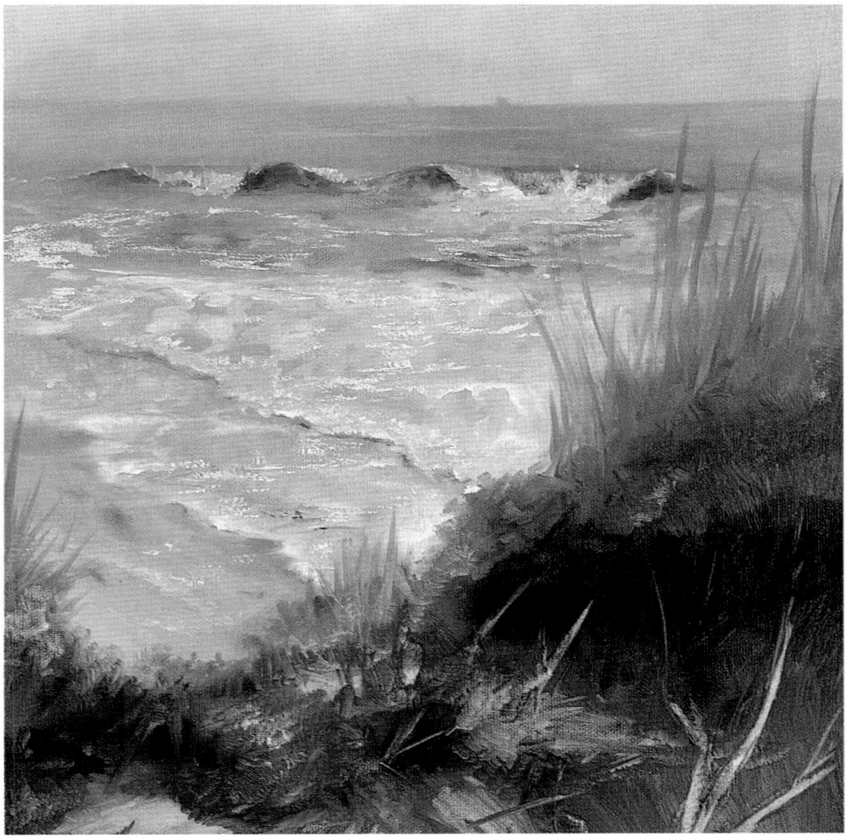

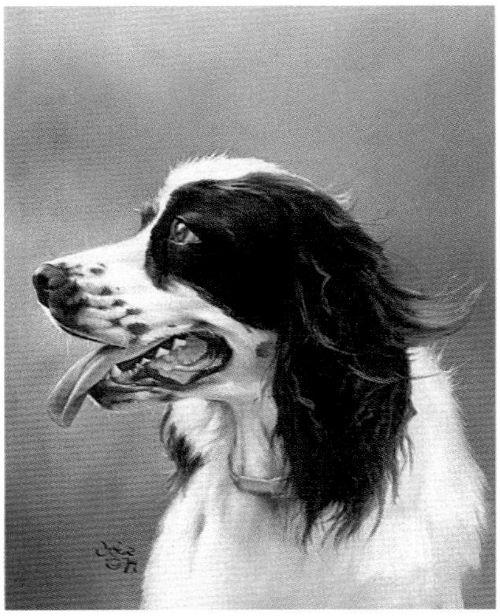

Cody, 1994
Oils, 15 x 20 in (38 x 51 cm)
Portfolio piece.

Untitled
Oils, 15 x 20 in (38 x 51 cm)
Portfolio piece.

Untitled
Oils, 15 x 20 in (38 x 51 cm)
Portfolio piece.

Longwood Gardens, Pennsylvania,
1996
Oils, 20 x 15 in (51 x 38 cm)
Portfolio piece.
Julie visited Longwood Gardens when she took a class in making bonsai trees and returned again with her paints to capture the feel of it. Julie was not too sure whether this was allowed without prior permission and neither, in fact, were the guards there, but they left her to get on with it. The picture is unfinished because closing time came along just a bit too soon.

Untitled
Pastels, 15 x 20 in (38 x 51 cm)
Portfolio piece.

My Teapot, 1996
Pastels, 11 x 14 in (28 x 32 cm)
Portfolio piece.
The teapot was a birthday present from Boris that suggested itself as a useful subject for exercising Julie's skills with pastels. The setting of this picture is a sun room in their house, which is lined with windows and filled with plants and fountains.

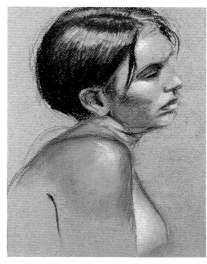

Untitled
Pastels, 15 x 20 in (38 x 51 cm)
Portfolio piece.

Untitled
Pastels, 15 x 20 in (38 x 51 cm)
Portfolio piece.

Kenny, 1978
Pencil, 15 x 20 in (38 x 51 cm)
Portfolio piece.
A portrait based on a photograph taken by
the subject's wife, Anne, drawn while
Julie was at college.

African Head, 1996
Ink, 4 x 6 in (38 x 15 cm)
Portfolio piece.
Julie takes a sketchbook with her to most
places and it became useful on a plane
journey when she found a photograph in
a magazine that demanded to be drawn.
The picture looks as if it has highlights
on the face but it is simply the background
colour of the paper heightened by the deep
contrast of the black around it.

Untitled
Pastels, 15 x 20 in (38 x 51 cm)
Portfolio piece.

Mother and Daughter, 1988
Pencil, 8 x 10 in
(20 x 25 cm)
Portfolio piece.
A picture that sprang straight
from the imagination and
proved enormously cathartic
because it captured aspects of
Julie's troubled relationship
with her own mother. Boris
was so moved by it that he
painted a version of his own
that is so far unpublished.

Untitled
Pastels, 15 x 20 in (38 x 51 cm)
Portfolio piece.

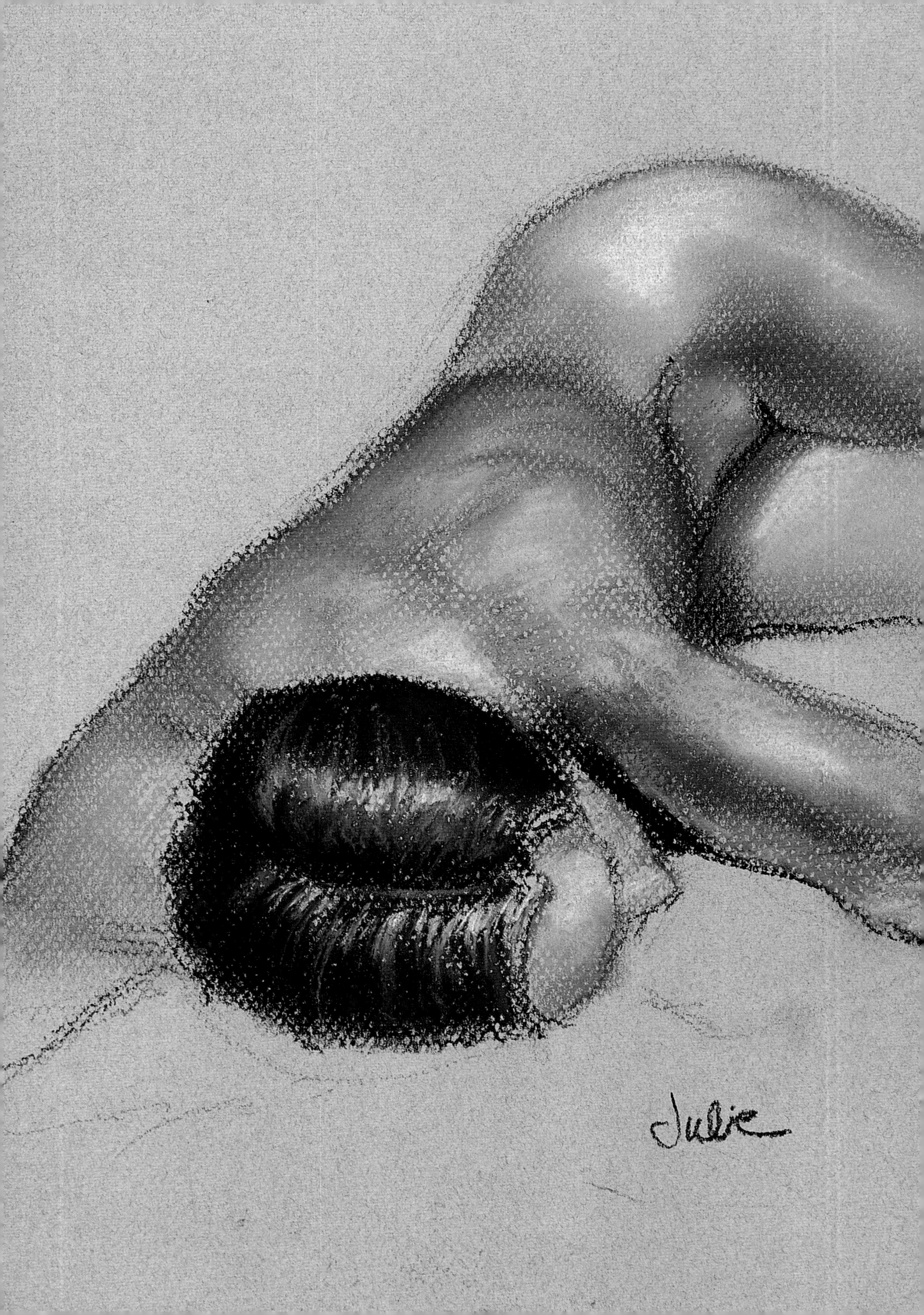
Julie

5 FIGURE STUDIES

ABOVE: *Ink*
Ink presents much more of a design problem because there are no colours or tones and no going back once you have made your mark.

OPPOSITE: *Pastels*
Using colour in figure studies adds another dimension; it has its own emotional language.

I N MOST OF HER WORK Julie portrays idealized figures but that is not all that attracts her. Certainly with her interest in bodybuilding and fitness Julie is drawn to physical perfection, but as an artist she is interested in all physical types, and in everyday, imperfect human beauty and sensuality.

All through her college years and even during high school, she studied life drawing and centred her interest in art around the human form. She still makes it a part of her weekly routine, attending classes and drawing groups with nude models. At this point, her knowledge of anatomy and

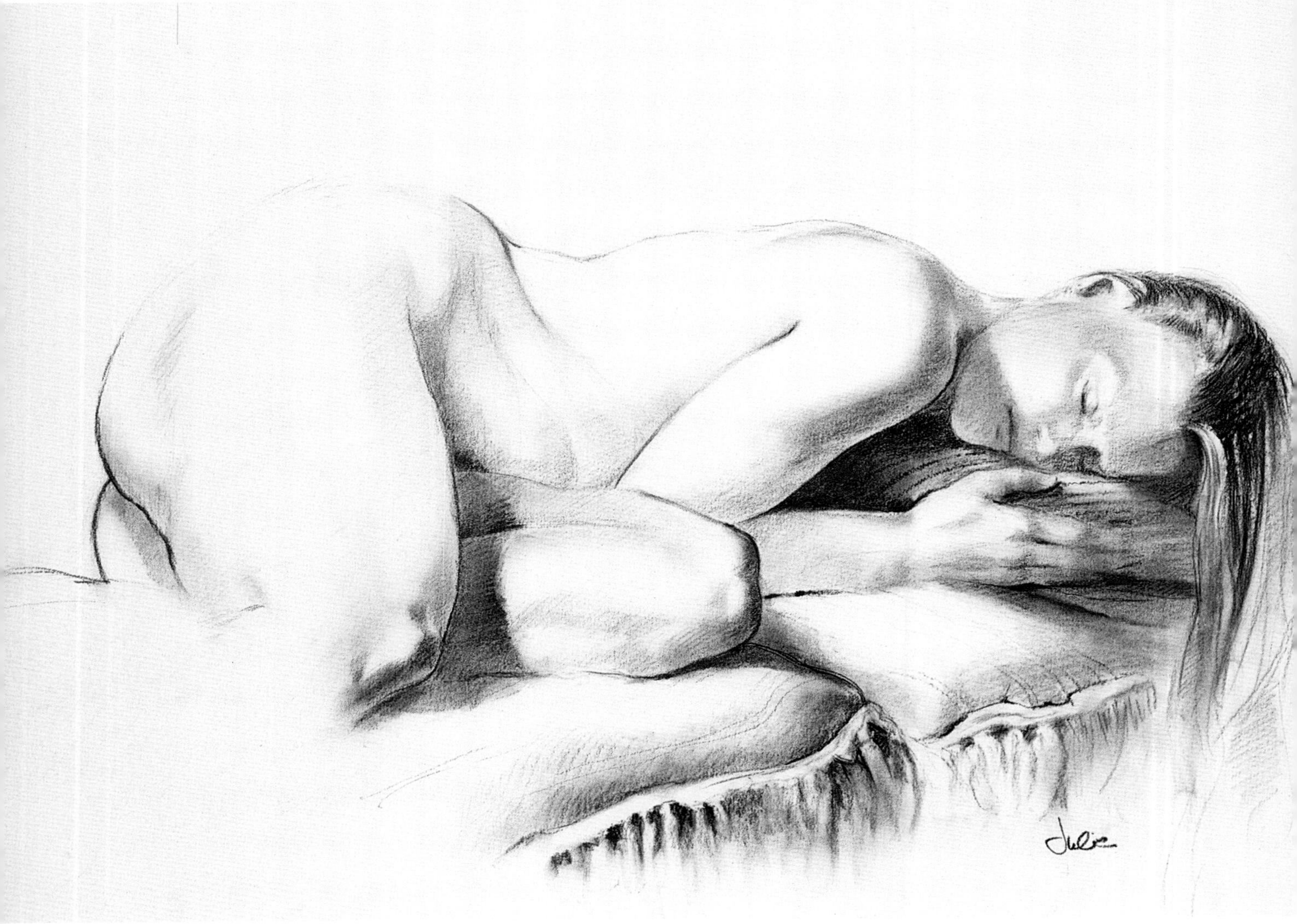

proportion is so developed that she can focus her attention on experimenting with different media and styles. She feels very strongly that figure work is the foundation of her art.

Julie and Boris work closely together in the same studio. They even place their easels side by side so they can see and comment on each other's work as it progresses. As a result they spend virtually their whole time together and very rarely squabble. They listen to music, usually classical, as they work and talk all day long.

The great thing about this companionship is that there is always someone to call on for an objective view of what is happening in a painting.

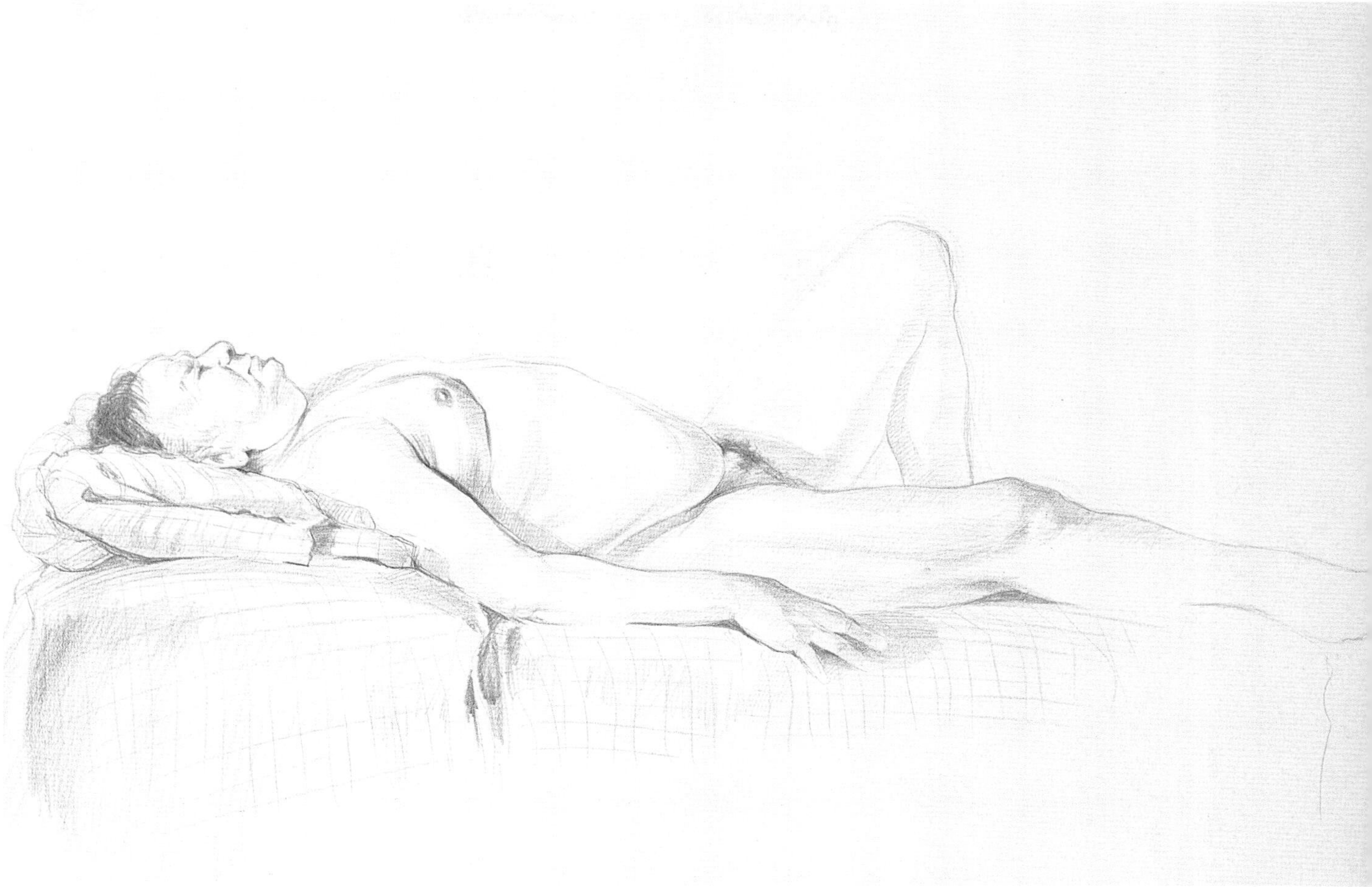

OPPOSITE: *Charcoal*
Intensity of outline is varied to draw the eye to whatever the artist wants to emphasize. The hair and cushion fringes are deliberately heightened to tie them together. Leaving breaks in the outline draws light into the figure and also blends it in with the surroundings.

ABOVE: *Coloured pencil*
There is just a suggestion of background, which only matters insofar as it relates to the figure.

RIGHT: *Coloured pencil*
Julie has emphasized here the heaviness of the figure by suggesting how it presses down into the fabric below.

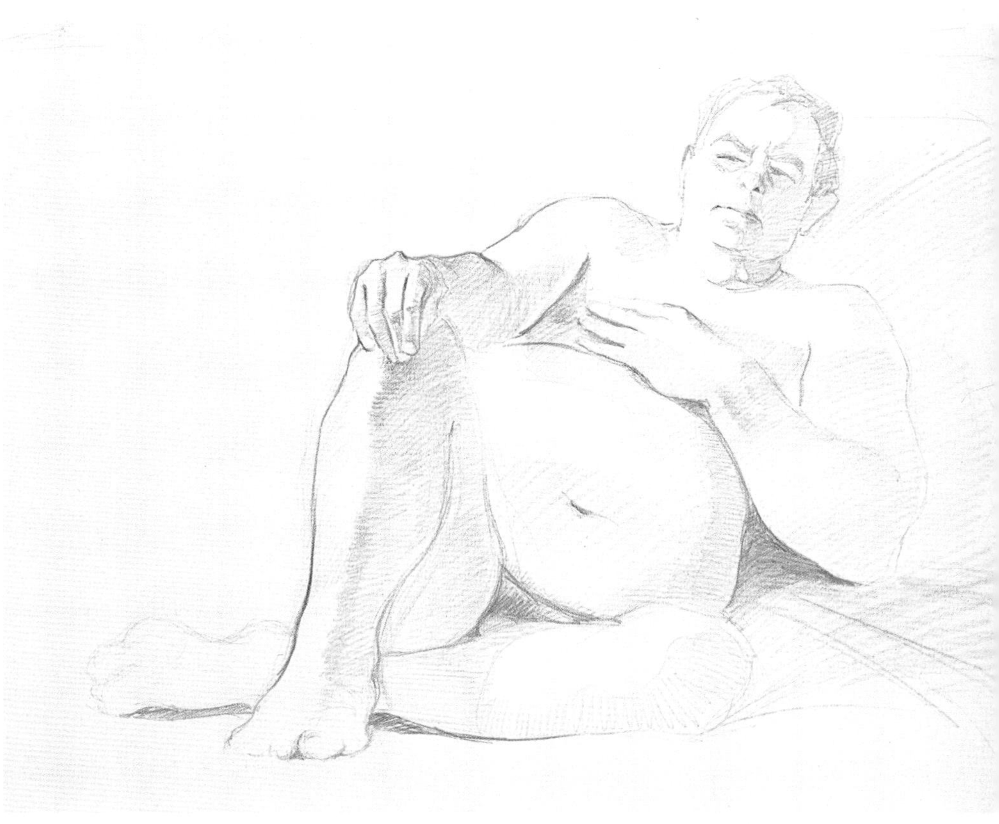

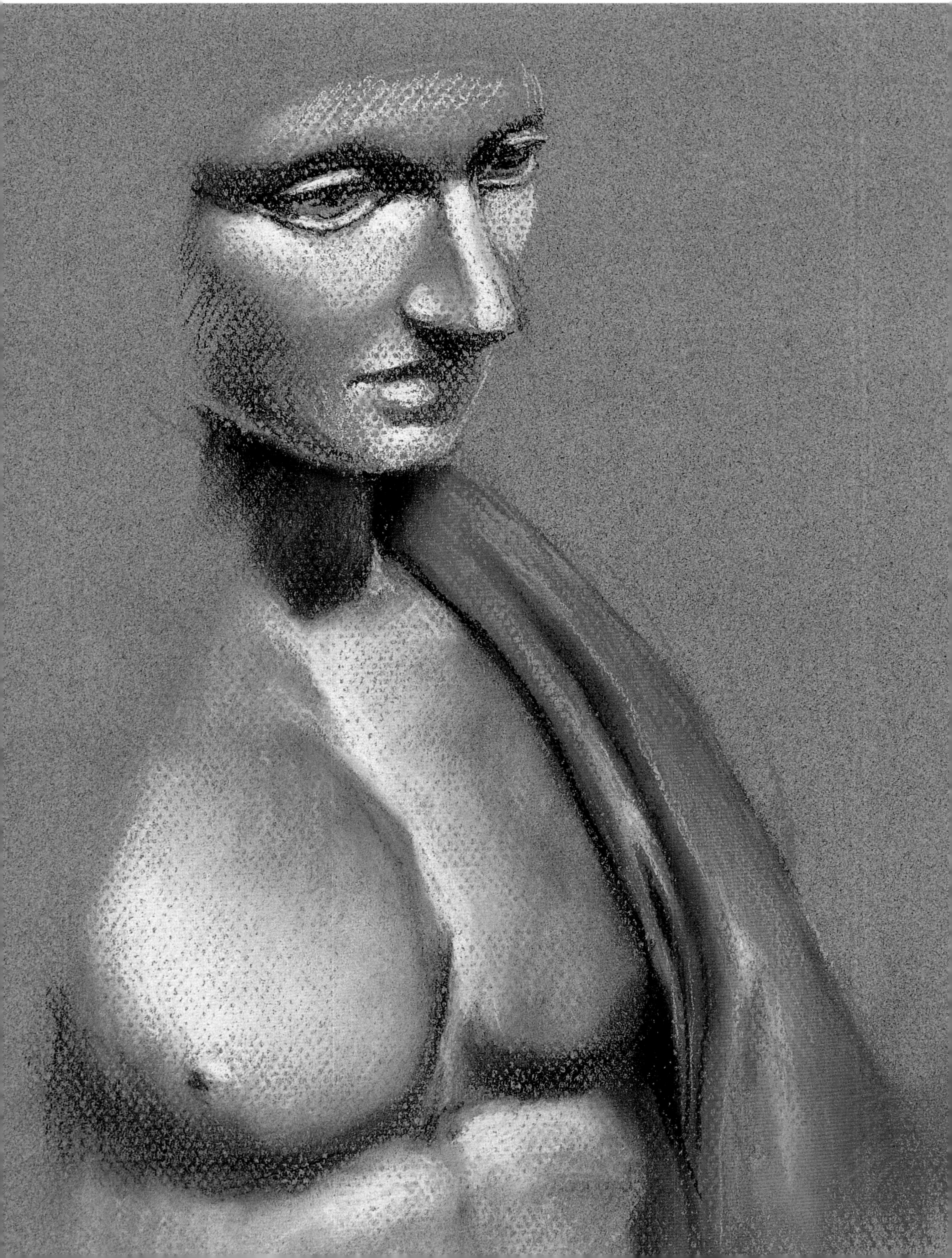

LEFT: *Graphite pencil*
Any work of art, even life drawing, tells a story so before she sets to work Julie tries to determine what it is and focus on that; whether it is the materials, the face, general pose or whatever. Here it was that all lines on the figure seemed to radiate from the centre, so all the shading was done with that in mind.

BELOW: *Ink wash*
Painting with ink presents a very different challenge to drawing. The brush can suggest long, flowing movement which perfectly suited the physique and attitude of this model.

OPPOSITE: *Pastels*
The model failed to turn up for one life-drawing session, so Julie draped a cloth over a Greek statue and set to work anyway. She used to hate the tactile dryness of pastels on the fingers, but loves their creaminess on the page and their beautiful colours so much that she has grown to accept this.

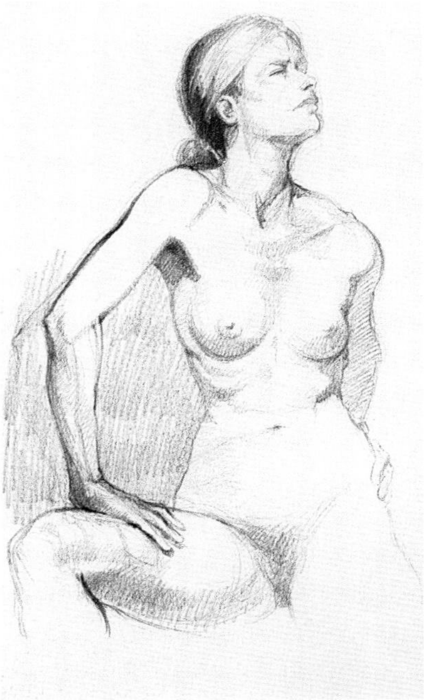

LEFT: *Charcoal*
There are no set rules in this work. Sometimes Julie aims for an exact likeness, sometimes a particular colour or tone catches her eye and she exaggerates that over the whole figure.

BELOW: *Red chalk*
There was a classical feel to the attitude and pose of this model, so Julie used a medium popular with many old masters.

OPPOSITE: *Inks*
Julie: 'I enjoy using inks because you have to be very loose. Once down it is set, you can't fake things or change them afterwards. You have to be willing to accept that and just let things happen more than with other media.'

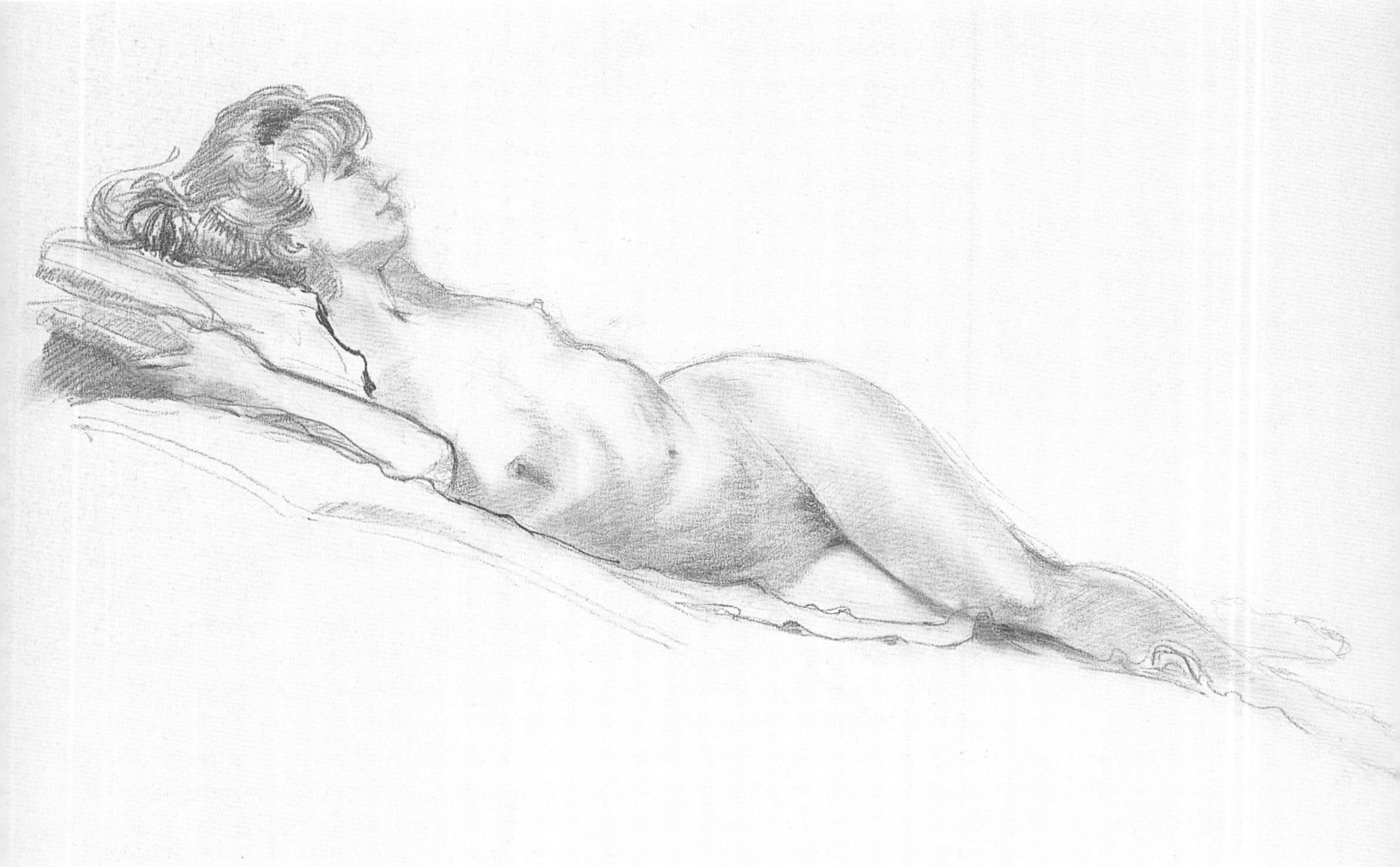

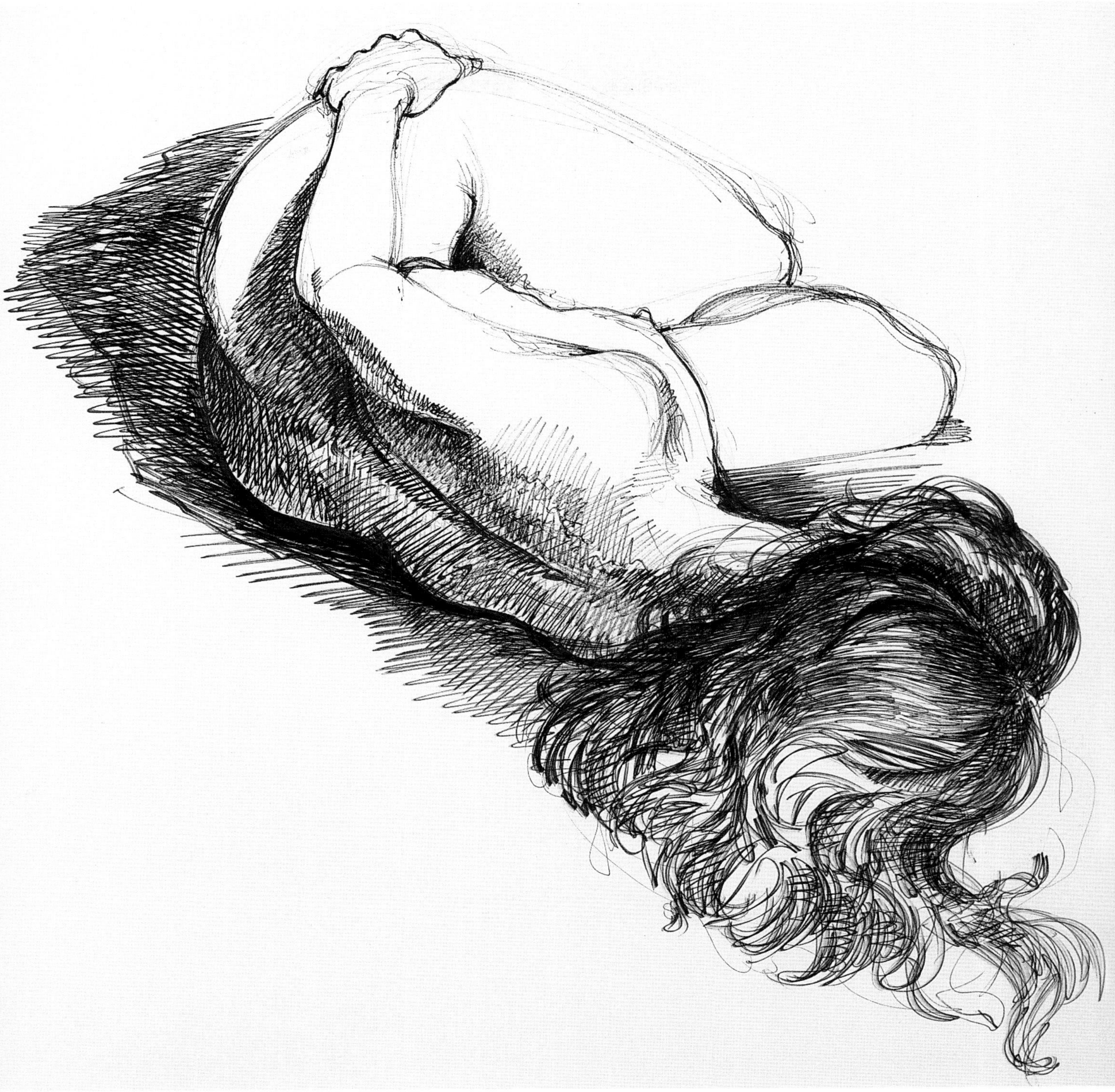

All artists have a problem with this every now and then. Some resort to looking at their picture in a mirror or just leaving it to one side until time has created the necessary distance. Getting an outside opinion can be tricky because most non-artists often can't quite see the problem and don't dare voice their opinion anyway. But the rapport Julie and Boris enjoy means that work can gallop ahead without such delays. Also when

one's painting is going well it tends to inspire the other with fresh ideas. All in all, they find that working together pushes both of them to new limits.

In a practical sense, this motivation often happens when one has a deadline to meet and the other does not. The one without a deadline then uses the same pressure to push their own work along and ends up doing a picture that might otherwise not have happened. Julie: 'Luckily we have the same amount of tolerance for work. We love what we do and being together as we do it. There's no power struggle. Neither is trying to prove anything. I can't imagine us being any luckier than we are.'

ABOVE: *Charcoal*
Here, the model's prop also proved a useful way of passing time while posing.

OPPOSITE: *Charcoal*
The spine strongly links the two main areas of focus. The face was deliberately left vague to create a depth between it and the hair.

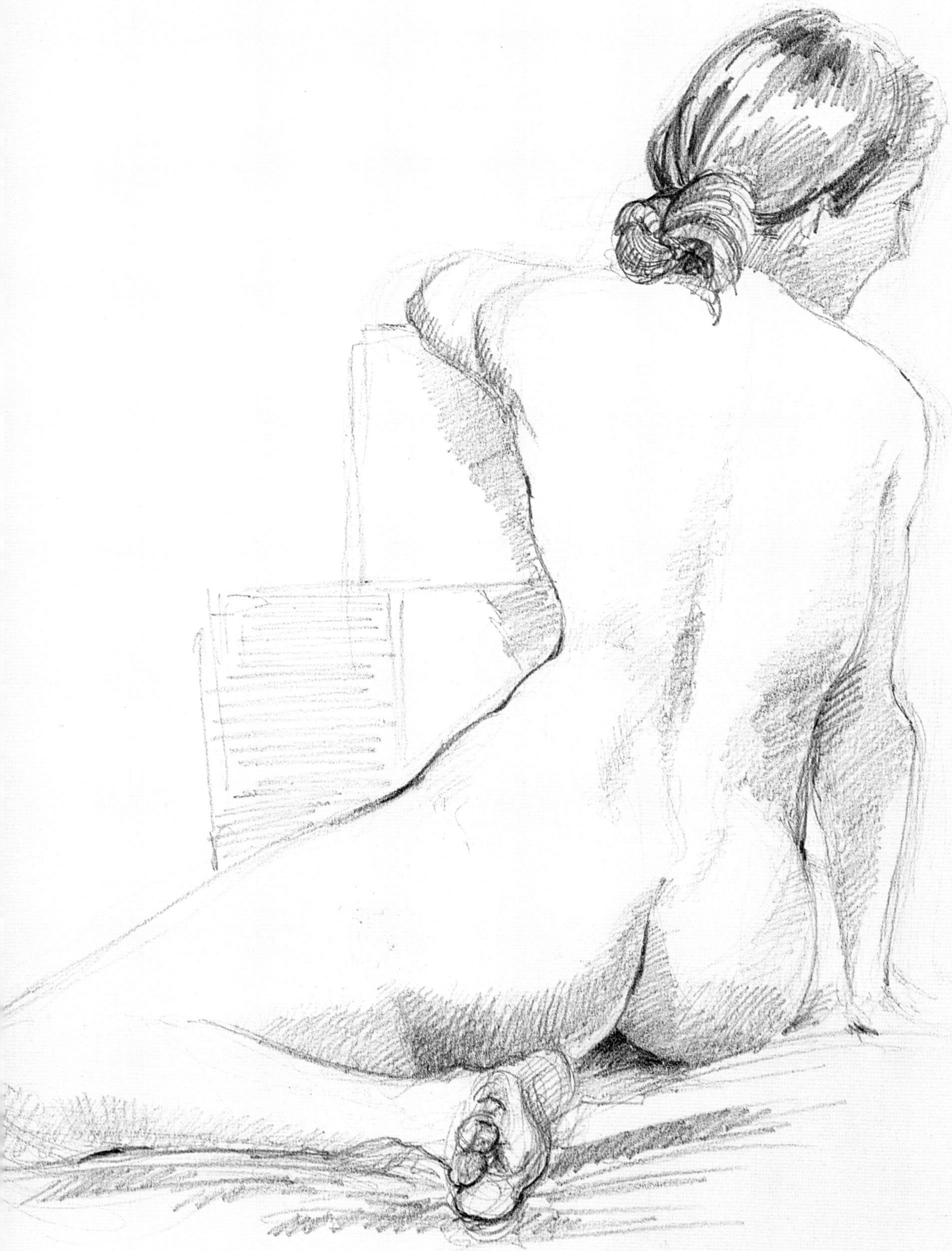

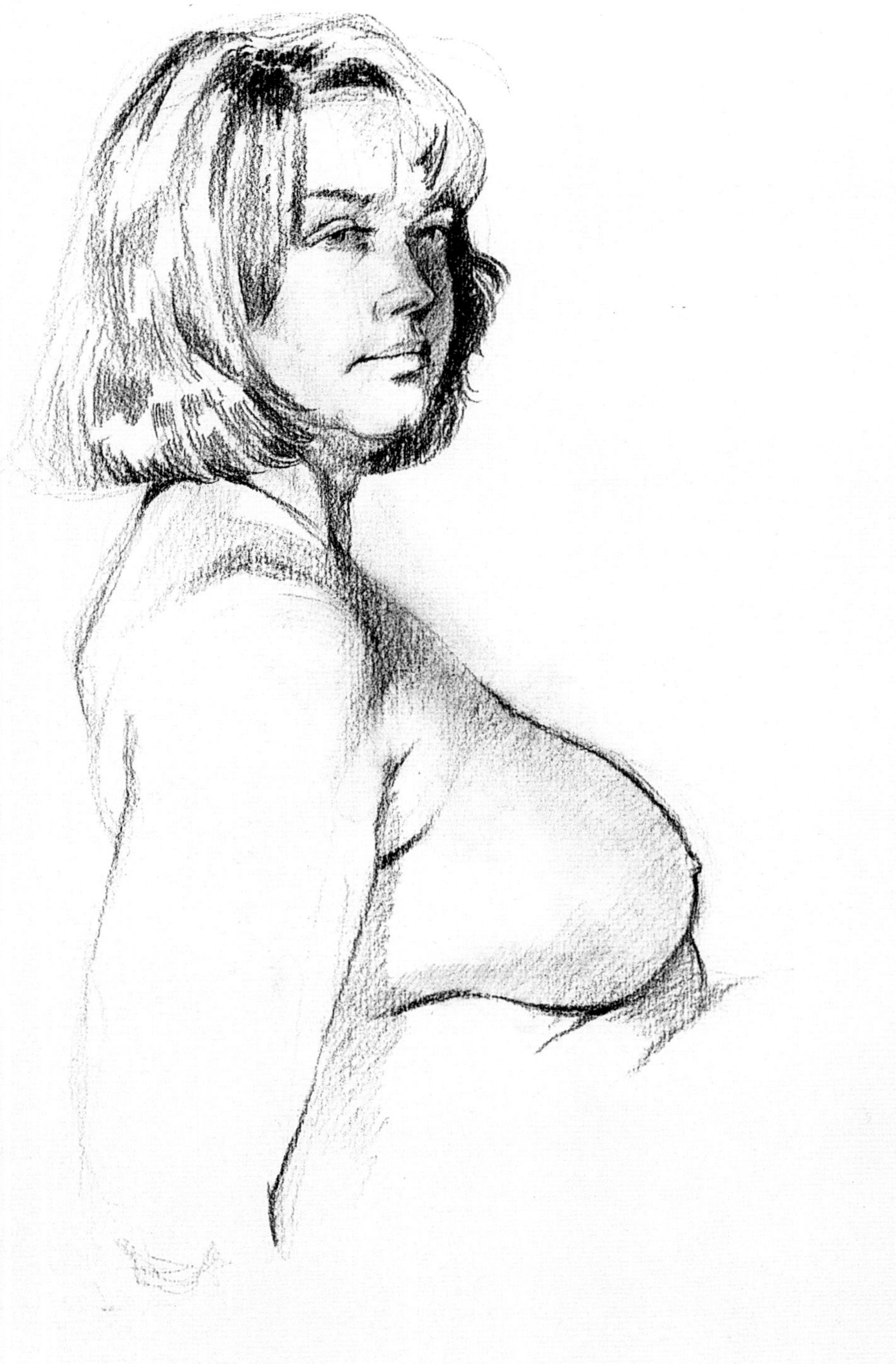

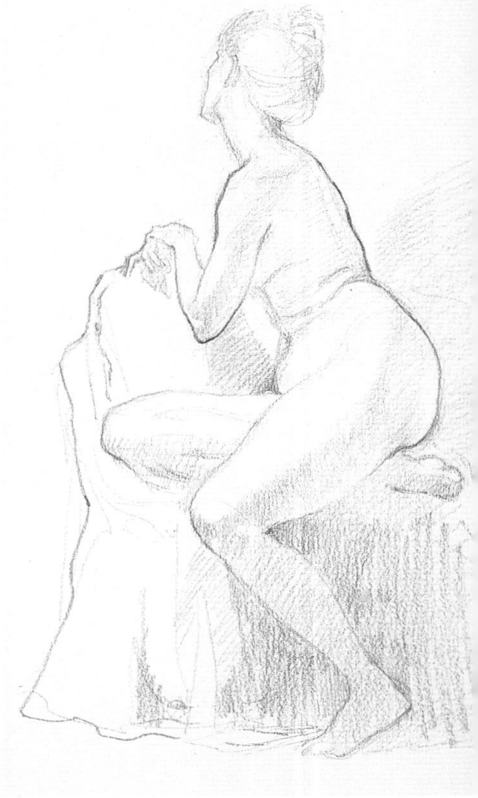

LEFT: *Charcoal*
In figure drawing sessions, Julie enjoys leaving the choice of pose entirely to the model. She will not even change her assigned viewpoint unless something is blocking the way. The challenge is to make a beautiful picture from whatever is presented.

ABOVE: *Red chalk*
Another classic life study pose for a classic medium.

OPPOSITE: *Coloured pencils*
The colours here are more impressionistic than usual, with certain flesh tones being exaggerated and spread over the whole figure. To strengthen the effect, smooth Bristol paper was used. The quality of the surface can make an enormous difference to the effect of a medium.

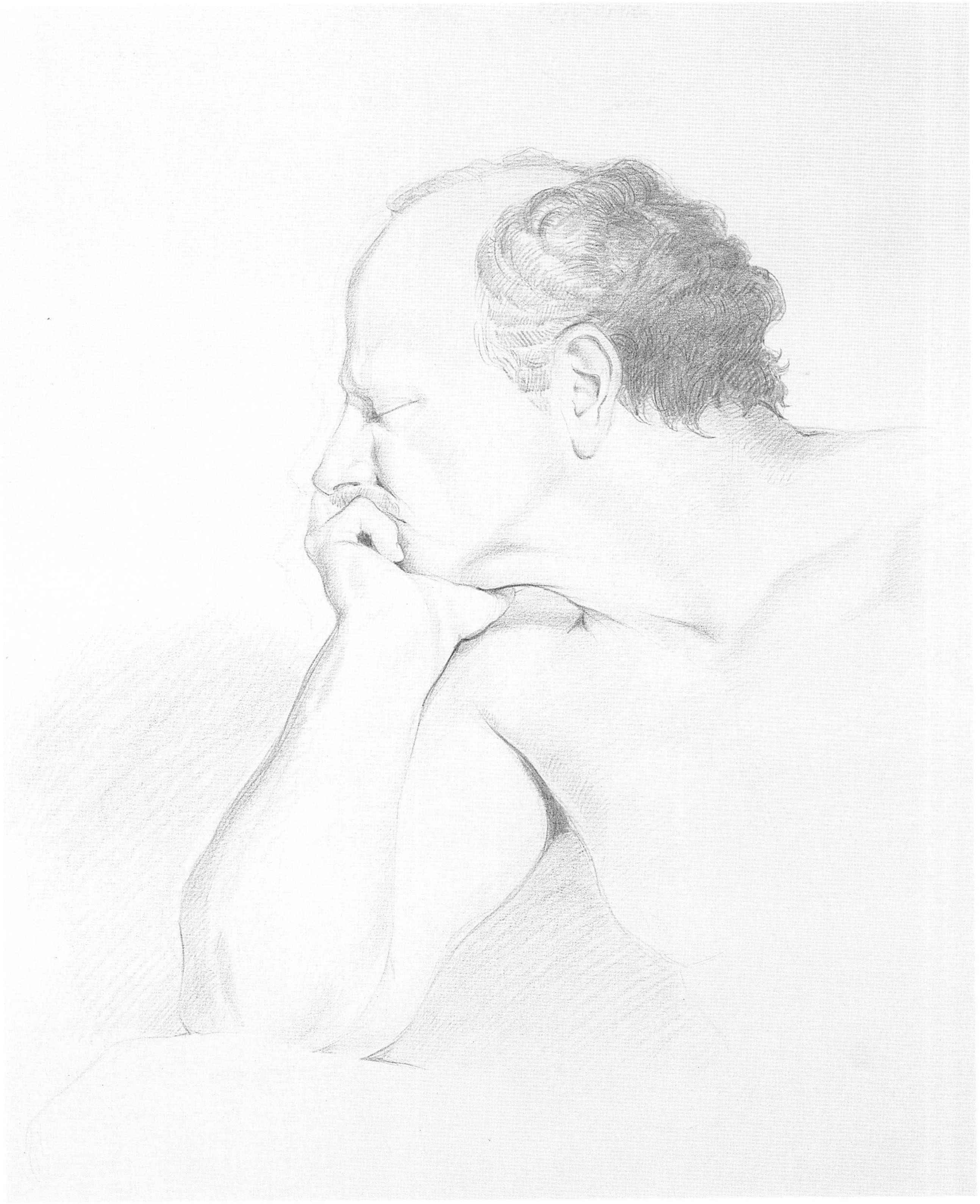

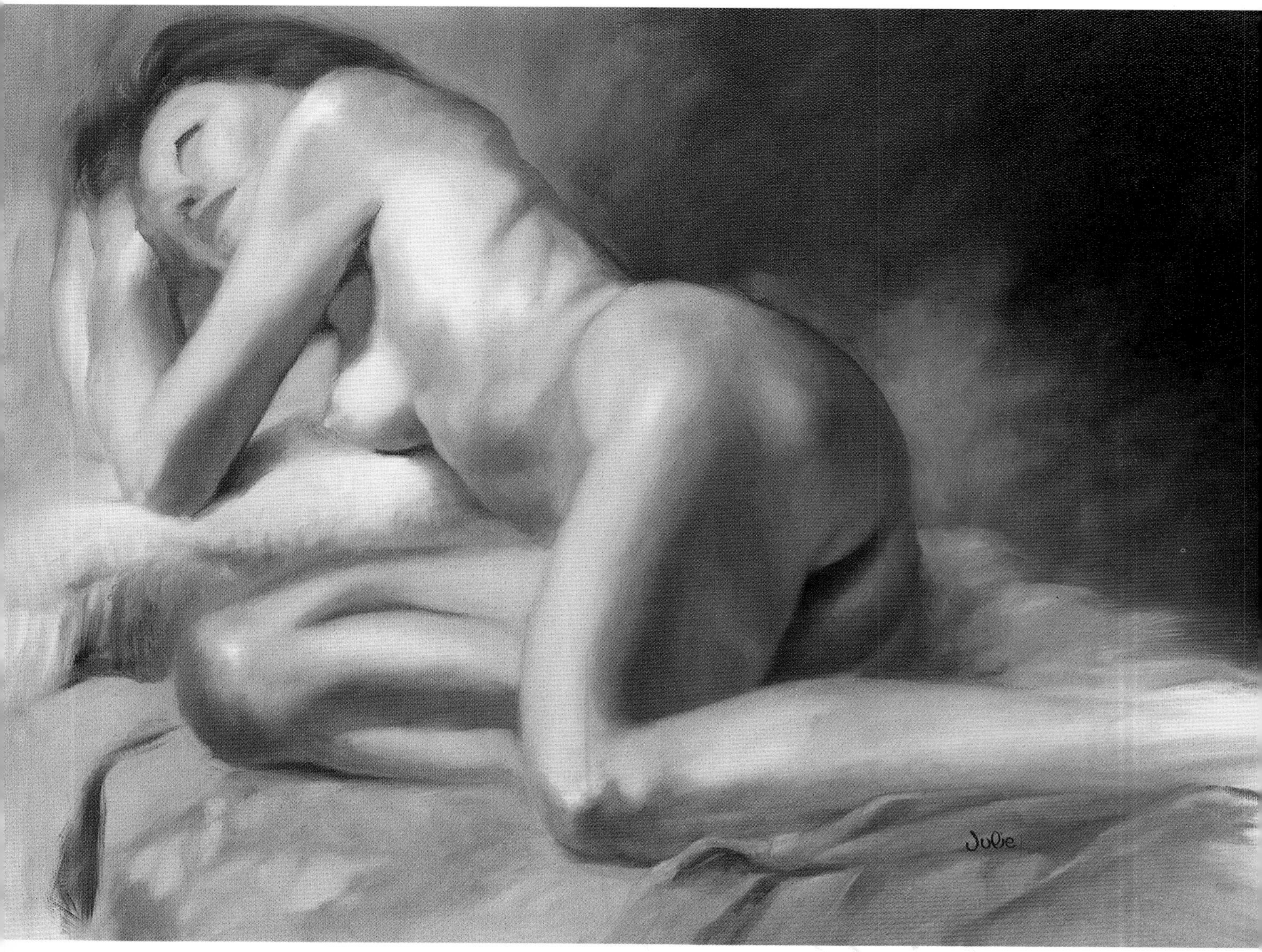
Julie

ABOVE: *Oils*
Julie: 'Oil painting from life is really fun, but very different from my usual work because of the speed. You are working with very wet paints and different brushes. With this picture, the model came for two sessions, but usually I try to finish a picture in one go. The mood changes if you try to come back to it and often it doesn't work.'

OPPOSITE ABOVE: *Charcoal*
In striking contrast to the drawing below, this sketch is full of shades and shadows, using the range of this medium to its full effect.

OPPOSITE BELOW: *Coloured pencils*
The theme of this drawing was the bright light flooding down onto the model.

Painting from life is a whole different experience to Julie's usual work where the composition is first sketched out in detail on illustration board. With life painting the sketching is done directly on canvas with thick brushes and this very rough outline is then progressively refined until the subject comes into focus.

Julie recommends canvas for anyone wanting to learn how to paint in oils because it is a far more forgiving surface than illustration board. The texture acts as a kind of filter for uncertain brushwork and has other charms that still attract her to it now. For commercial work, people generally prefer a sharper edge though.

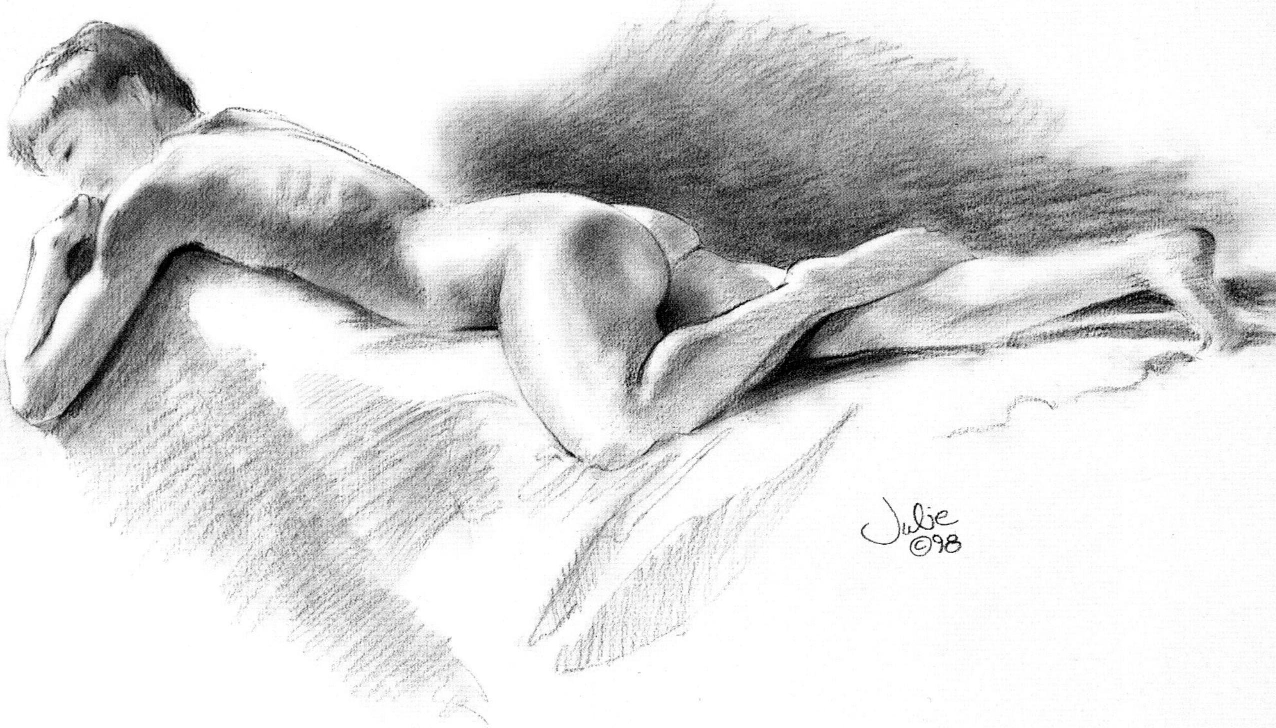
Julie
©98

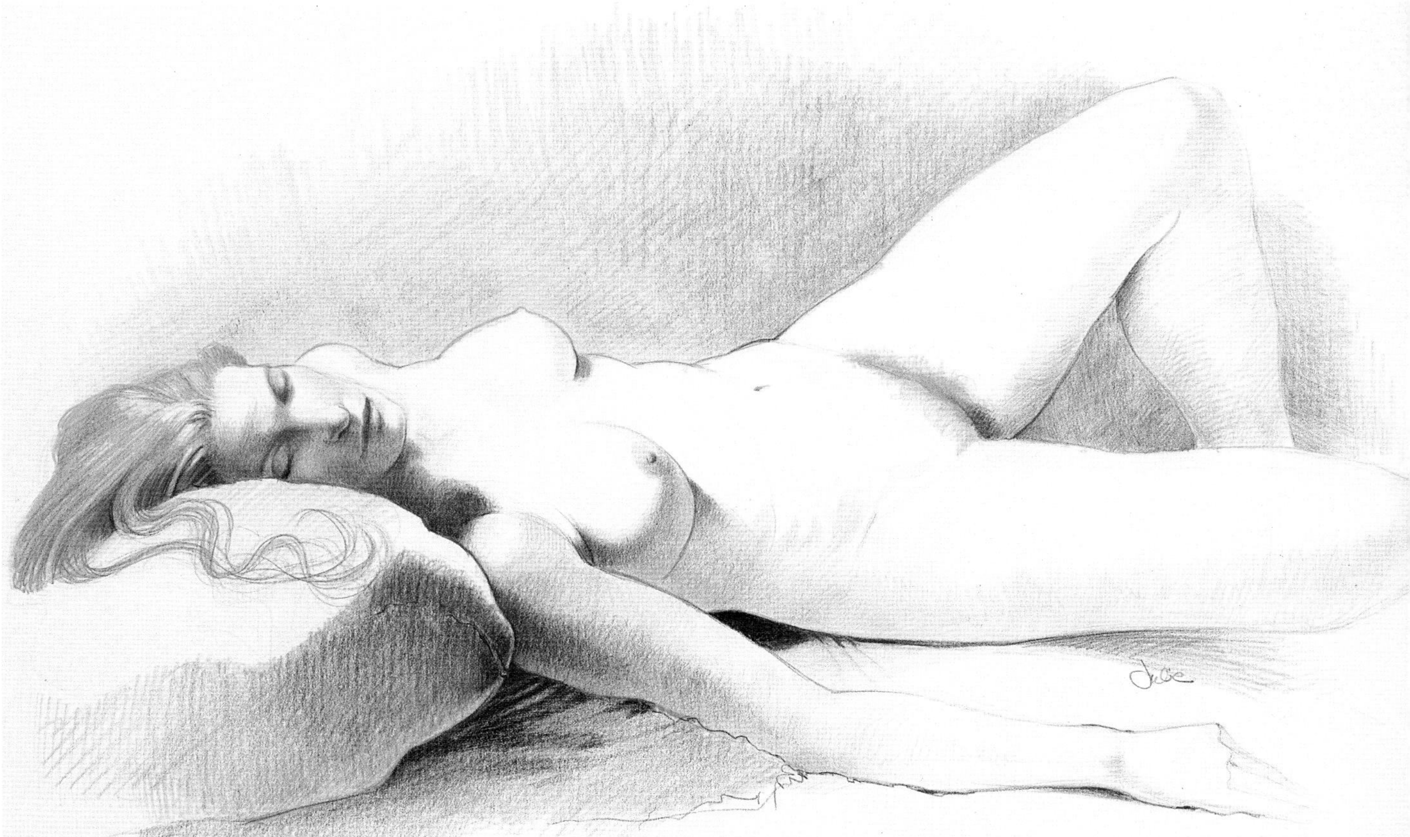
Julie

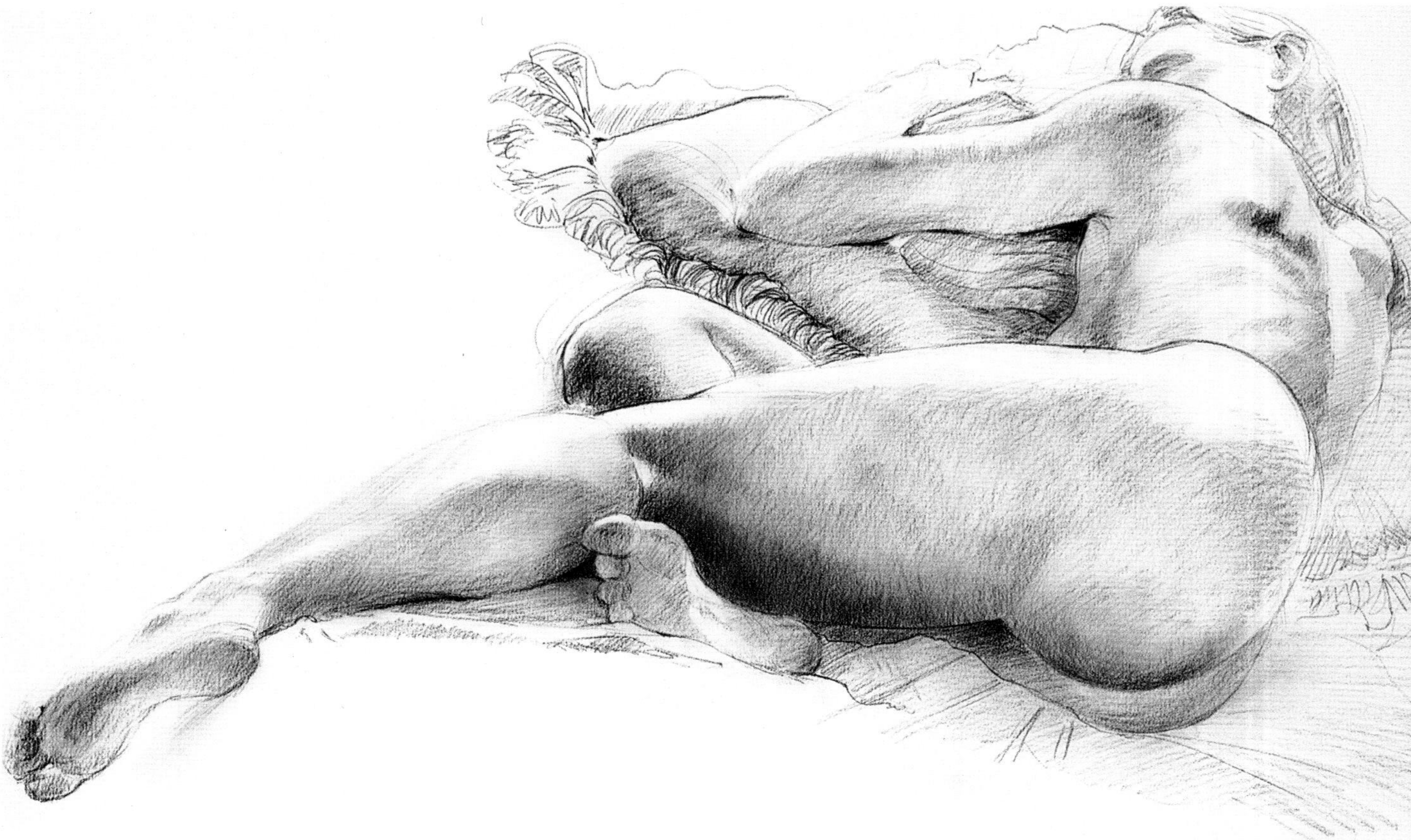

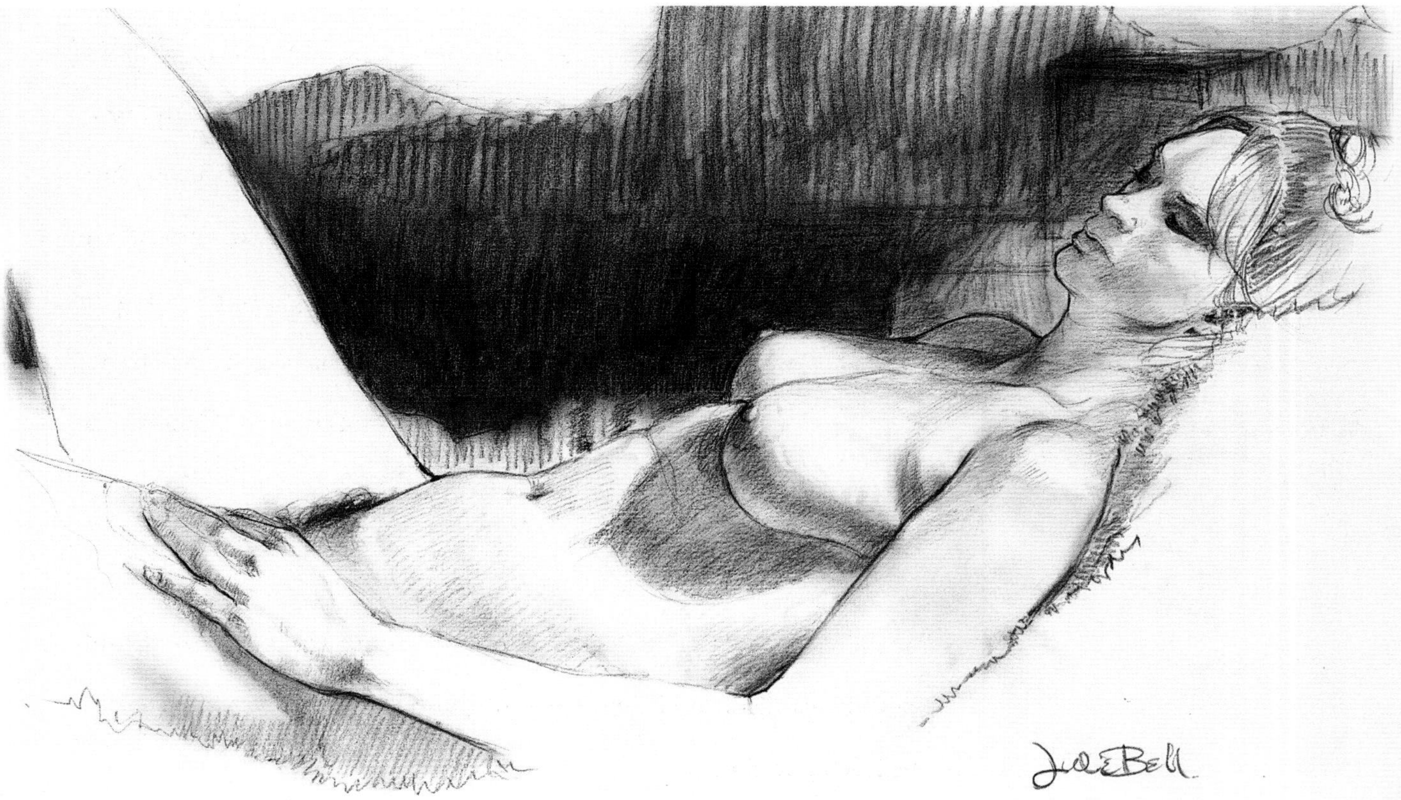

ABOVE: *Inks*
For ink drawings, Julie uses a flat-tipped calligraphy pen because the variation in line width injects life into a drawing.

OPPOSITE ABOVE: *Charcoal*
Charcoal is one of Julie's favourite drawing media because as with paint, you can get soft gradations of tone and very strong contrasts. Every medium has its attractions, however, and is particularly suited to certain themes.

OPPOSITE BELOW: *Sepia Conté*
This medium lies between hard chalks and soft pastels and is great for dramatizing skin colours and monotones.

As an artist Julie's great luck was meeting her teacher at the right moment. Boris' luck was finding a pupil with the imagination and determination to make such good use of his lessons. Boris himself says of the experience: 'It has been wonderful to see this happen, the way her style has evolved; and as she gets more confident and secure, her work looks more and more her own. She has such an individual character. It shows in the creamy softness of her figures, they have a sensuality which is her own brand. Her evolution has a great deal to do with self-assurance. She has grown in her sense of her own self and this is reflected in the work. Often she cannot see it herself, but I do, sitting next to her each day.'

That they married and managed to mingle their personal and professional lives so closely is one of those blessings that tempt one to believe in destiny.

ACKNOWLEDGEMENTS

Having a *third* book of my artwork published and distributed throughout the world is something that, as a child, I was almost afraid even to dream of (but, boy did I dream about it anyway!). This seeming miracle in itself has me spilling over with gratitude for the infinite and countless experiences, teachers (knowing and unknowing), and God-given abilities which have all added up to produce this art, and to allow me to tell you something about who I am. Rather than thanking individual people, I want to thank every person who has touched my life and every twist of fate that has led me to this magnificent place in my journey. I also have to thank all of you who are reading this now for allowing this art to communicate and connect with you, in whatever way it touches you, because, as an artist, that is my true purpose.

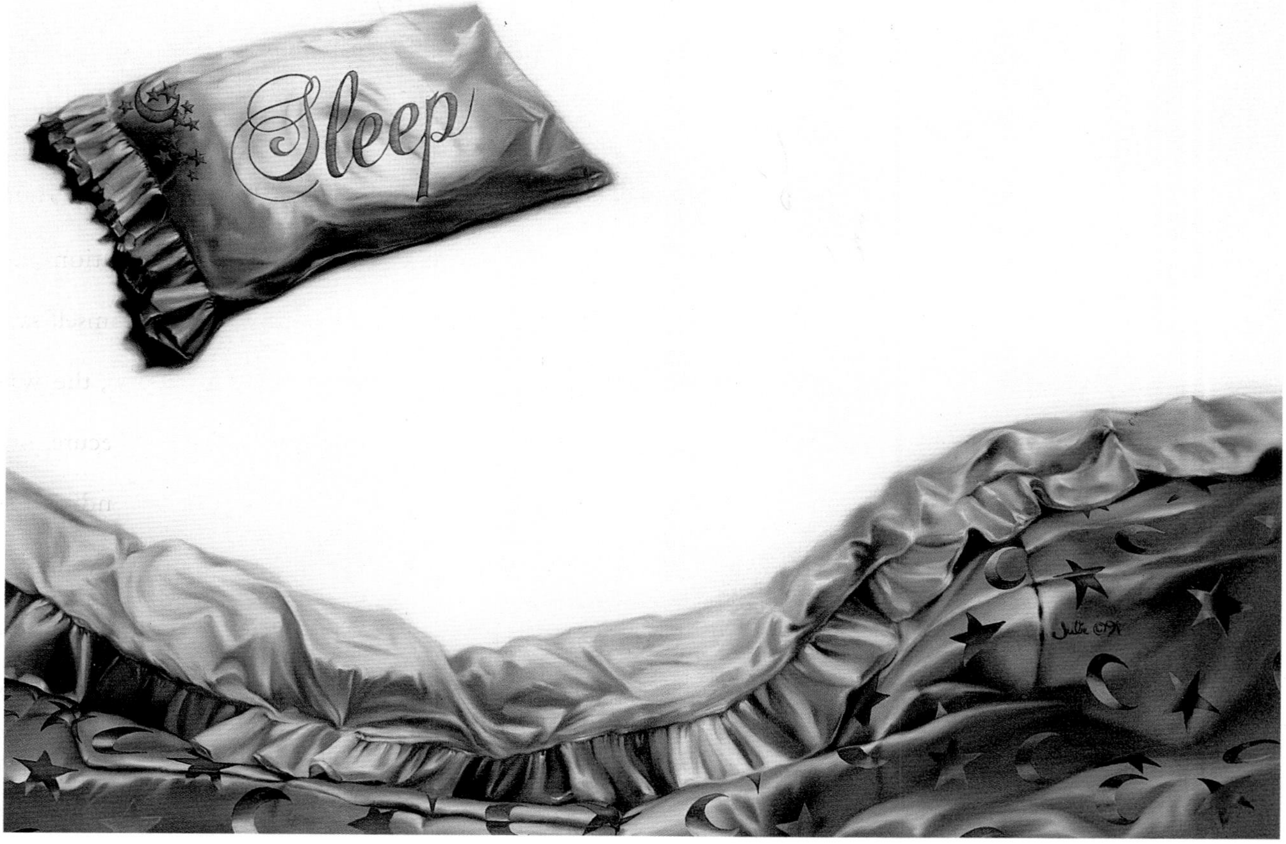
Sleep

Sleep, 1991
Oils, 15 x 20 in (38 x 51 cm)
Magazine illustration. Britton Advertising.